Love, Lies and Murder

Evelyn Cullet

Dedication

To my eldest sister, Jane, a very special lady for whom I named one of my characters. Love always.

I'd like to give a special thanks to editors Erynn Newman and Sirena Van Schaik, for their creative assistance in the writing and editing of this novel.

Chapter One

Threading her petite fingers through his strong ones, Charlotte Ross couldn't believe her good fortune. Here she was, on a plane taxiing to the runway. Everything was perfect: the wealth to which she'd become accustomed, the large house she'd soon call home, and the handsome man beside her.

She lost herself in his warm, brown eyes before they crinkled with laughter. She blushed, having been caught staring at her new husband. The man of her dreams had shared the perfect day when they had exchanged vows earlier. Now she yearned for their honeymoon. The Italian Riviera would be almost as amazing as her husband.

Life couldn't get any better. She sighed in contentment. A loud rumble filled the air, and a sense of impending doom clenched her heart. The plane jolted.

Charlotte gasped. "No," she murmured. "No." A second rumble wrenched her from the seat. Her hold on her husband's hand slipped—

Charlotte jerked awake. Her heart climbed to her throat as another rumble split the silence of the dark room. Thunder from a summer storm had turned her beautiful dream into a nightmare.

Lying still, she waited until her heartbeat slowed before opening her eyes. She turned over in bed and glanced at the man beside her. His muscular form was sprawled across the bedding in peaceful bliss. An occasional flash of lightning flickered through the room and caressed his handsome features, long eyelashes casting shadows on his chiseled cheekbones.

Charlotte stretched lazily beside him, her gaze following the contours of his slumbering form. The night before had been... magical. It was as though he knew what a woman—what *she*—wanted and needed, and he selflessly gave in to all her desires. Could there ever be another man as sensitive or as passionate? The blinking light on the nightstand tore her gaze from her lover's body.

"Five-thirty!"

She gently nudged him with her elbow. "You'd better get up. It's nearly dawn."

"Five minutes, sweetheart," he mumbled, his deep baritone rough with sleep, before he rolled over and slipped his arm around her waist.

It would be easy to snuggle up to his warm body and go back to sleep, but Charlotte bit down the impulse and nudged him again. "You'd better get up *now* or you'll be late. You have to go home and change for work."

He cuddled closer as his lips touched her ear. "I don't want to go to work," he whispered. "I'd rather stay here in bed with you."

"It's very tempting, and I'd love for you to stay," she said, "But..."

"Please, Charlotte, just a few more minutes."

She pressed a finger to his soft lips. "If you don't leave now, you won't have enough time. Don't forget, you still have to pack for your business trip this afternoon."

He groaned. "Why do you always have to be so practical?"

"Because it's part of my job as your administrative assistant." Now it was her turn to tempt him. "But if you hurry and come to work early, I'll bring something special, and we can enjoy a leisurely breakfast." Her fingers played across his chest. "In your private office."

"It's a date." He kissed her shoulder before climbing out of bed.

As he picked up his clothes and began to dress, Charlotte stared at the muscles on his six-foot-two, athletic physique. He gazed back at her, and his lips curved into a smile that revealed a hint of a dimple in his left cheek, and the most beautiful, straight, white teeth she'd ever seen.

After he slipped on his shoes, he bent down, his eyes darkening in passion, and placed a kiss on her lips. It seared through her body, and he shifted slightly, deepening the kiss until she clung to the collar of his shirt and ached for him to join her in bed.

Their lips parted on his chuckle, and he winked at her before heading out the door. Charlotte moved to the side of the bed where John Trent, her boss and the man in her dream, had spent the night. She pressed the side of her face into his still-warm pillow and inhaled the intoxicating, musky scent of him. Slowly letting her breath out, she glanced at the red roses he'd given her the previous night at dinner—one of his many thoughtful and romantic gestures. Rolling over in bed, she sighed. "He loves me."

Chapter Two

At half-past six that evening, Charlotte rushed to open the clear glass doors of the Torchlight Steakhouse. The chilled air was a welcome oasis from the scorching summer heat. She climbed onto a tall stool at the Victorian-themed bar.

"Gin and tonic," she told the attentive bartender as she glanced over his clean-shaven features. *Attractive, but he couldn't compare to John.*

Thinking of John, Charlotte rubbed her temples where a headache had taken root. Being the administrative assistant to the vice president of a small business was stressful enough when he was there. When he wasn't, like today after he'd left on his business trip, it was always a disaster waiting to happen. This afternoon had been that disaster. She really needed a drink to relax and take the edge off the day.

After a quick glance at the door, she checked her watch. Her friend was supposed to meet her here for dinner at six-thirty. Jane Marshall had resigned her job in the Human Resources Department of Longbourne and Payne Freight Consolidation, the company they worked for, and left town last year over a disagreement about her manager using her ideas to further his career.

Communications with Jane had slowed down to the occasional email as they went their separate ways. Jane's phone call last night, saying she was back in town and suggesting they meet for dinner, had come as a pleasant surprise. They'd been close in the past, almost like sisters, and it would be great to have her back. But whether or not this was a permanent move remained to be seen.

A warm breeze floated in through the open door. She caught a glimpse of a young woman in sunglasses wearing a pink knit blouse and beige chinos. Her body language screamed nervous. She slid the sunglasses up into thick dark hair before her delicate hands dropped to her waist and began wringing together. Her eyes darted around the restaurant, searching the crowd as her spine stiffened. After a moment, her gaze locked with Charlotte's, and she darted across the room to her.

"Hi," the woman said breathlessly.

"Jane?" Charlotte asked.

Jane nodded. "It's me. I've had a makeover."

Charlotte stared at the transformed woman before her. Not only did she appear completely different from the Jane she used to know, but she looked amazing. Her usually long black hair was now cut in a short, stylish bob that attractively defined her high cheekbones and delicate nose. Her frame was slight and airy, having lost the twenty pounds that had weighed her down in the past. And she was wearing eye shadow and mascara. This was a far cry from the woman who usually avoided makeup and only wore minimal amounts when she had to. Charlotte realized she was staring. "Well, you look great!"

"Thanks, I feel great. It's nice to see you again, too."

Charlotte gave her a quick hug. "I'm glad you're back. I've missed you. Are you staying?"

The distressed look on Jane's usually impassive face was hard to miss. "That depends on a lot of things." She climbed onto the stool next to Charlotte and ordered a vodka martini from the bartender. Charlotte was silent as she waited for the bartender to mix the drink. When he'd finished, he set it down and stood there with his fingers thrumming the bar. He glanced at both of them and then blurted out, "Have you ladies heard about Carlton Witherspoon? He was murdered this afternoon."

"What!"

Charlotte's shrill cry nearly went unnoticed above the restaurant clamor. Only a few curious onlookers turned in her direction. "Who would want to kill a sweet old guy like Carlton? He'd never hurt a living soul."

Jane's face was unemotional as she addressed the bartender. "How did you find out?"

"I just overheard two cops at the other end of the bar talkin' about the crime scene. Said they had to leave because they didn't want to contaminate it before the coroner showed up."

Charlotte gazed down the bar to the end as Jane leaned forward to peek at the two officers sitting there. The middle-aged chief of police and an older officer, Matt Bridgewater, stood at the bar with drinks in their hands. Probably colas. They never drank on the job.

Jane ducked back behind Charlotte.

"Things like this don't happen in Eldridge Corners," the bartender continued. "It's a good little town with decent, ordinary folk. We haven't had a murder here since..." He glanced at the ceiling and brought his gaze down to meet Charlotte's. "Since, I don't know when."

He leaned over the bar toward her and whispered in a conspiratorial tone. "I'll tell you something else I overheard."

She turned her face away to avoid the less than fresh smell of his breath. "And what might that be?"

"The police can't find the murder weapon."

Jane glanced at her. "But it was..." She hesitated. The bartender was staring, waiting for her to finish the sentence. "I mean, maybe they just don't know where to look."

Charlotte didn't expect to hear anything less from Jane. She always had her nose in a mystery. Giving Jane her best scowl, she warned, "Don't even think about it."

Tears glistened in Jane's large brown eyes. "I can't let this go. Someone murdered that sweet, old man, and they're not getting away with it." She slipped a tissue from her leather purse and blotted gently under her lower lashes. "I was genuinely fond of the old guy."

"Leave it alone." Charlotte kept her voice hushed, but emphatic. "Let the police handle it. There's nothing you can do for Carlton now except write him an amazing eulogy."

"Write, of course." Jane sniffled and blew her nose. Her demeanor changed from sad to enthusiastic in an instant. Not unusual behavior considering the manic-depressive life Jane led. "This murder will make a sensational story for my next novel. All I have to do is solve the case and write it."

"Oh sure." Charlotte rolled her eyes. "Solve the case just like that." She snapped her fingers. "And write about it in your next novel, like J.B. Fletcher. And what do you mean your *next* novel? I haven't seen a hard copy of your *first* novel yet."

"It'll be released in September. But I haven't been able to come up with a good story for my next one. Until now." Jane's eyes flashed in excitement.

Charlotte knew that look. It would only be a matter of time before she was talked into doing something against her better judgment.

"So, are you in on this investigation with me?"

And there it was. "Oh, no." Charlotte flashed back to the previous summer's vacation in England, when Jane's investigation into an ancient murder case had led them to stumble across a centuries-old corpse and had gotten them embroiled in more trouble than either cared to remember. That trip served as Jane's "muse" to write her first mystery novel, *The Body in the Wine Cellar.*

Charlotte gulped her drink, the alcohol burned a path through her body, steadying her nerves. "I don't think I'm ready for another one of your murder investigations."

"Ross, table for two," blasted out of the loud speaker in the bar, saving Charlotte from having to explain her reasoning, at least for a few moments. A young waiter led them to a small, round table in the middle of the crowded restaurant. After they were seated, he handed each of the women a black leather menu. "I'll be back to take your orders."

Dim lighting, hushed whispers, and the cold air blowing down from the vent above the table sent chills down

Charlotte's spine and gave the usually pleasant atmosphere a macabre feel.

Jane's dark eyes scrutinized the other patrons. She could be predictable at times, especially when she insisted on playing amateur sleuth, jumping from one improbable conclusion to another. And there was no doubt this was going to be one of those times.

Jane pulled a slim silver pen and a small notebook from her purse. "The first thing we'll have to do is line up our suspects. The top three reasons for murder are money, jealousy, and revenge. Let's start with money. Who stands to inherit Carlton's millions?"

Jane poised her pen over the book, her eyes giving Charlotte a thoughtful look, but Charlotte didn't know Carlton well enough to even hazard a guess. Shifting her gaze away from her imploring friend, she took in the diners scattered around the room. Someone here might know. Recognizing a familiar face, she gasped.

"John Trent?" she said, addressing a spot slightly east of Jane's head.

"I don't think John is related to Carlton." Jane twisted around. "Who are you staring at?"

"Don't move." Charlotte stiffened. "He'll see me."

"Who?"

"I just spotted John sitting in one of those corner booths with some woman. I can't see who she is. Her back is toward me, and this subdued lighting doesn't help. That rat! He told me he was going out of town this afternoon on business. I wasn't expecting him back until Monday morning." Tension filled Charlotte's eyes as she leaned over the table and whispered, "Why would he lie to me?"

"Maybe she's his sister." Jane shrugged, her pen taping her notebook. It was clear she would rather talk about Carlton's murder.

"He doesn't have one."

"A cousin?"

"I don't think so. He's kissing her cheek, that rotten son of a...!" Charlotte could barely breathe. "If he kisses her on the lips, I'll... Oh no! They're getting up!"

While it would be painful to face him, she resisted the urge to turn away. Instead, she tossed her honey-blonde hair over her shoulders and held her head high, even though the throbbing inside might cause it to implode at any moment.

As John headed in her direction, Charlotte stared at his strong, handsome face. A man with his incredible good looks and stature came around only once in a girl's life, if she was lucky. The tailored navy-blue blazer she'd helped him pick out for his thirty-second birthday made him look even more dashing than usual. A trill of dread at possibly losing him nagged at her, as pain stung her heart. Could she keep her emotions in check when his eyes finally met hers, and he realized she knew he wasn't out of town? She held her breath, her teeth grinding together.

John's soft brown eyes, which had reflected warmth when he looked at her this morning, were now as hard as glass as he moved past her table at a brisk pace with not even a glimmer of recognition or the slightest hesitation in his movement to confirm that he saw her. The familiar, musky scent of his cologne lingered in the air to torture her heart after he passed.

It had taken a few minutes, but Charlotte finally recognized the woman who'd been sitting at John's table. Her platinum blonde hair fell loose onto her shoulders. The tight, white tank top, revealing an inch of plump cleavage, was paired with snug blue jeans and spiked, steel-tipped, candy-apple red heels. Her surgically enhanced lips and pinched nose gave her oval face a permanent smirk, which was even more pronounced this evening, as if she had exaggerated the look to make a point. She waved four fingers at Charlotte as she sauntered past her table, a smug smile pasted on her cherry red lips.

Charlotte turned to glance at Jane, but she could barely get the words around the lump in her throat. "Susan Blanchard? I can't believe he's on a date with her. That woman has been with every man in town."

Jane scanned her menu. "Maybe he likes the trashy type. Why do you care who he's with, anyway?"

"John and I have been seeing each other for a while now." She paused at the surprise on Jane's face. "I was sure we were exclusive and in love before he left on his supposed business trip this afternoon. I couldn't possibly have been *that* wrong about us."

Jane sighed, whether in exasperation or pity, Charlotte wasn't sure. "Getting involved with your boss was a bad idea.

Jane unbuckled her seat belt, reached over, and flipped on the turn signal. "Come on, turn the corner."

Not in any mood to argue, Charlotte said, "All right. I'll drive past the house, but I'm not stopping." She turned the corner onto Treadwell Square.

The stately manor house, partially hidden by trees and dense shrubbery, loomed up before her like a huge black fortress against the golden haze of the sunset. Dusk hung sadly over the old Victorian mansion, as if it were aware of the tragedy that had taken place inside.

"Go around the corner, and park one block over," Jane said. "We can sneak in the back."

"We?" It was pointless, but Charlotte protested anyway. "I'm not going in there with you."

Jane glanced at her, fake innocence filling her wide eyes. "Okay, I understand. We could talk if you prefer. I mean, you haven't mentioned a word about what happened at the restaurant since we left, and I know you're angry about seeing John with another woman."

Charlotte pulled her car up to the curb and turned off the engine. She closed her eyes in an attempt to turn off the rush of emotions flooding her mind. And it almost worked. "I'm not angry. I just want to calmly go over to his place, rip out his heart, and run it through a meat grinder!"

"Calmly, huh?" Jane shook her head. "But it would give me more ideas for my third novel if you follow through."

Charlotte pried her eyes open and tore her hands from the steering wheel, giving Jane a withering sneer. "All right, I *am* angry. And hurt. But I have every right to feel that way."

"I understand what you're going through." Jane's hand rested on her shoulder. "I've been there. That's why I want you to come with me. It'll take your mind off your problems and give you a chance to cool down. By tomorrow morning, things will look different. There's probably a very good reason why John was having dinner with Susan. Since she works for your company, it might've been a business dinner."

Business? She grunted. From the way John acted toward Susan in the restaurant, it was more than just business. But Jane was right. She had to get her mind off them, or she might end up doing something she'd regret, like providing Jane with her next novel idea.

Jane gave her a playful nudge, drawing her from her thoughts. "Besides, you know you're as interested in this murder as I am."

Charlotte rubbed her temples in an effort to stave off the headache about to overtake her. At least it was something else to think about. She nodded slowly. "I have to admit, my curiosity has been piqued."

"Besides, helping me solve his murder is the least you can do for the man you were once engaged to."

Raising her gaze at that, she fought the urge to smack Jane in the back of the head with her purse. "I was never engaged to Carlton Witherspoon. I don't know how that rumor got started."

"Hmm. I suppose it was your mother who told everyone."

"I wouldn't doubt it." Charlotte was used to her mother spreading rumors about her love life, even outrageous ones like that.

Jane crossed her arms and settled back in her seat. "So, are you ready to go into the house now? If not, I'm prepared to sit here all night and wait until you change your mind."

Charlotte fixed her most determined stare at Jane.

Jane's grin told Charlotte it would be useless to resist. Instead of fighting, she opened the door and slid out of the car. Jane followed suit, and before she could change her mind, Charlotte was forced to follow the self-appointed sleuth to a wall of dense shrubs behind the house.

"I know there's an entrance here somewhere," Jane said. "I used to sneak in through a hole in the back of these bushes whenever I wanted to get away from my parents. Of course, that was a long time ago."

Charlotte couldn't understand Jane's reasoning. "Why would you come here?"

"The flowers in Carlton's greenhouse were gorgeous." Jane had a dreamy look in her eyes, as if she could see them as clearly now as she had then. "Their heavenly fragrance perfuming the air carried me to a place I'd never been before. It was the most glorious spot on the planet."

As Jane reminisced, she attempted to squeeze through a shrub-filled break in the black, wrought-iron fence. "The opening was right about here. Ouch!" Jane jumped back, grabbing the inside of her forearm. An angry red scratch ran down the length of it. "Either these bushes have grown a lot denser over the years, or I have. See if you can get in."

Pushing the bushes aside, Charlotte had little trouble slipping her five-foot-three, one hundred and ten pound body through the opening between the shrub and the fence. "I made it."

"Good, now go the gate and let me in."

The soles of Charlotte's sandals sank deep into the soft garden soil as she clumped along a dubious path through the uneven landscape. The air was filled with the rich fragrance of a garden in bloom. The scent of jasmine hanging in the air was heady, but Charlotte couldn't shake the unease tightening her shoulders.

She counted the steps that would take her out of the garden and onto the driveway, occasionally peering into the shadows. Funny how one's perception of a place changed when unpleasantness was associated with it. For as long as she could remember, this had been the loveliest garden in town, but now a sinister aura hung in the air and branded it as the deadliest.

She worked the latch on the heavy iron gate, muttering under her breath as rust kept it from opening. Finally, giving a noisy groan of dissent, it swung open.

Jane slipped in through the gate, and together they made their way to the mansion on the other end of the green expanse. The garden had always been a safe place that welcomed everyone through its carefully planned landscape, but now, every shadowed tree hinted at the horror that took place behind the heavy oak doors of the mansion. Charlotte repressed a shudder as they inched, silently, up the stairs leading to the house.

Jane ignored the yellow police tape across the back door and turned the knob. Surprisingly, the door opened. Climbing around the tape, she slid through and into the darkness inside. Charlotte took one glance over her shoulder before she followed.

Jane lead her through a cavernous, old-fashioned kitchen, down the dark burgundy carpeted hall, and finally into the huge, cathedral-shaped living room.

Why is Jane so familiar with this house? "Have you been in here before?"

Jane smiled and nodded slightly. "When I was eight years old, Carlton caught me huddled in a corner of his greenhouse hiding from my father. I forgot why my dad was so angry with me on that particular day, but Mr. Witherspoon asked what I was doing there. At first he was annoyed, but later, after I'd explained why I was hiding, he took me to his kitchen, and the cook gave me milk and cookies. He said he knew my dad, and he couldn't blame me for wanting to get away."

Jane's dad was a great guy when he was sober, but a mean drunk. No one wanted to be around him when he was in that condition, which happened more often as Jane got older.

"Afterward, Carlton took me on a tour of the place." Jane's voice was soft as she remembered her elderly friend. "After that, he said I could come here anytime. Occasionally we'd meet and have long talks about flowers and other things. I admired the old man's common sense, and he helped me through quite a few problems."

"In all the years we've been best friends, you never told me this story."

Jane let out a heavy sigh. "Carlton said I could tell my mother where I was, but no one else. He didn't want the place overrun with kids."

Charlotte eyed her friend with a new perspective. *I wonder what else she hasn't told me.*

A fire-gold sunset streamed in though the tall, rectangular living room windows, giving the room a temporary feeling of daylight.

"This place was magnificent when I was here last summer," Jane said. "It was tastefully done in Queen Anne furniture. The walls were full of tapestries and valuable paintings, and the floors were covered in Persian carpets."

Charlotte stood in the middle of the room and glanced around. "And this is all that's left—one easy chair, a grandfather clock, and that small end table. What exactly are we looking for, anyway?"

"A clue of some kind. Anything out of the ordinary."

From the way Jane checked every crevice in and around the fireplace and along the floor boards, Charlotte suspected she might be looking for something specific. But searching seemed useless. "I wouldn't know what a clue looked like if one came up and hit me between the eyes. Don't you think this would be better left to the professionals?"

Jane huffed out a long, slow breath. "Left to themselves, the police in this town will probably never find the murderer."

Glancing around, Charlotte didn't see anything in the room that looked even remotely like a clue until she looked at the floor. The smeared blood and the footprints leading from the chair to the front door were hard to miss.

"Have you seen these?" She placed her size eight foot next to one of the prints. "Looks like the murderer ran out in a hurry."

Jane glanced at the footprints. "They're not relevant."

"Wait a minute." Charlotte pointed to the floor. This didn't sit right with her. "Why aren't you interested in these footprints?"

"Because they're mine."

Air rushed out of Charlotte's lungs and up through her brain, leaving her dizzy. Jane made the confession like it didn't really matter, but it had to. She had been here. Thoughts raced through Charlotte's mind, and all of them pointed to one thing: Jane had a lot of explaining to do. "They're yours! How did *your* bloody footprints get here?"

Jane rubbed her forehead, a sure sign she was nervous, as the words came pouring out. "I was here this afternoon to see Carlton. The front door was unlocked, so I came in. This room was as closed up as a Royal Egyptian tomb, and I choked on the rancid copper smell, so I pulled the drapes aside to open the window for air. Carlton's head was just visible over the back of the easy chair, but he didn't turn to greet me when I called out to him. I thought he must have dozed off. That's when I noticed his hand resting on the side of the arm-chair. Something about its color and stillness didn't look right."

Her voice faded off in a tremble, and Jane took a deep breath. "When I ran up to him, he was slumped down in an awkward position." Jane closed her eyes and put her hands over her face as if she was seeing something different than this cold, empty room.

"He looked so frail, and there was blood spatter everywhere. On his shirt, his pants, and on the floor around him." Jane's voice cracked as though she was fighting back a sob. "God, it was horrific."

Silence filled the room. Charlotte could see it so clearly, Carlton's frail form slumped and broken in the chair. She wanted to comfort Jane, who stood there, motionless, her hands against her eyes as though she was trying to press the image from her mind.

After taking a moment to compose herself, Jane took her hands off, and stared into Charlotte's eyes, her gaze haunted. "I felt for a pulse, even though I knew there wouldn't be one. When I dropped his wrist, I saw the dagger, and I thought my heart would stop. It looked just like the one I pulled from the Duke of Demshire's corpse when we were on vacation in England last summer. But I only got a quick glimpse of it, so I can't be sure."

Charlotte had to ask. "Did you touch it?"

"No!" Jane shook her head adamantly. "But someone evidently did. Anyway, to get back to my story, I was just about to bend down to get a closer look when I heard the upstairs' floorboards creaking. The hairs on the back of my neck stood straight up. It sounded like the murderer might still be in the house. I panicked, flew out the front door, and kept running until I got to Main Street, where I called the police."

Charlotte gasped, and placed her hand on Jane's shoulder. "You poor thing." What else could she say after such an incredible story.

Jane walked over to the small end table and brushed her fingers along the top. "There's some white stuff on this table. It's probably just fingerprint powder, but I'm going to scrape a sample of it into a tissue. Have you got anything I can scrape with?"

Charlotte knelt down next to Jane, being careful not to touch the dried blood. "No, I hardly ever come prepared for these things." The tip of a black card was sticking up from the chair cushion. She slipped it out. "Use this."

Jane pulled a tissue from her purse and had just scraped the top of the table with the card when heavy footsteps clomped into the room.

"What are you two doing here?" The voice that filled the room was deep, full of authority, and familiar.

Charlotte's heart jumped into her throat as she shot to her feet, slightly ahead of Jane. She spun around and glanced up at Todd Shlagg, the owner of the voice. Tall, broad-shouldered, and well-built, the uniformed police officer was not a handsome young man, by her standards, but what he lacked in looks, he made up in presence. For some women around town, he was the image of a sexy police officer, with a pleasant face and blond hair that hung in attractive, loose curls across his forehead.

Her hand leapt to her chest as she let out a sigh of relief. "Oh, Todd, it's only you."

"How did you two get in here? You couldn't have missed the yellow warning tape on the doors."

Jane turned around to face him, challenge in her eyes. "We saw it, but the back door wasn't locked. And to me, that's practically an open invitation."

"I just went out to get some din...dinner," Todd stammered and dropped his clean-shaven jaw. "Well, well. If it isn't my ex. I heard you were back."

"News always did travel fast in this town." Jane said dryly.

Todd eyed Jane in the dim glow of the sunset and fixed her in a tight stare. "You look different, kind of thin, and what's with the short hair and all the makeup? Have you been sick?"

"No," Jane answered, clearly annoyed. "I've had a makeover."

When Todd didn't comment, she added, "What's the matter? Don't you like it?"

He looked down and shook his head as if he didn't know what to say.

"Let's get back to the situation at hand." His gaze turned into an icy glare. He tried to look intimidating, but his glares never had an effect on Jane. "Being involved with the law in the past, you should know better. This is a crime scene." He nodded toward the door. "So, out."

Jane and Todd's relationship was well-known to everyone in town. They'd been high school sweethearts and had dated on and off through the years since then. Their problems, or the solutions to their problems, always began and ended with a disagreement similar to this one.

Jane's eyes narrowed as she studied Todd's concerned face. "Why are you lurking around this house, anyway? Don't tell me you're waiting for the murderer to return to the scene of the crime?"

A blush crept up Todd's neck as it always did when Jane teased him. "You may be some sort of hotshot mystery writer now, but that doesn't mean you know everything."

"What's the matter, sweetie? Did I guess your strategy for solving this case?"

"That's police business." Todd's jaw tightened.

The sound of Jane's laughter echoed throughout the house as she doubled over. "Oh, Todd, if that's your strategy, you're in big trouble."

Todd reached for his cap and slipped it on his head, straightening the bill with an official flair. "I think it's time you were on your way."

Charlotte thought he was reaching for his gun, and she wouldn't have blamed him if he'd taken a shot at Jane. Even though Todd had always been crazy about her, there were times when Jane's abrasiveness was hard to take.

Todd ushered them out of the house. "It's getting too dark in here to see properly, and I've been instructed not to turn on the lights, so you'd better go."

When they reached the door, Todd's voice softened. "Will you do me a favor, Jane?"

She glanced up at him. "Anything within reason."

"Stay out of this murder investigation." He gave her a warning look before he slammed the back door.

Jane pursed her lips in determination and muttered, "Fat chance."

Chapter Four

Charlotte stepped out of her apartment into the warm Saturday morning sunshine and walked down the stairs to find her mother waiting at the bottom. The sun glistened off her short, gray-blonde hair as she leaned against the sliding-glass doors of their sprawling, red brick, bi-level home. Her arms were folded across her gold camp shirt.

"Come in and have some breakfast, dear."

"No thanks, I've already had breakfast."

"Isn't it awful about poor Carlton? Imagine a murder in *this* town." Mrs. Ross put a hand to her cheek and gazed at the street with a blank stare. "No one is safe here anymore. Not with a murderer running loose."

Charlotte nodded. What would her mother say if she told her she was investigating the crime with Jane? *It would be even worse than the time she found out I was drinking in a bar instead of attending my cousin's boring bachelorette party.* Even though her mother tried to act like a modern woman, deep down, she was still as old-fashioned as her grandmother, and she had strict ideas about what was the "proper" behavior for her only daughter.

Not wanting to discuss the subject of Carlton's murder at length, and from experience she knew it would be lengthy, Charlotte said, "I've gotta go."

"Where are you going in such a hurry? You usually sleep in on Saturday mornings."

Charlotte shaded her brow from the sun, especially bright this morning, possibly because she'd gotten up earlier than usual. "I'm on my way to meet Jane."

"What?" Mrs. Ross's voice was strained. "I thought we'd seen the last of her."

Charlotte plunged her hand into her shoulder bag, rummaged around, and came up with a pair of thin, silver-rimmed sunglasses. "Well, she's back."

"Is she staying long?" A worry line appeared between her mother's brows.

Shaking her head as she slipped the glasses on, Charlotte ignored the clipped tone. "I really don't know."

"I've never liked that girl." Mrs. Ross repeated this every time she heard Jane's name. Now she scanned the neighborhood and added, half under her breath, "I can't understand why you two have always been such good friends."

"You know we have a lot in common with school and work. And we both love a good mystery. Besides, she's fun."

"She's a bad influence on you." Mrs. Ross's voice was low and gruff. "Getting you in trouble with the law when the two of you were investigating her so-called mysteries. And don't get me started on those awful parents of hers. Their arguing could be heard all over the neighborhood. The best thing that family ever did for this town was to move away."

Charlotte huffed. She didn't need to be reminded of all that again. Her patience with her mother grew thinner every day. She didn't know what she was liable to do when the last of it was gone.

"I think Jane's done pretty well for herself. She's a respected mystery writer now. See if you can be gracious to her for my sake." Charlotte slipped her car keys from the pocket of her beige, walking shorts. "Oh, by the way," she hesitated a moment for effect. "I've invited Jane for dinner at your house Sunday night."

"You *what*?" Maggie Ross's eyes grew so large, they could have been mistaken for saucers.

"I said I've invited Jane to dinner tomorrow night." She opened the door of her new Mustang and slid into the driver's seat, a twinge of mischief making her smile widely. "Well, I have to go. I'm late. Bye."

Charlotte's father appeared at the front door. "Is that Charlotte's voice I hear?"

"Bye, Dad." Charlotte waved as she drove away. "See you tomorrow night."

In her rear-view mirror, she caught a glimpse of her mother bounding up the sidewalk as her mouth worked in rapid motion. *Sorry, Dad.*

Charlotte drove her Mustang to the Eldridge Inn where Jane was staying and parked in the white gravel lot. The inn was a beautiful piece of architecture. The Georgian-style building boasted red brick and double-hung windows with white wood shutters. It had been a family's stately home before the matriarch and patriarch of the family passed away. When that had happened, the two Eldridge sisters took possession of the home, renovated it inside and out, added a small tea room, and turned it into a Bed and Breakfast.

Vivie Eldrige's steel-gray eyes narrowed under thick dark eyebrows and caught Charlotte's gaze as she entered the oak-paneled lobby. Charlotte smiled. Vivie did not return it.

Jane met Charlotte at the door to the tea room.

"I love this old house," Charlotte said. "But I don't care much for Vivie's attitude."

Jane glanced back. "Don't mind her. She's what my mother used to call, 'a cranky old spinster.'"

In the tea room, they were seated next to a small window with rose-colored, gauze curtains. Jane gave the waitress her order: an egg white omelet and a cup of black coffee. Charlotte ordered a latte.

"So what's up?"

"Me." Jane's eyelids fluttered. "I've been up practically all night. I couldn't sleep thinking about Carlton's murder. Every time I closed my eyes..." She placed her hands over her face.

"I didn't sleep very well last night, either. And this morning, my mother caught me while I was getting into my car and wanted to talk about the murder, but I managed to get out of it by telling her I invited you for dinner at their house tomorrow night. So how about it?"

"Sorry, I can't make it. Todd and I are going to see a movie tomorrow night."

Charlotte wasn't surprised they were back together already, especially after the sparks that flew between them yesterday evening at the Witherspoon mansion. "When did this happen?"

Jane took a sip of water, probably to quell the loud growling noises emanating from her stomach. "Todd paid me a visit late last night after his shift was over. He thinks he can keep me out of this murder investigation by romancing me. Well, that strategy works both ways."

Charlotte could just imagine. "I don't want to get into an argument with you about starting up with Todd again, so I'm not going to say any more, but the dinner invitation is open. Todd's invited too. You know how my mother feels about him."

"Yes, and I also know how she feels about me. So forget it."

"Come on, Jane." Charlotte scrunched her face into a sad, pleading look that matched the desperation she felt inside. "You can't leave me alone with my mother for an entire evening. She'll drive me crazy with questions about my love life."

Jane peered across the table at her. "Speaking of your love life, you're not thinking about going over to John's place to have it out with him, are you?"

The waitress set down two steaming cups of fresh-brewed coffee. The women remained silent until she returned, a few moments later, with Jane's omelet.

"I've cooled down quite a bit since last night." Charlotte sipped the thick foam floating across the top of her mug. The latte felt soothing as it went down, and she needed as much soothing as she could get this morning. "I'm still angry, but I'm not sure if I want to go over to John's or even contact him right now. I'd probably just make a fool of myself."

She drummed her fingers on the warm mug as she thought about her options. "Besides, I have some things to do in town today. That should keep my mind off of him for a while, and then I've got to be at Jim Longbourne's for cocktails at six."

"The president of your company invited you to his home?"

"It seemed odd to me too. But he must have a good reason."

"I wish I could go to the Longbourne's with you." Jane dripped cold water from her glass into her cup to cool the coffee. "I wouldn't mind talking to Mrs. Longbourne again. She's such a sweet lady."

"I hate to tell you this, but Bessie Longbourne passed away last February."

Jane raised her eyebrows in surprise. "How did she die?"

"Well, there are some rumors. But I think it was under peculiar circumstances."

"You do? What do you consider to be peculiar?"

"Jim Longbourne said she tripped while walking down the stairs to the basement and hit her head on the cement floor. Died instantly. He remarried a month ago."

"So soon? Anyone I know?"

Charlotte shook her head. "I don't think so. She's an out-of-towner. From what I hear, Longbourne met her on one of his business trips. She's only twenty-three."

"The old wife's questionable death and a young, new wife so soon afterward, sounds peculiar to me, too. I may get more than one novel out of this visit." Jane gobbled down the rest of her omelet and gulped the last of her coffee. "Get the check.

I've got to go to the post office and ship this sample I picked up at Witherspoon's to my friend in Chicago."

"Why in such a hurry?"

"We've got to work fast. You know that homicides rarely get solved after the first forty-eight hours. After that, the trail gets cold. It's going to be cool enough by the time the inquest rolls around on Monday. I hope to get some information back, in case it can be used as evidence. You'll be at the inquest, won't you?"

"Sorry, I can't make it. Some of us have to work for a living."

"Take the day off. You have plenty of vacation time."

"I can't." Charlotte signaled the waitress for the bill. "I have to confront John."

Jane reached into her purse and pulled out the black business card. "Before I forget, here's your card back. You might need it."

Charlotte took the card from her friend. "This isn't mine."

"You gave it to me last night at the mansion when I asked you for something to scrape the table with."

Charlotte shrugged. "I saw it sticking out of the chair cushion."

"Why didn't you tell me that? It might be a vital piece of evidence." Jane snatched the card out of Charlotte's hand and examined both sides. "Unusual printing. I've never seen a business card like it. What company's logo has the letters SOT inside of a diamond?"

"I don't know," Charlotte said. "There's something inside the letter O too, but I can't quite make it out. The card's too smudged. Looks like some kind of bird, or it might be a flower. I'll ask around the office Monday."

"We may not have until Monday to find out. We're racing the clock, and the trail is getting colder by the minute. Why don't you ask your dad? His family's been here for generations."

Charlotte checked her watch. "I'll catch him at his office. He works until noon on Saturdays, and after that, he's off to the country club for a round of golf. If I find out anything, I'll let you know. Where will you be?"

"I'll be around," Jane said vaguely, a sure sign she was up to something. "I have some serious investigating to do."

"Try not to get into trouble."

"Don't worry. I never look for trouble, but if trouble comes looking for me... Well, you know the rest."

That old cliché certainly fit Jane. Actually, in Jane's case, the cliché was an understatement.

Chapter Five

Charlotte walked into her dad's knotty-pine-paneled office with its large, square windows overlooking the Ross Stone and Granite's vast quarry. Her father sat at an oversized, mahogany desk, his body bent over the keyboard, completely absorbed by what he was reading on the screen. "Dad?"

Oscar Ross glanced at his daughter. "What is it, dear? I've got a lot of work to do."

"I only need a few minutes."

"Can we talk later at the country club?"

"No, Dad. I have to be at the Longbourne's for cocktails at six, and I still have some things in town I have to do. Please, I need to talk now."

Mr. Ross turned away from his computer screen and folded his hands on his black desk pad. "Okay, what is it?"

Charlotte took the business card from her shoulder bag and handed it to him. "Do you recognize this?"

Mr. Ross glanced at the card and flung it into his wastebasket. Surprised, Charlotte retrieved Jane's vital piece of evidence. "Why did you do throw it in the trash?"

"Because it belongs there. Where did you get it?"

"I picked it up," Charlotte hesitated, "Somewhere, but I don't know what company's logo is on it."

"It doesn't belong to any company."

"To what does it belong?"

"Forget about it." Mr. Ross turned to his computer screen and resumed typing.

"Please, Dad. Why won't you tell me?"

"Because it caused a lot of trouble in this town, and it's best forgotten." He glanced up at his daughter. "When I saw that card, I thought it had resurfaced."

"What resurfaced?"

Mr. Ross stared at his daughter, his eyes hard, measuring as though he was deciding whether to talk or return to his work. After a few moments, he nodded his head firmly and sighed. "All right. I'll tell you. But only because I don't want you going around town asking a lot of questions."

He put a hand to his jaw. "Let's see. I don't know if I can recall everything. It was a long time ago, around the early seventies, just about the time all those hippies and cults were popping up around the country."

Charlotte settled herself in the chair next to his desk.

"The letters 'SOT' stand for the Society of the Tri... Triumvirate," he began. "A religious sect started by Carlton Witherspoon's father, who appointed himself as the head minister or leader. Said he'd seen the light in the stars, and they showed him the way to salvation. His group believed in something they called Seventh Dimension Astrology. Seemed harmless enough. You know, a bunch of young, small-town folks with nothing better to do with their time."

Charlotte leaned closer to her dad as he continued. "They used an old, abandoned storefront on Main Street as the society's meeting place. The cult went on for several months, and about a quarter of the town's people were avid followers. Of course, our town was a small community back then, not like it is now."

"I can imagine." She rolled her eyes, and stood. "Now, please get on with your story."

"Where was I?" Mr. Ross glanced out the window and then he turned back to his daughter. "Oh yes, I remember. On the surface, this new society appeared to be a quiet bunch, at least they didn't bring a lot of attention to themselves. But as time passed, the members of the Society began to buy things they shouldn't have been able to afford. New clothes and shoes, new fences and farm equipment, a lot of little things, but back then those little things added up to big money. Suddenly, everyone wanted to join this society, including my own father. I remember my parents having a big argument over it."

He leaned back in his leather office chair. "Your grandmother didn't want anything to do with them, but Dad was determined. He needed new things too. So one night, in spite of my mother's protests, he went over to the old Witherspoon mansion and tried to sign up. He was told the membership was closed. My father was furious."

Charlotte nodded. "I remember Granddad's temper."

Her dad grunted. "He got the local sheriff and some other concerned citizens together to investigate the Triumvirate. What they discovered was a shocker. Every adult male member was obligated to drink a small glass of juice before every meeting. They claimed the juice gave them the power to see into the future. But what Witherspoon didn't tell his loyal followers was they were drinking the juice of the poppy."

Charlotte sucked her breath through her teeth. A soft hiss echoed through the room. "Opium?"

Mr. Ross nodded. "As it turned out, the meeting place was nothing more than an opium den full of hippies and free love and whatnot. I heard from my friends that all the men were addicts. Not only were they addicted to the stuff, but Witherspoon had them trafficking the drug out of state. After old Witherspoon and his gang of drug dealers were uncovered, a few were convicted and sent to prison. The ones who weren't jailed were sent to a hospital for rehabilitation, but many of them didn't make it."

Charlotte shuddered.

Mr. Ross slipped out of his chair and walked around to the front of the desk. He placed his large hand on her shoulder. "So, now do you see why I don't want you to get involved in this?" The concern in his voice was unmistakable.

"Don't worry, Dad." Charlotte patted his hand in reassurance. "I'm not involved in anything." *Yet*.

"Good."

"So, what happened to Carlton? Was he mixed up in it?"

Mr. Ross took his hand from Charlotte's shoulder. "Carlton was working as the CEO of some small corporation in another state at that time, not sure where. He and his mother didn't appear to be involved. At least nothing was proven. When the trial was over, Carlton moved his mother to Chicago. I think she had family there. Then after a few years, he moved back here.

He remodeled that crumbling old mansion from the ground up. And over the years, he's done a lot to revitalize this town. His money was behind the new shopping mall, and he's been a huge contributor to the new hospital. It's equipped with all the latest technological advances. Something this area has needed for a long time."

Charlotte kissed her dad's forehead. "Thanks, you've been a wellspring of information."

No one at the Cut 'N Curl Beauty Salon, the Sharp as Nails manicure parlor, or the two shoe stores Charlotte visited in the mall remembered anything about the Society of the Triumvirate, but they all appeared concerned and saddened by Carlton's death. Someone had hung a black wreath on the front door of Witherspoon Manor, probably a member of her mother's garden club.

On her way home, Charlotte stopped at the corner of Ridge Avenue and Broad Street. Glancing down the street toward the Collingswood Townhouses, which filled a three-block radius, and the small-manmade lake in the center of the cul-de-sac, she sighed. *Should I turn the corner or go home?*

The chance of seeing John entering or leaving his condo made her heart flutter. She wasn't sure if the sight of him would ease her pain or make it worse. Most likely the latter. She turned her car onto his street, anyway.

A light breeze brushed Charlotte's face through the open window as she drove her car around the cul-de-sac and approached John's building. A young woman stood near his front window, giving the building a once-over. Something tense and vigilant about the tall, well-dressed woman made her look suspicious.

Charlotte pulled her car up to the curb across the street and turned off the engine. After waiting a few moments, she stepped out and softened the sound of her footsteps until she was right behind the woman. Her heart raced as she asked, "Are you lost?"

The woman made a sharp turn as if startled. Her shoulder-length, auburn hair swung around, almost obliterating the look of alarm that flitted across her round, freckled face. "I'm not sure if I have the right place. All of these buildings look alike."

"Who are you looking for?"

There was an infinitesimal pause. "My, um, friend's condo."

"Maybe I can help."

"Oh, no. I mean, thanks anyway." She pulled her cell phone from her pocket. "I'll just make a call."

Charlotte nodded. "Okay, if you're sure." She turned away and strolled toward her car. For a split second, she considered walking up to John's door and ringing the bell to see if he was home. Second thoughts made her keep walking.

She tried to keep an unconcerned attitude on the drive home, but the look of alarm on the woman's face troubled her. What was she really doing there? Was John the friend she was looking for? And if so, who was she? *Come on Charlotte, you're starting to think like Jane.* With a chuckle, she tried to ignore the worry niggling at the back of her mind.

At her apartment, she checked an excited voice mail message from Jane. "Where are you? I've been trying to reach you all afternoon. Call me."

"What is she talking about?" Charlotte slid her cell phone from her purse and noticed it was dead. She'd forgotten to charge it. *Sorry, Jane. I'll call you later. Right now, I have to dress for cocktails.*

Charlotte arrived at the Longbourne estate at six-fifteen, not exactly on time, but what she considered fashionably late. A middle-aged woman in a maid's uniform answered the door and escorted her to the lounge. "The Lounge" sounded like a good place to have drinks before dinner.

As she entered the room, her feet sank into the soft pile of new white carpeting. Subdued lighting accented the original oil paintings that lined the walls. In one corner, a large gold ceramic vase of white lilacs sent eddies of perfume wafting toward the open door.

The only person Charlotte recognized was the new Mrs. Longbourne, who stood alone near the entrance, wearing a designer evening gown of pale pink chiffon cut so low in front, it was just a hair's breadth away from indecent. In animated Barbie doll fashion, she had one thin hand splayed against her slim hip and held a half-empty martini glass in the other, while acknowledging her guests with a toothy smile.

"Hello, Alyssa." Charlotte found it hard to address this young girl as Mrs. Longbourne, in deference to the first Mrs. Longbourne, whom she had always admired for her modesty, graciousness, and hospitality.

"Hello, um, now don't tell me, you're…"

"Charlotte Ross"

"Charlotte, right. And you are?"

"I'm the vice president's administrative assistant."

"Oh, you're just one of the office staff." The woman tossed back the rest of her drink and set the glass on the end table, rounding her shoulder in an indifferent stance.

Charlotte resented her attitude, but she could understand it coming from a young woman with little breeding who'd been thrown into society without being prepared to take such a huge step. She almost felt sorry for her, so she offered a kind smile. "You look lovely this evening."

Alyssa passed a well-manicured hand over her long, fair hair. "Thanks. Her glazed-over, baby-blue eyes fixed on the toes of her delicate, pale pink evening slippers. "I can't wait until I can sit down and take off these shoes. They're killing my feet."

"Too bad. They're beautiful."

"They're the best I could do. Honestly, the stores in this dumpy little town are pathetic."

Charlotte had to get away from this conversation before she said something she might lose her job over, so she scanned the room hoping to catch someone's eye.

But Alyssa wasn't through with her yet. "Have you ever seen my engagement ring, Char?" The new Mrs. Longbourne extended her long, thin hand for Charlotte's inspection.

Only every time I see you, Alyssa. "It's impressive." She tried to keep the exasperation out of her voice.

Alyssa nodded. "Ain't it, though?" Her half-closed eyes did a slow scan of the crowded room. "Some party, huh?" She commented with the same enthusiasm she might have used in discussing a dental appointment.

"I wouldn't know. I've just arrived." Charlotte continued to check the room for a familiar face. "Ruth," she called out.

Mr. Longbourne's longtime administrative assistant, Ruth Truhart, turned her head at the sound of her name and motioned for Charlotte to join her.

"Excuse me," Charlotte said to Alyssa, but the woman was so mesmerized by her expensive jewelry, she hardly noticed Charlotte leave.

Charlotte rushed to join her coworker, who was standing in front of a large, antique tapestry depicting a colorful garden scene. Ruth, the consummate professional, had worked for Jim Longbourne for twenty-five years. This evening, instead of her typical business suit, she wore a white silk, sleeveless floor-length gown.

Ruth glanced at the doorway. "I noticed you were talking with Alyssa. What do you think of the new Mrs. Longbourne?"

"She appears to be vain and shallow, but perhaps I'm not giving her a chance. Once I get to know her, she might be almost tolerable."

"Tolerable?" Ruth raised her eyebrows. "She'll never be tolerable. She a total nincompoop. The woman has no idea how to throw a party. I had to put this one together for her. She has no manners, no tact, no... no... anything." Ruth waved her hands in frustration. "I don't know what Jim Longbourne sees in her."

Harsh but true. Charlotte shrugged. "Except for her gorgeous face and fabulous figure, I don't either."

Ruth peered at Charlotte through delicate, wire-rimmed glasses. "Men can be so blind when it comes to looks."

Her boss's actions at the restaurant proved that. "You're absolutely right."

An awkward silence fell between them. While she worked in the same office as Ruth, they weren't friends, so outside of the usual office gossip, they had very little to talk about.

"By the way," Charlotte fussed with the thin, gold chain around her neck. "Why was I invited to this party? I don't know any of these new society people."

"Don't you? Take a good look around the room. While you're looking, I'll get you a glass of champagne. You're going to need one."

As Ruth walked away, Charlotte spotted John Trent standing near the white marble fireplace, holding an empty cocktail glass. *Thank goodness he's alone. I'll finally have a chance to talk to him.*

John's gaze met hers, and his eyes widened as if he was surprised to see her there. She took a few steps forward, but before she could reach him, she bumped into a short, heavy-set, balding man in his early sixties.

Jim Longbourne planted a heavy hand on her shoulder. "Charlotte," he said in the hoarse, raspy voice that always grated on her nerves like sandpaper. "So glad you could make it to our little get-together. I've got some exciting news, and I knew you'd want to hear it firsthand. Stay where you are. I'm going to make an announcement."

Maybe he's retiring to spend more time with his new bride and leaving the business to John. Charlotte's fears were

quelled as excitement took over. She could definitely see herself as the wife of a company president.

"Everyone gather round," Jim Longbourne shouted. "Your
attention, please."

A murmur spread through the crowded room before it
diminished to silence. "You're all probably wondering why I've
invited you here this evening. Well, I have a big announcement to make. Last night, our company's vice-president, John
Trent, became engaged to Miss Susan Blanchard. "

The room filled with stifled gasps, followed by short,
intermittent applause. The air suddenly became too thin to
breathe. Charlotte's heart fluttered as if she was on a roller
coaster that had just plunged two hundred feet straight down.
Her stomach followed. She clutched her throat and swallowed
hard to prevent everything she'd eaten that day from coming
up.

"Here." Ruth held a glass of champagne out to Charlotte.
"We're drinking a toast to the happy couple."

Charlotte's knees went weak. Tears welled in her eyes.
She shoved Ruth's hand aside, knocking the champagne flute
to the floor as she pushed her way through the now exuberant
crowd and darted, blindly, out the front door.

Chapter Six

Running toward her car, Charlotte fumbled through her purse for the keys, but she could barely see through her tears. "Where the hell are those damn keys?"

She could probably find them a lot quicker if her hands weren't shaking so much. Her fingers finally touched metal and plastic. Pressing the button to unlock her car door, she slid behind the wheel. A headache throbbed in her temples as sharp pain knifed through her heart. John was getting married to someone else.

She took deep breath to steady her nerves, and pulled a tissue from her purse to blow her nose. Then she rammed her foot down on the gas pedal. The car shot out of the driveway and into the street.

The shrill sound of the doorbell ringing woke Charlotte. She opened her sleep-filled eyes and sat up to discover she'd passed out on the living room sofa. Not in the mood to see anyone this morning, she called out, "Go away!"

"Charlotte, open the door."

In a desperate attempt to stop her head from throbbing, Charlotte pressed her fingers to her temples and squeezed hard. "Stop ringing the bell and go away."

"It's Jane. Open the door."

Charlotte leaned back on her brown velvet sofa with neither the strength nor the inclination to move.

"Will you please open the door?" Jane tried again.

"God, that woman's persistent." Charlotte pried herself off the sofa and staggered to the door. She turned the lock slowly so the noise wouldn't add to the drum solo beating inside her head.

Jane pushed the door open. "I was getting worried. I've been trying to call you all morning. I left a million messages on your cell phone."

"All morning?" Charlotte tried to focus her eyes on the small black numbers of the kitchen clock. "What time is it?"

"Nearly noon."

"Is it Sunday?"

"Yes."

"Oh, good." Charlotte rubbed her eyes. "For a minute, I thought I'd slept through an entire day."

"No wonder I couldn't reach you. Your phone's turned off." Jane looked up from Charlotte's discarded phone on the end table. Her eyes narrowed, and she tilted Charlotte's face upward, examining it.

"You look like you've had a rough night." Jane picked a piece off lint off her friend's shoulder. "And you slept in your dress, didn't you?"

"I didn't feel like changing." Charlotte glanced down at the wrinkled, pale-crimson beaded cocktail dress she'd worn the night before.

"I'll make coffee." Jane's voice trailed off as she headed toward the small kitchen. She picked up the empty gin bottle and tossed it in the trash. Then she sloshed three cups of spring water into the old, electric coffeemaker on Charlotte's white Formica counter. "That must have been some party," she said as she measured out the coffee grounds. "I don't think I've ever seen you this bad. How much did you have to drink?"

"Don't yell." Charlotte held both hands across her fragile forehead. "I didn't have anything to drink until I came home. I ran out right after Jim Longbourne announced..." Her voice trailed off. *This can't be happening.*

"Announced what?" Jane came back to the living room.

The words caught in Charlotte's throat. "I can't even say it."

"You don't have to. Here." Jane tossed her cell in Charlotte's lap. "Susan's posted it all over the Internet. That's why I was worried about you. I thought you might have done something crazy."

Charlotte held the phone straight up in front of her and focused her burning eyes on the screen. As she read the words, she winced. "Oh, great! Now the whole world knows." A slow flame of anger sparked inside her. She slammed the cell phone down on the end table.

"Hey, be careful with that." Jane snatched the phone up.

"What?" Charlotte stared in a daze at the floor. Jane waved a hand in front of Charlotte's face to get her attention. "Do you want to talk about it?"

"Talk about it? I don't even want to *think* about it."

"Then I'll check to see if the coffee's ready."

Without much enthusiasm, Charlotte drifted into the kitchen. She slid the pine captain's chair aside and dropped down onto it as Jane poured coffee into a black mug and set it on the table. "Here, drink this. It'll help you feel better."

Charlotte grabbed the hot mug by the handle, lifted the cup to eye level, and stared at the rising steam. "Coffee is not going to solve my problem."

"Alcohol's not the answer either."

Jane was right, but at the moment, alcohol was all she had to numb the pain.

"Don't abuse yourself over John. He's not worth it. I know you're hurting right now, but you'll get over him. One day, you'll look back on all this and wonder what you ever saw in that guy."

She patted Charlotte's hand. "What you need is a diversion. Something that will take your mind off of...well, you know." Jane thought a moment. "Why don't you help me solve Carlton's murder? It'll be like old times. Holmes and Watson back on the case."

Charlotte slammed her cup on the table, coffee splashing. "My life's falling apart, and you want me to play detective?"

Jane's face was taut with irritation. "I'm just trying to help. For goodness sake, put things into perspective. Forget about John. He's a lost cause and quite frankly, he doesn't deserve you."

Charlotte could only stare at her friend.

Jane rolled her eyes in exasperation. "Okay, even if he does deserve you, it's not like you're going to get him back now. He's getting married, so whatever you had wasn't the real thing for him."

Charlotte opened her mouth to argue, but Jane cut off her words, "Look, you might as well get on with your life. Hard work is what you need right now, and hard work is what it's going to take to solve this crime."

Charlotte tried to keep the sadness and pain from showing on her face. Jane had to know it was hard for her to think of a murder case or anything else this morning. But whatever Jane saw there seemed to temper her annoyance. Charlotte took a cautious sip from her cup. The warm liquid, along with Jane's words, did a good job of reassuring her.

She put a hand on Jane's arm. "You never pull your punches, do you?" Charlotte gave a weak laugh at Jane's grin. "Okay, maybe I needed that little pep talk. Thanks."

Jane squeezed Charlotte's hand. "Any time. After all, you *are* my B.F.F. Now drink your coffee, and when you feel like talking, I'm here for you."

Getting everything off her chest would be a relief. So Charlotte didn't hesitate to relate what had happened at her dad's office and then at the cocktail party, as Jane sat across the kitchen table and listened with wide-eyed interest.

"Take a shower and change," Jane said. "I know just how to cheer you up."

Charlotte ordered dry toast and herbal tea for lunch. Her stomach wasn't ready to accept anything more substantial.

"This is your idea for cheering me up—Shorty's Diner?" Charlotte scanned the walls of the old rail-car-turned-restaurant jammed with booths. The tall stools at the long counter that wrapped around the kitchen area were like giant chrome mushrooms sprouting from the gray tile floor. Nothing better for depression than surrounding yourself with the color gray.

Jane stirred a spoonful of artificial sweetener into her black coffee. "It beats sitting in your cramped apartment while you feel sorry for yourself. Besides, everyone in town passes through this place eventually. We might even catch a glimpse of," she lowered her voice to a dramatic whisper, "The murderer."

"Here?" Charlotte resisted the urge to laugh.

"Why not? It could be any one of these people." Jane's voice softened as she leaned in close. "It's easy to kill as long as no one suspects you. And it sometimes turns out to be the last person anyone suspects. So look around and tell me who you think the murderer could be."

In a casual gesture, Charlotte checked the familiar faces of the two waitresses behind the counter, the seven people seated in front of the counter, and each person she could see in the booths without making herself look conspicuous. She dismissed each one in turn. Most of these people she'd known her entire life. Finally, she glared into Jane's eyes. "You."

"Me?" Jane placed a hand on her ample chest, feigning despair, and leaned back in her seat.

"Yes, you. You're smart and knowledgeable about murder, even though it's academic. You're friendly but forward, always speaking your mind. Everyone thinks they have you figured out since they've known you for so long, but you do keep secrets. And I don't think anyone would ever suspect you."

"I don't know whether to be flattered or insulted." Jane straightened the collar of her crisp, white cotton blouse. She crossed her arms in front of her. "But what motive would I have to murder Carlton Witherspoon?"

"Did someone mention murder?"

Charlotte glanced up at the hefty man in his late fifties, with short, salt-and-pepper hair, as he leaned his thick, hairy arm over the top of their booth. The substantial bags under his pale blue eyes gave her the impression he hadn't been getting much sleep.

"Hi, Chief," Jane said cheerfully. "Having your usual donut and coffee?"

"As a matter of fact, I just finished."

Charlotte forced a smile. "How's the investigation's going?" she asked, trying hard not to think about John.

Joe Holland peered down his thick nose at her. "It's early yet. But we've got a few leads."

Charlotte exchanged glances with Jane, then she looked up at the police officer. "If you had a choice of any of the people in this diner, who would you think would be the most likely suspect?"

Not hesitating for a moment, he said, "If I had to lay money on my choice of anyone here planning a murder and getting away with it successfully, I'd put my money on Jane."

Jane raised an eyebrow. "So, the two of you think I'm the kind of woman to commit an ideal murder?" She leaned an elbow on the table and rested her chin in her hand. "I find that fascinating."

Charlotte tried to stifle her amusement over Jane's obvious annoyance.

"After all," the Chief chimed in, "You did come back to town just before the murder, and Todd told me he found you checking out the murder scene. Maybe I need to take you down to the station for questioning to find out what you know about all this."

"Don't bother," Jane replied. "I can tell you right now, at the time the murder was committed, I was in my room at the Eldridge Inn. Alone."

Charlotte's surprise at Jane's answer quickly turned to quiet understanding.

"Really?" the Chief said. "I'll have to check that out."

"I also don't have a motive."

"Don't you? Wasn't it Carlton who gave your father that bad financial advice? He not only lost most of his money, but he lost his job, too."

Jane frowned. "My father eventually recovered from both losses."

"Yeah, but he was never the same man after that."

Jane shifted in her seat, obviously uncomfortable with this conversation. "He never blamed Carlton."

"Since your dad is no longer in town, I guess I'll have to take your word for that."

The Chief's tone was dismissive, but to Charlotte, it sounded ominous.

"I've got to go on duty in a few minutes." He checked his watch and placed his cap on his head. "I'm looking forward to reading your new novel when it comes out. Most folks in town are." He pulled his cap down and slipped on his polarized sun glasses. "Be seeing you ladies around." The police chief turned and lumbered toward the door.

"Speaking of your novel," Charlotte said. "I read the manuscript you sent me. It was so good, I couldn't put it down. I had no idea you were such a talented writer."

Jane appraised the large tanzanite stone in the gold ring on her finger. "Well, to tell you the truth, I'm really not what you'd call a brilliant wordsmith."

"You're being too modest. The novel was very well-written."

"Yeah, it was great. I came up with the original idea, but my publisher wrote most of the copy. Actually, we collaborated on it. You remember Albie, don't you?"

Charlotte had met Albert Alan Chastain, the debonair young man with the sandy blond hair, last summer while she and Jane vacationed in England. Albie was also known as the roguish younger son of the Duke of Chalisbury. "How is the adorable rascal?"

"Rascal is an extremely polite word for Albie."

"He let you take all the credit for writing the novel, didn't he?"

Jane twisted the ring he had given her around her finger. "He had to give me the credit. If his father ever found out he wrote a murder mystery involving one of the old man's peers and put the family name on it, the duke would have had the British government shut down his publishing house on some technicality or other."

Charlotte huffed. She'd gotten a taste of the British aristocracy's power first hand. "I'm sure he would."

Jane slipped a pale green compact out of her purse, checked her face, and applied a fresh coat of Ruby Red lipstick. "Albie talked me into getting this makeover." She picked at her hair, and closed the compact with a loud snap. "He took me to an exclusive salon in London where everyone was exceedingly friendly, especially to him. I don't think I was the first woman he'd taken there."

"He gave the impression he didn't stay in any relationship very long."

Jane sighed. "Ours may have been one of his longest."

"I knew you two were friendly, but to get romantically involved?"

Jane leaned back in her seat and toyed with her empty coffee cup. "We did a lot of research for the novel together. My funds were running low, so he invited me to move into his apartment in London, and one thing led to another. You know how these things sometimes morph into more than you originally planned. But once the novel was finished, so was Albie's interest, and he moved on to his next author."

Charlotte shook her head. "It's too bad you couldn't make a go of it."

"We might have, but family interference and class differences got in the way."

Charlotte recalled the same situation happening to her the previous summer, when she had fallen in love with the Earl of Bredon. After a brief, unsuccessful relationship, they had parted for the exact same reasons. And that's where John had stepped in, to lovingly put the pieces of her broken heart back together, only to shatter it again.

"I'm really sorry." She said the words, but she wasn't sure if they were for Jane's sake or her own.

"Don't be." Jane shrugged. "He's nothing more to me than my publisher now, but he's pressuring me for another novel. That's the real reason I came back to town. I wanted to talk to Carlton about helping me with it, but since I can't do that, the least I can do is to find his murderer."

Charlotte cupped her hands over her face. "There ought to be some easy way of telling who the murderer is." She glanced around the room again, trying to search for answers to their quandary.

The door to the diner opened, and a redheaded woman walked in. Charlotte grabbed Jane's forearm. "Quick, turn around. That woman picking up the takeout order was suspiciously hanging around John's condo yesterday afternoon."

Jane craned her neck to get a better look. "Did you tail her?"

"I didn't have time."

"We've got time now." Jane slid out of the booth. "I'll pay the check. Go get your car."

Charlotte slid into the driver's seat as dark clouds swirled overhead, threatening a storm. The humidity in the air clung to her skin and made it difficult to breathe, so she switched on the air-conditioning.

Jane hurried out of the diner and jumped into Charlotte's car, gesturing to the woman who was sitting in a sleek, black sedan. A moment later the sedan raced out of the lot. Pressing on the gas, Charlotte arrowed the car in her direction, tapping the steering wheel in irritation at the thought of losing her.

They finally caught up with the woman at the stop sign on Timberlake Lane, just down the road from the Longbourne estate. From there, the redhead took them on a slow cruise around town that ended an hour later at the Eldridge Inn, as if she suspected they were tailing her.

They had just pulled into the parking area when rain began to fall—lightly at first, but after a few moments, the raindrops were hitting the ground, hard. Jane waited for a break in the storm as they both eyed the woman still sitting in the sedan.

"That woman's been everywhere there is to go in this town. I wonder what she's up to."

"Maybe she couldn't find her friend." Charlotte said.

"When I see Todd tonight, I'll have him run her Virginia license plates through the DMV. We'll find out who she is, and possibly, why she's really here."

Chapter Seven

Early Monday morning, Charlotte sat at the desk in her cubicle, the first in a block-long, rectangular office building filled with identical cubicles at Longbourne and Payne Freight Consolidation. Holding a freshly brewed latte in her hand, she stared at her blank computer screen while trying to come up with a tactful way to question John without sounding like a jealous, nut case.

Ruth Truhart walked in and stopped at her desk. "So, how was your weekend?"

It was that thoughtless, requisite question asked by office personnel every Monday morning. And if it had been any other Monday, it wouldn't have bothered her, but this morning, she had to tamp down the urge to scream.

"Great! Fantastic. Just wonderful."

Ruth, impeccably dressed in a beige linen suit, scrunched her eyes into a sympathetic look. "You're not still upset about that surprise engagement announcement, are you?"

Charlotte raised a speculative eyebrow. "Why should I be upset?"

Ruth leaned over, her hand calming on Charlotte's tense shoulder. "Of course you are. I could tell by the way you ran out of Longbourne's house Saturday night." There was a slight sarcastic tinge to her usually bland-sounding voice.

Charlotte went for her tissue box before the tears she knew would eventually be there began to fall. It was empty, so she grabbed her purse. As she rummaged for a tissue, her lipstick fell to the floor along with the black business card. Charlotte took a deep breath in an attempt to bring her emotions under control. "Do you think they'll both be in today?" She bent down to pick up the fallen items.

"I'm sure they will. After all, they work here, too."

Charlotte grabbed the tube of Rose Petal Pink lipstick and shoved it in her desk drawer. Then she handed Ruth the black business card.

Ruth brought it up to her bifocals. "This is an unusual card. Wherever did you get it?"

"I picked it up when I was with Jane."

Ruth tapped her fingertips with the card. "I didn't realize your friend was back in town."

"She came back a couple of days ago. Do you recognize the logo?"

"No." Ruth cleared her throat. "Any reason why I should?"

Charlotte shrugged one shoulder. "I just thought you might be able to tell me something about it."

Ruth made a quick adjustment to her glasses. "Sorry, I've never seen it before." She checked her gold designer watch. "I've got to get back to my office. Longbourne likes the morning mail on his desk as soon as he arrives."

"Right, you'd better get to it."

Ruth scurried away, and Charlotte remembered she still had the black business card, so she went to Ruth's office. "I'd like the card back."

"The card?"

"The business card you had in your hand."

Ruth shuffled around her desk, moving papers as though she couldn't find it. Charlotte narrowed her eyes. *What's wrong with her this morning?*

"Oh, here it is. Sorry, I'm getting so forgetful."

Charlotte walked back to her desk and shook her head. *Short-term memory loss—another thing I have to look forward to when I reach fifty.*

A moment later, John Trent flew past her on the way to his office. "Morning, Charlotte."

"Morning, John." It was an automatic response. "I've got to talk to you," she added, her face hot and her heart pounding as she followed him in.

He sat down at his desk. "Is it work-related?"

"Not exactly."

"Then I don't want to be disturbed. I've got some important things I have to take care of right now." He motioned for her to leave with a flip of his hand and turned toward his computer screen.

She stomped out of his office and went back to her cubicle. *Fine.* If he didn't want to talk now, she'd try again later.

Susan walked into the office wearing a white, short-sleeved polo shirt, a size too small, with the company logo emblazoned across the pocket. It was neatly tucked into tight-fitting slacks. She shuffled up to Charlotte in her black, steel-toed boots and thrust out her left hand. "Isn't this the most magnificent engagement ring you've ever seen?"

The first thing Charlotte noticed was Susan's long, red, manicured nails. The second thing she noticed was herself getting hot under the collar. The pain in her heart only intensified when she saw the ring. It *was* magnificent, the kind of ring she would have loved to get from John.

"He must have paid a fortune for it," she whispered.

Susan grinned. "The diamond is a full carat, and the three baguettes on either side are a half carat each." She pulled her hand away and stared at the ring. "It's so beautiful, I can't stop looking at it. Imagine me with a ring like this and with a guy like John. I'm so lucky."

Charlotte attempted to control the green-eyed monster that was now devouring her from the inside. She wanted to shout out that John was *her* boyfriend and by rights the engagement ring should be on *her* finger, but instead she swallowed back the words. "Yes, you are. Congratulations."

"Bet you wish this was yours."

"Huh?"

"Don't think I haven't noticed the way you look at John. Fixing his tie, bringing him breakfast. Well, all that's got to stop! And if I ever see you putting the moves on him again, I'll have you fired. And you know I can."

Charlotte caught her breath and held it as she nodded. She'd never realized anyone in the office knew about her relationship with John. She cringed when she realized that he probably told Susan.

"And no more of those cozy little business dinners," Susan said, adding insult to injury.

Her words sparked Charlotte's anger. "He told you they were *business* dinners?"

"Yeah, that's what he told me. But I know better, don't I?" Her voice trailed off as she sauntered through the office, waving her hand around for everyone to notice.

The sharp ring of the telephone didn't faze Charlotte. She picked up the receiver. "John Trent's office." Her voice sounded harsher than she'd intended.

"Hi, it's Jane. Are you having a bad morning?"

"Oh, Jane." Charlotte changed her tone, even though she was still shaking in the aftermath of her confrontation with Susan. "Is the inquest over already?"

"It is, and I think it may have been the shortest one in history. The verdict was 'murder by person or persons unknown.' They adjourned after evidence of identification and the medical evidence were given. I'll call my friend in Chicago to see what he's found. Did you get a chance to talk to John?"

"No. He's hiding in his office rather than facing me—the coward. I'll have to catch him after lunch."

Jane huffed into the phone. "Good luck."

The morning dragged on for Charlotte as she tried to get through her work. Every time she checked the clock, only a few minutes had passed, and each time, her tension grew. She couldn't concentrate on her work, couldn't concentrate on the emails she needed to answer or the letters she needed to send out. Not even thinking about Jane's murder investigation held her attention for long. Instead, her mind kept going over what she would say to John when she had the chance to talk to him.

For lunch, she stuck to her desk and managed to choke down a ham and Swiss sandwich. John hadn't left any instructions when he had breezed past her desk on his way to lunch with Susan.

After she ate, Charlotte sat staring at a blank computer screen, watching the clock slowly slide toward the end of the day, impatient for John to return. It was two when he finally strolled in.

"Come into my office and close the door," he said.

Charlotte followed him in and pointedly sat down in the chair opposite his desk.

His dark, searching eyes met hers. "I know what you want to talk about."

Concealing the anger in her voice was impossible. "How could you get engaged to someone else?"

He paused to straighten his pale blue tie and clear his throat. "Now look, Charlotte. You've always made more of our relationship than there actually was. Sure, we've had some great times, but we were both single. There's never been any commitment on either of our parts. We've always been free to see other people."

The coldness of his words surprised her. "You mean you've been seeing other women the entire time we were together?"

"Of course not. I mean, only Susan. But she happens to be the girl I've been looking for all my life."

If he had punched her, it would have hurt less. Charlotte couldn't control the tears surging up from the hollow ache in her heart. They erupted from her eyes and slid down her cheeks as her words caught in her throat. "I can't believe it. Not after everything we've been to each other."

John closed his eyes as his body tensed. "I wanted to break the news to you on Saturday morning. I stopped by your apartment, but you weren't home. I couldn't reach you on your cell phone and I didn't want to leave it on a voice mail. I'm sorry you had to find out about the engagement the way you did."

She sobbed into her hands as her chest convulsed.

He got up from his chair and handed her a tissue. "Please don't make this harder than it already is. I'm engaged to Susan now. The sooner you realize that, the better for everyone concerned."

His harsh words fell on her heart like a sledgehammer. Her knees nearly gave out as she rose unsteadily from her chair. She resisted the urge to slap his face and call him every nasty name her mind could conjure up. Instead, she opened the door and stormed out.

Stunned, Charlotte sat at her desk and stared into space, her hands resting lightly on the computer keyboard, his words whirling around in her fevered brain. Whenever someone approached her desk, she put her telephone receiver to her ear and pretended to be on a call. When the telephone really did ring, she assumed the best professional manner she could summon at the moment.

"Good afternoon... John...Trent's office."

"It's me again." Jane's voice sounded excited. "I've got news for you. Meet me for dinner at the steakhouse."

"Great," Charlotte said. "I can't wait to get out of here." She hung up the phone as a surge of impatience replaced her pain for an instant. She needed Jane and her distraction.

Charlotte left the office at five to meet Jane for dinner, and read the sign posted on the front door of the building: "Employees who wish to attend the funeral of Carlton Witherspoon on Tuesday may do so but must return to work immediately afterward."

Overheated, Charlotte walked into the restaurant. The cold air lowered her outer temperature a few degrees, and seeing Jane in the corner booth, calmed her nerves. Only a few early diners were in the restaurant this evening. The usual dinner crowd didn't gather until well after six. The same waiter who served them on Saturday walked up to her.

"Table for one?"

Charlotte cringed. She hated those words. "No." She speared her finger in Jane's direction. "I'll be at that corner booth with my friend."

"Can I get you something to drink?"

"Yes." Charlotte rubbed her hands over her face. "I really need one. It's been an excruciating day, and my head is splitting. I'll have a double gin and tonic, easy on the tonic."

After he left, she went to Jane's table and sat across from her.

"So, how did it go?"

Those were the last words Charlotte wanted to hear. She brought the white linen napkin to her teary eyes. "If you don't mind, I'd rather not talk about it."

"Of course I mind," Jane said. "I'm your best friend. I want all the details."

Charlotte lowered the napkin and sniffled. "There *are* no details. He brushed me off as if I was nothing more than a speck of dandruff on his shoulder. He said he finally found the girl of his dreams in Susan."

Jane leaned back in her seat and rolled her eyes. "You mean he's been looking for a tramp all his life? Does he know about her involvement with all those men?"

"I guess so." Charlotte shrugged and pulled a tissue from her purse to blow her nose. "Unbelievable, isn't it?"

"I can't see them together. I mean, they're practically social opposites."

A sudden idea made Charlotte feel a little better. "You don't suppose she's the murderer, do you?"

"Unlikely."

"Well, you said it's sometimes the most unlikely person."

"I don't think she has a motive," Jane said.

"Maybe she does. We just don't know what it is, yet."

Jane nodded but didn't seem convinced. "It's something to check into."

Charlotte wadded her tissue and squeezed it tight. "I'll go down to the shipping office and see if I can find anything incriminating."

The waiter arrived with her drink and set it on the table. Charlotte took a large gulp. The alcohol helped to ease the pain in her heart, and the coolness of the drink soothed the heat that still clung to her. She held the wet glass up to cool her forehead. "That's better." She sighed. "So, what's your news?"

"I spent the entire morning looking through old newspaper files, but I didn't find anything, so I asked the editor. He knew even less than your dad. It was as if the Gazette deleted the entire record of everything that had to do with the Triumvirate incident."

"You have to remember, they didn't have the advancements in telecommunications we have today, so it was a lot easier to hush things up in those days, especially if some of the town officials were involved."

Jane stared into her half empty martini glass. "You could be right, but I'll try the library archives tomorrow, right after the funeral. Are you going?"

"I might as well. Longbourne is letting everyone have the morning off if they attend. By the way, what did you learn from your friend in Chicago?"

Jane leaned in closer and brought her voice down to a whisper. "According to his findings, the white powder I scraped up was just fingerprint powder mixed with a little dust."

Charlotte took another sip of her drink. The relaxing properties of the alcohol were finally taking effect. "So we're back to square one?"

"Shhh," Jane hissed, her eyes darting around. "Not necessarily. My friend said we should take samples of Carlton's hair and fingernails in order for him to do a better analysis."

The warmth drained from Charlotte's face. "Do we have to go back into the house to get them?"

Jane smiled. "We can go right after dinner. Todd's on the second shift."

"Gives me something to look forward to." Charlotte shuddered. "What did you find out about the redhead?"

Jane dropped her napkin in her lap. "Not much. She's an unemployed actress. Her name is Catherine Effingham. She's never been involved with the law, so there isn't much to go on."

"What's she doing here?"

"She's probably looking for her friend like she said."

Charlotte gulped down the last of her drink. "Maybe her friend isn't a woman. Maybe it's John. I'll bet she's tracking him down. Come to think of it, I really don't know that much about him, except that he's a college graduate, an only child, and I think his parents live in Virginia."

Charlotte hesitated a moment. "Virginia!" She practically shouted, drawing a few curious looks from the other diners around the room. "Isn't that where her license plates are from?"

Jane nodded, but Charlotte continued on without allowing her to say anything. "The redhead is probably his ex-wife, looking for back alimony or God-only-knows what. She looks like the type, you know, semi-attractive, but really needy. Why don't you make friends with her? You're good at getting people to talk. She's staying at the Eldridge Inn. You could break into her room and look around for something that links her to my boss."

The amazed look on Jane's face made Charlotte ask, "What?"

"I think that gin has gone straight to your brain. We'd better order dinner before you get any more crazy ideas."

Charlotte didn't think they were crazy. It all made perfect sense to her. "I'll bet she's involved in all of this. Maybe she's Carlton's illegitimate daughter. She probably murdered him for his money, or she could be..."

Jane made a frantic gesture to get the waiter's attention as Charlotte continued to spin her own theories on who the mysterious redhead was.

Chapter Eight

Charlotte cheered up a little after dinner. She'd confessed all her suspicions, and now she was more at ease and better able to handle the visit to the mansion. They drove in silence to the house on Treadwell Square, both engrossed in their own thoughts. Once there, Jane unlocked the back door with a key.

They walked into the living room, and Charlotte caught her breath. Officer Matt Bridgewater, her dad's friend, was the last person she expected to see there this evening.

When he spotted them, the officer jumped and made a grab for his gun. "How did you two get in here?"

"The back door was open," Jane said.

"No, it wasn't." He slipped the gun back into its holster.

"It was when I turned the doorknob." Jane put her hands in the pockets of her white linen slacks, cleverly concealing the key. "Come up with anything new on the murder?"

"Well," he said, and then hesitated. "Things are coming along, but don't think you can get anything out of me, like you do Todd."

Jane fluttered her eyelashes at the seasoned police veteran. "I would never trick you into divulging police information." She sauntered over to the grandfather clock and addressed its face. "Where's Todd? Isn't he on second shift?"

"So that's why you're here." The officer gave her a sly glance and wheezed. "Todd and that rookie Billy Price are setting up traffic signs and barricades along Main Street for the funeral tomorrow. We're expecting a crowd."

Jane turned from the clock and glanced at him. "I imagine there will be. Do you mind if we look around upstairs?"

"What for? There's nothing up there to see. Besides, this house if off-limits. You'll have to leave."

This was fine with Charlotte. She turned around and headed back the way they came in, but when she got to the kitchen, Jane grabbed her arm and pulled her in another direction.

"This way," she whispered, leading Charlotte toward a narrow, polished oak staircase at the back of the kitchen. She pointed upward.

At the top of the staircase, there was a series of doors along a wide hallway. The door at the end was open. Charlotte peered in to see a king-sized bed and an antique dresser next to a tall, oval floor mirror. A large, mahogany, roll-top desk stood in the corner.

Jane pushed her in and followed. "This is, I mean, this was Carlton's room. We might find something useful in here." She walked up to the dresser and peered at the various photographs covering the top.

Charlotte grabbed the brass knobs of the roll-top desk and pulled the top up. It opened to reveal numerous mementos. She fingered a royal blue ribbon with Carlton's name on it, picked it up and went over to sit on the bed. Jane sat down next to her and glanced at the ribbon.

"We may have to spend a lot of time here, and even then, there may not be any—"

"I don't think the master wants you in his room, touching his things," an elderly voice warned.

Charlotte jumped to her feet and turned around, knocking a large photograph to the floor. "Crofts, you frightened us."

Unaffected by her words, the elderly butler walked over and picked up the photo with one veined, gnarled hand. As he stood up, Charlotte glanced down at the photograph he held. It was one of an aging Carlton Witherspoon, forever frozen in time, standing in front of a gray brick building, along with two much younger men. The sign on the building said, "Witherspoon, Longbourne, and Payne Consolidation."

"Look at this old photo." She motioned to Jane.

The butler looked down at it, too. "It's the three of them when they first went into business together." Crofts's voice was full of nostalgia. "It was a real sad day when they had a parting of the ways. A difference in 'business practices' they called it, but I knew better. It was over some actress."

Charlotte exchanged looks with Jane. "I'd heard they were all partners at one time."

But Crofts, lost in reverie, didn't seem to notice what she said. "The two of them, old Witherspoon trying to impress her with his money, and young Longbourne with his good looks and charm. Like schoolboys they were, always trying to outdo each other. Acted like a couple of fools. It was a shame, it was."

Crofts's shaky hand returned the photograph to the table. "As it turned out, she chose Mr. Witherspoon, but she swindled him out of a lot of money, and then she disappeared. I don't think Mr. Witherspoon ever got over it. But I say she was just no good. Never did see her in any movies."

Jane's conspiratorial smile signaled to Charlotte that they might have tapped into an unlimited source of information. "Is there a picture of the woman anywhere?"

Crofts straightened the picture he placed on the dresser, until it was in the right position before his frail hands drifted to a sepia-colored photograph of a young lady in a gaudy dress. She wore a feather boa and stood with one hand resting against a wooden doorframe. The now faded photo made her small features nearly unrecognizable, and the sharp, scripted signature, "All My Love, Adeline," was almost unreadable.

Jane motioned to Charlotte. "Does this face look familiar?"

Charlotte studied the picture. "Vaguely, but it could be anyone."

"I don't think the master wants you in his room, touching his things." Crofts repeated. He seemed to have recovered from his daydream of the past as he snatched the picture from Jane's hand and placed it back on the dresser.

Jane pulled the black business card from her purse and held it in front of the butler's eyes. "Do you remember anything about this?"

Crofts gave the card cursory glance. "Ah, yes." He took the card from Jane's hand. "I believe this is Mr. Witherspoon's." Then he promptly shoved the card into his inside jacket pocket.

Jane huffed. "Well, of all the... Listen, the master has died. His funeral is tomorrow. He doesn't care about worldly things anymore. So I'd like the card back, please."

Her comments had no effect on the butler. Without deigning to look at either of them, he turned and left the room.

Jane's gaze followed him out the door. "Well, there goes my only clue."

"You were pretty rough on the old guy."

"I was only trying to shock him back to reality. How can he recall an incident from that long ago so vividly, but not recall what happened only two days ago?"

Charlotte shook her head. "His memory is pretty unstable. Do you think he knows something about the murder he's not telling?"

"I think he knows a lot of things. He just can't remember any of them. What's he doing here, anyway? We'd better have a talk with Matt."

Charlotte trounced down the back stairs, slightly ahead of Jane, and walked through to the living room. The sight of the officer sitting in that easy chair unnerved her. "How can you sit there?"

When he saw them, he lurched to his feet. "Hey, I thought you two left."

"We were leaving." Charlotte racked her brain for an excuse. "And then we met up with Crofts, the butler. What's he doing here?"

"He lives here." Matt shrugged his shoulders.

"You're actually letting him stay in the house?"

"He said he doesn't have anyplace else to go."

"What about the housekeeper?" Jane asked. "Is she still here, too?"

"Nah, she caught a plane for New Jersey right after the inquest. She has a daughter there."

"I thought this house was off-limits to everyone."

The officer settled back into the easy chair. "There's always one of us on duty. So it's not as if he's going to take off with anything. Besides, he makes a great sandwich."

Jane gave Charlotte a nudge. "I think we've heard enough. Let's go."

After a short drive in complete silence, Charlotte pulled her car up to the front of the Eldridge Inn and glanced at her friend. "I don't like it when you're this quiet. What's on your mind?"

Jane unbuckled her seat belt. "If the police searched the house so thoroughly Friday, how did they miss the black business card? You found it, and you weren't even looking." She turned her gaze to meet Charlotte's. "I'll bet the card was deliberately placed there after they'd already searched."

"But no one was in the house except you and me." Charlotte hesitated while she thought of who else had been there. "And Todd."

"Crofts must have been there, too. He's the only other person who had access to the house."

It might sound like another cliché, but Charlotte had to say it. "You don't honestly think the butler did it, do you?"

Jane's eyes held a look of serious contemplation. "He may not have had anything to do with the murder, but I do think he stuck the card in the chair."

"I don't understand. Why would he do that?"

Jane opened the car door and stepped out onto the pavement. "That, my dear Watson, is what we have to find out."

Chapter Nine

The hot summer sun burned through the clear morning sky as Charlotte backed her Mustang out of the driveway and onto the street. Temperatures were due to soar today.

"We forgot to pick up hair and fingernail clippings at the mansion last night," Jane said from the passenger's seat. "Our only hope is to get samples at the funeral this morning."

"I'll do a lot of things for you, but not that." Charlotte adjusted her rear-view mirror and shifted into drive.

"Don't worry. You don't have to do the distasteful deed."

Charlotte made a right turn and headed toward Main Street.

Jane glanced out the side window. "I don't know if you realize it, but you just drove through a stop sign."

"Damn!" Charlotte glanced around in case a police car was hiding along the side of the road. "It's only been up for a few days, and I'm not used to seeing a stop sign on that corner. But the town council had to do something. The early mornings were getting to be a nightmare with all the traffic from the new subdivisions. It was getting impossible to pass that corner during rush hour with everyone trying to get to the train station at the same time."

Charlotte made a left onto Main Street and another left turn onto Second Avenue.

"Looks like everyone in town is here this morning," Jane observed. "There's no place to park."

Charlotte spotted Todd standing on the corner ahead of them, directing the long line of traffic into the large, empty lot across from the Shady Haven Mortuary. She motioned to Jane.

A few moments later, they entered the mortuary through the thick, oak doors and were greeted by Officer Billy Price, who pointed them to the main viewing room. Large, elaborate stained glass windows decorated the walls while the plush wall-to-wall carpeting and Baroque music gave the room a touch of elegance.

They were the last in a long line of people paying their respects that started at the back of the room and moved slowly along the west wall in the direction of the casket. The air conditioning seemed to be in a constant struggle to cool the heat generated by the crowd. As they passed the casket, Jane touched it and let out a quiet sniffle and then a louder one, and another, louder yet. She shoved a hand into her shoulder bag, pulling out some tissues. She blew her nose into one of them, and with the casual motion of an expert pickpocket, she snatched something from one of the flower arrangements, using the other tissue as a cover.

Charlotte chose to ignore Jane's actions as she inspected the red rosebuds on a large heart-shaped arrangement. "I've never seen so many flowers at a funeral. It would almost be indecent, but considering how much Carlton loved flowers, I think it's only appropriate."

After a half-hour, the long procession finished passing the casket, and everyone was finally seated. Jane crossed her arms and legs, fidgeting in her chair.

Charlotte tried to distract her. "Don't you love this music? It's one of the Bach Brandenburg Concertos."

Jane shrugged. "It's okay, if you like the classics. I never really understood what attracted you to them."

"It's the romantic in me."

Jane tapped an impatient finger on her purse and reached into the side pocket. She slipped out a card and handed it to Charlotte. "Does this look familiar?"

"I thought I saw you grab something from one of the flower arrangements. It's another black business card."

"Or it might be the same one. Do you see a connection here?"

Charlotte didn't feel Jane's enthusiasm for finding clues just as Jane didn't share her enthusiasm for classical music.

Jane slipped the card back into her purse. "Someone representing the Triumvirate sent a basket of flowers."

Charlotte glanced at her. "Do you think it was Crofts? But why would he do something like that?"

"Maybe he meant it as a symbolic gesture from Carlton's past. But then again, it might represent something from the present—something more ominous. I wonder if it was added to that flower arrangement for someone else to find. Or it could have been put there as a warning or a signal. There has to be a connection to Carlton's murder, somewhere." Jane surveyed the crowded room, taking in all the possibilities. "I've got to figure out how to get these people out of here so I can collect samples of Carlton's hair and nails." Suddenly her gaze fell on an object that made her eyes widen, as if she'd had a brilliant idea. "Carlton once told me if I was ever in trouble, instead of yelling for help, I should scream, fire. That'll get everyone's attention."

"No." Charlotte shook her head. "I've done a lot of outrageous things for you, but I refuse to do *that*."

"Relax, I wouldn't ask you to yell fire. Just go over to the wall and pull the handle on the fire alarm. But wait until I get near the casket. I'll give you a signal."

Charlotte walked to the back of the room where the fire alarm was located and waited for Jane's signal. *This is going to be a disaster.* There had to be other ways to get excitement into her life. *I'm getting too old for this.*

Jane approached the casket and paused in front of it, her hands resting on the top of the dark metal, her gaze locked on an arrangement of flowers. To anyone looking at her, she was the image of a grieving friend, down to the white tissue she waved. *The signal!*

Charlotte took a deep breath to calm her racing heart, glanced around the room to be sure no one was watching, and pulled the red handle.

An earsplitting alarm shot through her. She pushed her hands against her ears to muffle the sharp shrill as she stepped away from the fire alarm. As far as she could tell, no one had seen her pull it. Instead, mourners in the room glanced at one another, as if no one knew why an alarm had gone off.

Vivie Eldrige was the first to scream, "Fire!"

People shot to their feet. The word spread as surely as the noise from the alarm pierced their ears. They all scrambled toward the exit doors. Charlotte pushed her way into the ladies' room, before she got trampled in the crowd, and waited for everyone to leave. Then she ran out the front door, nearly bumping into the two firemen who pushed past her on their way in.

In the street, a fire truck was parked in front of the funeral home. Todd and Officer Price did their best to control the ghoulish crowd who watched and waited to see smoke and flames that were never going to materialize.

Charlotte was still breathing hard when Jane came up behind her and pressed a reassuring hand to her shoulder. "Great job."

"I hope you managed to get what you needed."

"It was the hardest thing I ever had to do." Jane grimaced. "But the samples are in my pocket."

Charlotte shuddered. "Ugh!"

The two firemen came out of the funeral home and signaled an all clear to the Fire Chief. One of them yelled, "False Alarm!"

Low murmurs of relief came from the mixed crowd as the mourners meandered back inside. Once the crowd had thinned, Charlotte began walking toward the door. A firm hand gripped her forearm, and she was shocked when Todd pulled her back.

"What are you doing?" She asked in outrage.

Todd's eyes narrowed at the challenge, his jaw rigid. Then his eyes turned cold with suspicion. "You'll have to come with me to the station for questioning."

Charlotte's mouth dropped, and she tried to shrug Todd's hand from her arm. "Questioning about what?"

He wiped beads of perspiration from his forehead with the back of his free hand. "Susan Blanchard fingered you as the person who pulled the fire alarm."

The drive over from the funeral home had been tense, and Jane hadn't offered any advice on what to say. As they waited for Todd to return with coffee, Jane glanced through a few of the files sitting on his desk.

The coffee cup Todd placed in front of Charlotte was filled with dark sludge. He gave her a slight grin of apology before he sat down. "All right, tell me what happened. From the beginning."

Charlotte glanced across the desk at the officer and sighed. "I thought there was a fire."

Todd rubbed his forehead in quick, brisk strokes. "A fire?"

"Well, I saw smoke, and where there's smoke..." She let her voice drift off.

"The smoke was coming from the smoker's lounge."

"I didn't know there was a smoker's lounge." Charlotte squirmed in her seat. She'd never found it easy to lie. "I thought they'd passed a law against smoking in public buildings. I just assumed it applied to Shady Haven."

"Well, you assumed wrong. Anything else you want to tell me?"

Charlotte looked down at her fingers, which were entwined together. "No. It's like I said. I saw smoke, so I panicked."

Todd moved around to the front of his desk. Charlotte inched back in her chair, but there was no place to go, he was in her personal space. There was nothing she could do about it. She took in Todd's angry eyes and the hard slash of his lips. He was doing everything he could to appear menacing. The apologetic and smiling cop who brought her bad coffee a moment ago was gone.

"Don't you realize someone could've been hurt? You're lucky the people in this town are a laid-back bunch. I ought to lock you in a jail cell overnight to teach you a lesson." He leaned toward her. "But since neither the owner of Shady Haven nor the Fire Chief are pressing charges, I don't have any reason to detain you."

Relieved, Charlotte closed her eyes. "Can we go now?"

She opened them and glanced at Jane, who had been unusually quiet through the whole inquisition. The officer didn't answer, so Charlotte stood. Jane did as well, and they both took a step toward freedom.

Todd's heavy hand fell on Jane's shoulder, causing them both to jump.

"Not so fast." He turned Jane around. "This sounds like one of your crazy escapades. You're not doing your own investigation of this murder, are you?"

Jane widened her eyes. "Would I do something like that behind your back?"

"Because if you are," Todd wagged a finger at her, "I'm giving you fair warning not to get involved in this. It's not like the petty crimes you helped me solve in the past. Murder is big time, and it affects people and things you could never imagine. Whoever was willing to kill Carlton Witherspoon might be willing to kill you, too."

"Okay, okay," she said in defeat. "You've convinced me." She shot a brief smile at Charlotte, and they both quick-stepped it toward the door.

"Wait, Jane," Todd said as he bent down. "This fell out of your purse."

Jane snatched the black business card from his hand.

"You took this card from one of the flower arrangements at the funeral, didn't you?" He didn't wait for an answer. "There was a card just like it on one of the arrangements this morning."

"Okay, you caught me. So I took it. But there's no law against lifting a card from a flower arrangement, is there?"

"There's a law against stealing," Todd said. "But I know you wouldn't steal anything unless you had a good reason. This must be some sort of a clue, or you wouldn't have bothered with it. Okay, Jane, what've you found out?"

Jane scowled. "Nothing... really."

Todd put an impatient hand on his nightstick. "Don't toy with me, sweetheart."

"The only reason I took this card was because it looked unusual." Jane stepped backward, inching toward the door.

Todd glared at her, mistrust in his eyes. "You know who sent those flowers, don't you?"

Jane shook her head. "No. Don't you?"

"Not yet, but we're looking into it."

"This is all very interesting," Charlotte said. "But unlike Jane, I've got to get back to work."

"You go ahead." Jane eyed Todd who was now standing next to her. "I'm going to hang around here for a while."

"If you think you're getting any more details about this case out of me," Todd said, "Think again."

Uh-oh. He shouldn't have said that. Charlotte opened the door. Challenging Jane was like waving a red flag in front of a bull. *I'm not sticking around to referee another one of their arguments.*

Chapter Ten

Charlotte was the last to return to work, having missed the entire funeral because of the time she spent at the police station. On the way to her cubicle, she passed John's office. His door was nearly closed, a small crack tempting her to peek in.

With his telephone receiver pressed to his ear, he was so involved in the conversation, he didn't notice her return. She slipped into the chair behind her desk and sighed with relief as she switched on the computer.

"Damn it!"

Charlotte's heart thumped as she turned to see Jim Longbourne standing in the doorway of her cubicle with a large bloodstain on his white dress shirt.

She caught her breath. "Mr. Longbourne, what have you done?"

"It's just a small cut, but I'm bleeding like a stuck pig. Have you got a bandage?"

"Judging from all the blood, you may need stitches."

"Don't be silly. It's just a scratch. A big bandage will do."

Charlotte opened her top desk drawer and pulled out the emergency first aid kit she kept there. She selected the largest bandage from the box and took out a bottle of antiseptic, soaking a cotton ball with the liquid.

"Let me have your hand."

She dabbed across the top of the businessman's left hand. "How in the world did you get a cut like this?"

"I did it with this letter opener." He produced the instrument from his pocket. "It's a nice piece of work, isn't it?" He held it up to the florescent lights with his right hand and stared at the gemstones embedded in the gold handle. "Looks like a real dagger, but I didn't expect it to be as sharp as one."

Charlotte glanced up at it.

"Ouch, careful." He sucked in a breath through his teeth.

With her eyes on the dagger, she hadn't noticed she'd been pressing the cotton into the wound, hard. Relaxing her grip on the injured hand and the cotton, Charlotte tried to focus on tending his wound, but the dagger kept drawing her eyes. She knew that dagger. It was just like the one she'd seen the previous summer.

The one that had been sticking out of the throat of a two hundred-year-old corpse.

She fought hard to swallow the alarm down. She'd never expected to see that dagger again. As farfetched as it seemed, could it be the same one? And if it was, could it be the murder weapon?

"What's the matter, Charlotte? You look like you've seen a ghost."

She pointed to the dagger. "Where did you get the new letter opener?"

Jim smirked. "I found it on my desk this morning. Must have been a gift from a grateful client."

"I wouldn't fool around with that dag...lett...er... thing if I were you. May I suggest you put it in your desk drawer and leave it there?" Charlotte picked up a plain, silver-plated letter opener and offered it to the wounded man. "Here, use mine."

"Nonsense. What good is it sitting in my desk drawer? Besides, I like using it." He flipped it over in his hand as she finished with his bandage.

Of course he likes using it. Who wouldn't? If that's the same dagger I saw before, it's worth a fortune. He doesn't know what he has there. As he walked back to his office, Charlotte put a cool hand to her hot forehead. And then she grabbed the telephone and punched in Jane's number.

"Hello?"

"You have to come to my office, right now."

"Why?"

"There's something I think you should see."

"I can't. I'm on my way to the lawyer's office for the reading of Carlton's will."

"You're in his will?"

"Yes. But I don't understand why."

"Stop off here before you go," Charlotte said.

"I was practically out the door, and I'm already running late."

The phone went silent for a moment, and Charlotte could tell Jane was planning. "Okay, the reading shouldn't take too long. I asked Todd to drive me, and I'll see if he can drop me off at your office afterward. I should be there by three at the latest. Will that work?"

Glancing at the clock, Charlotte nodded. "Yeah. I'll see you then."

As Charlotte placed the phone in its cradle, the police chief stormed into the building along with Officer Billy Price. The Chief had a commanding presence about him when he meant business.

Charlotte smiled. "What can I do for you?"

"I have a few questions for Jim Longbourne. Is he in his office?"

Charlotte's smile slipped. "Yes, he's in there. I'll announce you."

"Don't bother." The Chief turned on his heels and started toward the office.

Officer Price leaned over Charlotte's desk. "Hi babe."

"Hi," Charlotte muttered as she backed away. What an ego he had.

Billy Price, aka Billy the Schoolyard Bully, had grown into a devilishly handsome man. Six feet of pure muscle, and neatly trimmed, black hair. He was a guy women flocked to, and when he smiled at them, his white teeth gleamed in his tanned face. But Charlotte had never found him attractive. There was something about him that felt snake-like. He was a little too slick, like a human python slithering through life, catching and devouring all the ratty elements and attracting the undesirables.

"Come on, Billy," the Chief said. "This ain't no social call."

"Coming, Chief." Billy's sensual wink made Charlotte shudder.

At the sight of the police, John rushed out of his office, and several coworkers gathered around Charlotte's cubicle.

"What are the police doing here?" John demanded.

"They want to ask Longbourne a few questions." Charlotte tried to keep the coldness out of her tone.

"Questions about what?"

"I don't know. You'll have to ask him yourself."

John's warm, brown eyes narrowed into cool depths as he stared at her. Then he went back to his office doorway, where he stood, obviously waiting for the police to finish.

A few moments later, Jim came out of his office and announced he would be gone for the rest of the day. He leaned into Charlotte's cubicle. "Call my wife, and tell her not to expect me for dinner. And please call Ruth to let her know."

After he joined the officers, quiet murmurs could be heard throughout the office, where wild rumors flew, and speculation grew as to why Longbourne was being taken away by the police. Susan Blanchard ran up to John and threw her arms around his neck.

"I heard Jim Longbourne's been arrested. What's going to happen now?"

John tilted Susan's chin and gazed into her eyes. "Don't worry. Everything will be all right. Go back to work. I'll see you later."

The look of concerned affection he gave Susan made Charlotte nauseous. She closed her eyes and turned her head, waiting for the feeling to pass. After a few moments, she glanced at the tranquil blue ocean screen-saver on her computer screen. It reminded her that she needed to water the ivy plant on top of her filing cabinet. The glossy leaves of the once vigorous plant looked dry now, their luster as faded as her hopes of ever having a future with John. *Looks like you're suffering right along with me.*

Trying to take everything in stride, Charlotte glanced through the window as Jim Longbourne climbed into the squad car. Behind her, John watched until it was out of sight before he walked out to the middle of the office.

"I know everyone has a lot of questions," he said in a clear and commanding voice. "And I assure you, I will get the answers. But right now, I need you all to do your jobs. So please, everyone go back to work, and I'll let you know the details as they become available."

Does he actually think anyone will get any work done this afternoon? Charlotte shook her head as her coworkers returned to their desks. She turned to her computer screen, but her thoughts weren't on the spreadsheets. Instead, they were on the dagger in Longbourne's office. Was it the same dagger? Had it been used in the murder? And if it was, why was Longbourne so careless about using it? Unless he was hiding it in plain sight. But was he clever enough to think he could get away with it? Or confident enough?

Giving up on the work in front of her, Charlotte picked up a few papers from her desk and walked to Jim Longbourne's office. She went to his confidential file cabinet. It was locked. But she expected that. Luckily last summer, she'd discovered where he hid the key.

Skimming through the files to see if she could come up with a motive, she found a folder with a notice inside that Carlton Witherspoon had bought up the controlling shares of stock in Longbourne and Payne. This confirmation from Jim's lawyer informed him that Carlton had sold his shares to a large conglomerate in Chicago. *It sounds like Carlton was selling the company right out from under Jim. This could be a motive for murder.*

Glancing around, Charlotte placed the sheet on the photocopier and ran it. Then she tucked the copy into the stack of papers she had and stuck the original back in the drawer.

At her desk, questions reeled in her mind, and she spared another glance at the clock. There was no way she could get much work done now. Picking up the phone, she flipped open her contact book and began making the phone calls Jim had requested of her.

There was no answer at Alyssa Longbourne's cell number, so she left a message. The same with Ruth's cell. Trying her condo's number, Charlotte listened to the endless ringing before she placed the telephone receiver back on its cradle. *Guess she doesn't have voice mail.* If Ruth wasn't at home or accessible by cell, where was she?

"Okay, Charlotte, I'm here. What do you want?" Jane's voice scattered Charlotte's thoughts in every direction.

"You startled me." She'd been so distracted, she'd almost forgotten Jane was coming.

"From the look in your eyes, you were a zillion miles away."

Charlotte pushed out a breath. "Longbourne's been taken in by the police."

Jane raised her eyebrows in surprise and then lowered one. "Was he arrested or just taken in for questioning?"

"What's the difference?"

"There's a big difference." Jane pulled out her cell phone. "I'll call Todd and find out."

Charlotte swung her chair around to see John standing in his doorway, staring at her with an intense look she could only construe as lethal.

"If you can tear yourself away from your personal business for a moment, will you please come into my office?"

She leapt from her chair. "Right away." Charlotte walked into his office and stood next to his desk.

He sat back and rattled off a list of things he needed her to do. She jotted them down on a pad of paper, but only a few of the items sunk in. How could she concentrate on what he was telling her and listen to Jane's phone conversation at the same time?

"Have you got it all?'

"Oh sure, I'll email you the information."

"One more thing," he said.

Charlotte stood, poised to make a dash toward her desk.

"What's the name of that new French bistro across the street from the courthouse?"

"Chez Pierre."

Charlotte was about to sprint back to her desk when John picked up his phone. Walking out of his office, she could barely hear what he said, so she stopped to listen as he made reservations for two for the following night.

His words fell on her heart like a grand piano that was dropped from a ten-story building. Even though she was crushed, she screwed up her courage and walked back to her desk with her head held high. She reached it in time to see Jane drop her phone into her purse, her eyes wide in a stunned expression.

"It's official. Longbourne's been arrested for the murder of Carlton Witherspoon."

"I was afraid he'd been arrested." Charlotte moaned and tumbled into her chair. "He came to my cubicle earlier today all bloody and holding that dagger. He—"

"Wait a minute," Jane interrupted. "He was bloody? And he had a dagger?"

"He said he cut his hand when he opened his morning mail with it, and he needed a bandage." Charlotte grabbed her friend's arm. "Jane, it looked like the dagger you pulled out of the Duke of Demshire's corpse last summer." She tapped her pen on the desk. "But it can't possibly be the same one. I mean, what are the chances? You sent the original back to England, didn't you?"

Jane seemed at a loss for an answer to that question. A quivering smile crossed her lips. "I was going to send it back, but I couldn't part with it. I didn't have the heart to see it end up in a museum."

Charlotte couldn't believe Jane could be so selfish. But this was only one of many surprising things she'd discovered about her friend lately.

"My apartment was robbed last month, and the Duke's dagger was one of the items stolen," Jane finally admitted.

"Did you report the stolen dagger to the police?"

"No. How would I explain that a woman of my limited means was in possession of a museum quality, priceless artifact? They might think I stole it. Then they'd investigate and find out that..."

"You did."

"Actually, I found it." Jane sounded stressed.

"It's not as if you found it lying on the ground, Jane. You pulled it out of the throat of a two hundred year old corpse. It's not the same thing. You should've returned it when you had the chance."

"Well, it's too late now, so let's not argue the point. I'd better go to the police station and check it out."

As Jane scurried toward the front door, Ruth Truhart strolled in and went straight to her desk in the large room next to Jim's office.

Charlotte picked up a folder, but closed it again as Jane approached and stopped in front of her desk.

"You noticed Ruth come in too, didn't you?"

Charlotte nodded. "I'd better go in and tell her what happened."

She pushed her chair back and went to Ruth's desk with Jane trailing a short distance behind.

"I'm surprised to see you here, Ruth. I thought you were at home, sick," Charlotte said.

Ruth adjusted her glasses. "I told Jim I wasn't feeling well, but I would be in later. He only hears what he wants to hear, and lately he's getting worse. What can I do for you?"

"There's something I have to tell you. It's probably going to be shocking, so brace yourself."

Ruth leaned against the back of her chair and tilted her head to one side. "Well?" She shrugged her narrow shoulders.

With a heartfelt sigh, Charlotte broke the news about Jim being arrested.

Ruth stared into space a moment with a complacent face, and then she inspected the nails on her left hand. "Was he? How interesting."

She studied her nails for another moment before her eyes darted up at Charlotte. "I've had my suspicions about Jim. He's been acting quite erratic since the murder, kind of nervous and watchful, almost as if he was rushing to get his affairs in order. I knew it would only be a matter of time before something like this happened."

"How can you be so calm? If my boss had been arrested, I'd be frantic."

"Oh, I am, Charlotte. I'm frantic inside." Ruth nodded her head for emphasis, but without much sincerity. "But you see, Jim hired me to be competent and not lose my head under unusual or stressful situations." There was little doubt that she was directing a barb at her. "Now, I have a lot of work to do and arrangements to make. So, if you'll excuse me, I'll get to them."

Charlotte turned to leave and spotted Jane standing outside of Ruth's office. "Some acting job," Jane said as they walked toward the front door.

"She didn't seem the least bit concerned about Jim, but she had to be."

"Don't worry, Charlotte, you're concerned enough for the both of you. Don't let her behavior become an issue. We've got more important things to think about, like that dagger. Which reminds me, I'd better go to the station and have a look at it."

As Jane put a hand on the door to leave, Charlotte said, "Wait. In all the excitement, I forgot to tell you. Carlton was buying and selling off large portions of this company. That could be all the motive Longbourne needed."

Jane's eyes sparkled with interest. "Do you have proof?"

Charlotte nodded. "I copied the letter from Longbourne's attorney. Do you want it?"

Jane shook her head. "No, you hold onto it. We might need it later, but for now, hide it."

Charlotte glanced around. "Okay. By the way, what happened at the lawyer's office? What did you inherit?"

"Millions."

"Aren't you excited?"

"I said I inherited millions. I didn't say it was millions of dollars."

"Millions of what, then?"

Jane opened the black canvas bag she carried and pulled out a large white envelope. She handed it to Charlotte. "Here's my inheritance."

Charlotte slid the contents out. "Millions. *A biography of and by Carlton Ambrose Witherspoon.* Not exactly what you were expecting, is it?"

Jane put a hand on her slim hip. "Why would Carlton leave me a manuscript of his autobiography?"

Charlotte flipped through the pages. "He probably left it to you because you're the only one in town who's been published."

"But why would he do that when he could easily have self-published it himself?"

"Judging from all the typos and corrections in this manuscript," Charlotte said as she perused the pages, "I don't think Carlton owned a computer. This looks like it was done on a typewriter."

Jane nodded. "I have to agree with you. He was very fond of that old Smith-Corona in his library."

"Have you read much of it?"

"I scanned a few pages when Todd was driving me here, but all I've found out is that he had a shrewd business savvy, and he was quite the Casanova, only the names were changed to protect the 'not so' innocent."

"Maybe you have to read *between* the lines." Charlotte drew a set of imaginary lines in the air. "You know, like Hemmingway, where he implies more than he spells out, trusting in your instinct to understand the true meaning."

Jane shook her head. "Don't get me wrong. Carlton was a good friend and a wonderful mentor, but the man was no Hemmingway. Take the manuscript home. See if you can read between the lines."

"I'll try." Charlotte closed the cover and placed the manuscript back in the white envelope. "So, if you didn't get all of that money, who did?"

"According to his will, Carlton Witherspoon's closest living blood relative will get everything except the house, which he left to his butler, Crofts, and a hundred thousand dollar endowment he left to his housekeeper. He also left a slightly smaller one to Crofts. His staff was well taken care of."

"Don't keep me in suspense. Who is this relative?"

"No one knows." Jane adjusted the shoulder bag that was slipping down her arm. "His lawyer is waiting for someone to claim the inheritance. Then, if no one can prove a relationship within one year, it all goes to charity. After he takes his cut, of course."

Charlotte sighed. "I guess that rules money out as a reason to kill Carlton. Unless it really is Longbourne. He'd be the big loser if the company was being sold out from under him." Even as she said the words, they didn't sound right to her.

Jane grasped the door handle to leave. "There are more aspects to greed than just money, but let's forget money for now. And Longbourne as well. Let's try the jealousy and revenge angles. I'll come to your apartment later tonight to go over the manuscript. Maybe there's something in it about either of those two reasons that will give us a clue to who the murderer is. I hope you're better at reading between the lines than I am."

Chapter Eleven

Charlotte sat on her living room sofa paging through Carlton's manuscript as dusk settled over the small town. Trying to read through the Xed-out words and typos was bad enough, but there was no continuity, and a portion of the manuscript was disjointed, like pages were missing.

While he described his business savvy as equal to Donald Trump's, there was no mention of his father's involvement with the Triumvirate, but there were several pages describing his relationship with the actress, Adeline Adams.

Crofts had gotten his facts wrong. The actress didn't swindle Carlton out of money, he intended to marry her and had deposited twenty-five thousand dollars into her bank account, so she could start up her own production company. But after she traveled to Chicago to meet with her other investors, she didn't return.

When he found out she'd closed her account and withdrawn all the money, he hired private detectives to look for her, but none of them were successful. She was pregnant at the time she left, and Carlton was frantic, but he never gave up hope that one day she'd return to him with their child.

Sadly, she never did, nor did he ever find out what happened to the child. Over the years, he tried compensating by romancing other women, but none could compare to his beloved Adeline, so he never married.

Maybe she didn't want to marry Carlton or to have him find her or their child. Could someone or something have warned her off?

It appeared that he left the manuscript to Jane to add the missing pieces and put it in some kind of publishable order.

Where was Jane, anyway? She should have been there by now. Try as she might, Charlotte couldn't shake the feeling of uneasiness. It could be nothing, just a manifestation of anxiety over reading the manuscript of a murder victim. Or it could be something else. She'd always trusted her gut, so she set the manuscript down and went out the front door to check the street.

Scanning the area, her eyes widened as they came to rest on the still form of Jane lying on the pavement, her limbs akimbo around her prone form. Choking on her breath, Charlotte couldn't even call Jane's name as she ran down the stairs. She pulled the cell phone from her jeans' pocket, and tapped out nine-one-one.

The ambulance pulled up to the emergency entrance at the Ridge Clinic, and the paramedics wheeled Jane out on a gurney. Charlotte caught up to them as Jane was being pushed through the automatic door.

Jane's eyes were open, and while they weren't their usual brightness, at least they were alert.

"You're awake," Charlotte said, breathing hard. "I was so worried about you. What happened?"

"I'll tell you about it later. Right now, I have to see if I can talk my way out of spending the night here, But first, I have to throw up."

Inside the clinic, Charlotte fidgeted while leafing through a worn, outdated fashion magazine. The antiseptic smell assaulted her sinuses as she looked around the large waiting room, noting its cool beige walls lined with colorful abstract prints hanging above a row of upholstered black leather chairs. Two elderly ladies wearing casual summer dresses sat in a corner, each reading a paperback. Charlotte tossed the magazine onto a polished maple table and headed for the water fountain.

Todd stood at the emergency entrance, chatting with a nurse. He must have spotted her, because he suddenly headed in her direction.

Oh no! Her mind went blank, but she knew one thing for certain: he would freak if she told him about Jane.

"Charlotte, what are you doing here? Where's Jane?"

"I..." She suddenly glimpsed Ruth walking through the lobby. "I was waiting for Ruth to get off duty. She's a volunteer here, you know."

"I didn't know." Todd glanced at Ruth, who paused to look back at the officer as she walked by. "I just finished with my annual checkup," he said. "But I have to get back on duty now. If you see Jane, will you tell her I'll call her later?"

"I certainly will. If I see her."

Todd exited through the front door, and Charlotte let out a sigh of relief.

Ruth walked up to her. "What on earth are you doing here?"

"Waiting for a friend. I'd almost forgotten you were a volunteer. I didn't think you were so altruistic."

"Altruistic? Me? Don't make me laugh. The only reason I volunteer here is because my mother insists on it. We wouldn't want anything to besmirch the name of Truhart, would we?" The disdain in her voice made it clear that Ruth cared nothing about the Truhart name.

Ruth leaned closer. "Nan's not my biological mother, you know, and Truhart's not my real name. My mother put me up for adoption when I was only hours old. Funny, I hadn't thought about her in years."

This was news to Charlotte. She didn't know how to respond, so she didn't.

Ruth glanced at her watch. "Well, I can't stand here and chat. I have to meet um... my mother, in a few minutes. I'll see you tomorrow morning. And do me a favor? Try not to walk around the office with your heart on your sleeve. It's pathetic."

Charlotte's shoulders dropped in resignation. *Is it that obvious?* She watched Ruth disappear down a hallway, and turned back to the lobby.

A few moments later, Jane was wheeled in, seated in a black and chrome wheelchair pushed by Ruth's mother, Nurse Nan Truhart. Charlotte strolled up to meet them.

"Jane just needs a hearty dinner and a good night's sleep," the nurse said. "She'll be fine."

"I promised Nan you'd take care of me." Jane stood and motioned toward the exit sign.

Charlotte grinned. "You can count on me."

"Let's get out of here." Grabbing Charlotte's arm, Jane dragged her through the front door.

"My car's in the emergency parking space," Charlotte directed. She followed Jane at a brisk pace. "Stop running. I've got something interesting to tell you. Did you know Ruth Truhart was adopted?"

"No, I didn't." Jane climbed into the passenger seat of Charlotte's Mustang while Charlotte rushed around to the other side and slid in behind the wheel. Jane glared at her. "Why did you call an ambulance?"

Charlotte turned the key in the ignition. "When I saw you lying on the ground in the driveway, I panicked. At first, I thought you were dead, but when I noticed you were still breathing, I couldn't imagine what happened to you. Then I spotted this paper in your hand."

She removed a slip of paper from her purse and unfolded it. The note was hand-written in large block letters on a half sheet of plain, white paper: *"Stop investigating now, or the next time you won't wake up."*

Jane scanned the note and crushed the paper into a ball.

"Hmm. It appears I'm making someone extremely nervous." She shoved the ball of paper into her purse. "Whoever followed me came up from behind and drugged me with ether. You must have startled the person when you came out of your apartment."

Charlotte backed the car out of the parking space. "Before he had a chance to kill you."

"If he was going to kill me, he would have done it instead of sticking a warning note in my hand."

Although Jane's demeanor was calm, she had to be as uneasy as Charlotte was, considering everything that'd happened.

"I have a weird feeling about all this," Charlotte said. "It's like we've blundered our way into the middle of a *Murder She Wrote* episode, and the scary part is that we don't know what happened at the beginning."

Jane glanced at her. "I never thought of it that way, but you're right. Now all we have to do is figure out what's really going on before things get any worse."

Charlotte slammed her foot on the brake pedal, bringing the car to a screeching halt.

"Things are going to get worse?"

Chapter Twelve

The night had been a long one for Charlotte with so many thoughts going through her mind. At dawn, before the sky had even lightened, she had given up the effort to sleep and gotten up for work.

The office was dark and quiet, the only light coming from her computer screen. It was the perfect setting for her to reflect on everything before she got lost in the daily work routine.

She propped her drowsy head up with one hand and stared down at the early edition of *The Gazette* spread out on top of her desk. After getting a jolt of caffeine from a hot cup of freshly brewed French Roast coffee, she read the newspaper headline out loud. "Longbourne Arrested."

Why would Jim Longbourne want to murder a harmless old guy like Carlton Witherspoon? If it had to do with the company, they could have come to some kind of agreement. But if he'd killed once, a second murder might be easier. Was his first wife's death really an accident? She was beginning to have doubts. In any case, he couldn't possibly have assaulted Jane, because Longbourne had been in jail yesterday afternoon. But what if he had an accomplice?

Charlotte turned to her computer as footsteps approached her desk. She checked the office clock. "You're in early this morning, John." Her breath caught in her throat. "Mr. Longbourne! I thought you were..."

"In jail? It's all right, you can say it. I was in jail, but my lawyer got me released yesterday evening."

"Yesterday evening?" The pulse in Charlotte's temple pounded. *That means he was out when Jane was attacked.*

"Yes, Charlotte, yesterday evening." His raspy voice sounded annoyed. "I came to the office to pick up a few things. When John comes in, please tell him I'm going to work from home today. And tell Ruth I need her to... Never mind. She just came in. I'll tell her myself."

As he walked to his office, Charlotte dialed Jane's cell number.

"Hello." Jane's voice was thick with sleep.

"Longbourne was released from jail yesterday evening."

"Do you have any idea what time it is?" Jane grumbled.

"Oh, sorry, did I wake you? I didn't realize you were up late last night. Out dancing and carousing with Todd after you got back from the clinic, I suppose?" Charlotte tapped her pen on the desk as she waited for an answer.

"Yes, we were out, but we were doing surveillance work."

"On whom?"

"I can't tell you that now."

"Why?" Charlotte paused. "Is Todd in bed with you? Wait! Don't tell me. I don't want to know."

Jane's voice sounded muffled as she muttered something indistinguishable.

"Why didn't you call me last night?" Charlotte asked. "At least I would have been prepared when Longbourne walked in this morning."

"I was going to call you, but we didn't get in until nearly... What time is it now?"

"Never mind." Charlotte glanced up. "Oh great!"

John and Susan strolled into the office arm in arm.

"What is it?" Jane asked.

Charlotte cupped her hand over the receiver and whispered, "John just walked in with his fiancée."

The couple stopped at the door of John's office where Susan wrapped her arms around his neck and leaned into him.

"Hello? Hello?" A muted voice shouted at the other end of the phone line.

"Hold on a second," Charlotte whispered. "I want to hear something. It might be important." She turned her head and had to strain her neck, but her keen sense of hearing managed to pick up what was being said.

"So it's settled." John smiled. "I'll pick you up at five-thirty. We can talk about it at Chez Pierre tonight."

"Mmm, sounds good. I'll see you later then." Susan leaned in and brushed her lips against John's before she moved down to his jaw, her red lipstick leaving a blush of color every place her lips touched. Charlotte's stomach flipped.

Susan finally let go of John and headed toward the shipping dock with a spring to her step. As she sauntered by Charlotte's desk, swinging her hips, Susan wrinkled her nose in a mocking way. The scent of her cloying, cheap perfume filled the surrounding air as if she'd taken a bath in the flowery fragrance. Charlotte detected the slight stench of body odor mixed in. *How can he stand her?*

Charlotte put her mouth close to the telephone receiver. "John's taking Susan to dinner at Chez Pierre tonight." She sighed and leaned back in her chair. "Why is he wasting his time with her? I don't understand what they could possibly have in common. I wish I could be a fly on the wall of that cozy bistro. I'd love to hear what those two have to say to each other."

"If you're really interested," Jane said. "I think I know a way. I'll meet you at your place at five. Right now, I've got to get some sleep. Goodnight."

"Morning," Charlotte muttered as she put the receiver down carefully. *I hope Jane knows what she's doing.*

At six that evening, Charlotte parked her car a few doors down the street from the restaurant. Getting out, she smoothed her skirt. "I hate this dress. It makes me look like a flamingo."

Jane gave her a sideways glance. "Quit complaining. You look fine."

John's silver Corvette was parked right in front of the bistro. Charlotte stopped walking to check out the large, ugly crease in his back fender. When did that happen? It must have occurred early today, because she was positive it wasn't there yesterday when she left work. *Why am I still concerned about his things? It's not as if I'll ride in that gorgeous car again.* A sigh slid past her lips, and the futility of her actions brought a sudden tightness to her stomach.

"Why am I doing this? I'm an attractive and intelligent woman. I could have any man in town."

Jane shook her head. "Except the one you really want."

A determined growl burst from Charlotte's throat. Jane was right. If she wanted to know what John and Susan were up to, she'd have to go through with this deception.

"Let's go."

Jane glided into the bistro in a floor-length, olive green evening dress, covered with large, faded, red and yellow flowers. Her rented orange Orphan Annie wig was a snug fit, and some fake teeth gave her the appearance of someone much older.

Charlotte tugged at her short, pink, form-fitting, satin dress, trimmed in white feathers. And then she adjusted the long, black wig that swung loosely around her shoulders, smoothing the bangs behind a pair of dark glasses.

They walked further inside the restaurant, and Charlotte pulled her glasses down so she could look over the top. There were only a few patrons here tonight. This was atypical. The people in Eldridge Corners usually swarmed new restaurants. Especially one so conveniently located. Then again, it was still early.

Jane walked confidently up to the maitre d'. She turned and glanced at Charlotte, who was still standing near the door trying to spot John. "Hurry along, Petunia," Jane called in a high-pitched, British accent. Charlotte nearly burst into laughter but caught herself before anyone could see.

"Do you have a reservation?" The maitre d's French accent sounded far from genuine.

Jane surveyed the nearly empty room. "Do we need one?"

The man glanced sideways at the ladies and then up and down. He pursed his thick lips. "We have a limited number of tables. I cannot seat you without a reservation."

Jane narrowed her eyes in a tight stare. "Then we have one."

The disdain on the man's narrow face spoke volumes. "Under what name?"

"Gertie Antwhistle," Jane said.

Charlotte threw a hand over her lips to cover a smile.

The man checked his reservation book and then looked up. "Oh, yes. This way please."

He led them to a table in the center of the cozy, dimly lit, but nearly-empty room. A thin red candle in a star-shaped silver holder sat in the middle of a table that was so small, it was obviously for two.

"Is this the best you can do?" Jane asked in an icy tone. She impersonated a disappointed old lady so well, Charlotte almost believed she was one.

The man stood with his hands clasped in front of him. He appeared to be talking to no one in particular when he said, "Your reservation was made so late, this was the only table available."

"Young man," Jane said, discreetly handing the maitre d' a twenty-dollar bill. "Do you think we could have one of those corner booths instead? The one next to that lovely couple over there looks inviting."

"Come to think of it," he placed a slim finger on his narrow brow, "I believe that particular booth is available. If you will, follow me please."

The back-to-back booths lining the walls were waist high with red velvet seats. Separating the top of each booth, large green plants wound their variegated leaves around short, white, wood trellises to ensure diners the minimum amount of privacy. Jane wasted no time situating herself in the booth with her back against the seat opposite John's. Charlotte slipped into the seat across from her.

A hefty young man with a slim black mustache sidled up to their table and filled each of their delicate crystal goblets to the brim. A few moments later, another man approached. "My name is Alfonse. I will be your waiter this evening."

Jane's eyes shot to Charlotte. They smiled at each other as the waiter handed each lady a short wine list. After he walked away, Charlotte whispered, "Wasn't that our high school language teacher?"

Jane nodded. "Yeah, it's Mr. Durand all right. He must be working here for the summer. I loathed him. He made my life miserable in French class. I can't wait for the satisfaction of having him serve me dinner."

"He never gave me a hard time when I had him for Spanish."

"Of course not. You were always the teacher's pet."

Charlotte sighed, refusing to give in to Jane's petty jealousies. "Let's get back to why we're here."

Jane composed herself and leaned flush against the back of her seat to listen to John's conversation with Susan.

After a short time, Alfonse appeared at their table and handed each girl a hand-written menu.

"What wine would you like with dinner?"

Jane glared at him. "We haven't decided."

He turned and walked toward a pair of swinging doors. Charlotte gulped down half of her water and drummed her long, fake, red nails on the white linen tablecloth. "I can't stand it," she whispered. "What are they talking about?"

"Shhhh. It sounds like they're getting ready to leave."

As the couple stood, Charlotte slid the menu in front of her face and held it there until they passed. "We just got here. They couldn't possibly have eaten already."

"Maybe they came early, or they only had a drink."

"You don't suppose they recognized us, do you?"

Jane shrugged. "It's possible."

"Well, did you manage to hear anything?"

"Something about meeting at the courthouse on Saturday morning."

"The courthouse?" Charlotte felt the blood drain from her heart. "I didn't think it was open on Saturdays."

"Ours is open from eight to noon."

"I bet they're getting a marriage license." Charlotte slid her dark glasses to the end of her short nose and stared at Jane over the top.

Jane shook her head. "It didn't sound like that to me."

Charlotte slipped the glasses off and flung them on the table. "What else would they be doing at the courthouse? Maybe they have to get married in a rush because she's pregnant." *Please God, don't let it be that.*

"People don't get married for that reason anymore." Jane picked up her napkin and checked the delicate embroidery along the edge. "But I think you'd better do some investigating before you go off half-cocked and make a fool of yourself."

"All right, I will. But I happen to know what I'm talking about. You should see those two at the office." Charlotte wrinkled her nose. "They're absolutely disgusting."

Jane set the napkin in her lap. "Let him go, Charlotte. He's not worth the aggravation."

Charlotte glared at her. "I love John, and I'm not giving him up to... to her," she finally managed.

"Suit yourself. But you're going to an awful lot of trouble for a lost cause." Jane scanned her menu, dismissing the subject like she always did. "Oooh, this Cassoulet looks delicious."

Chapter Thirteen

Charlotte walked in the front door of Longbourne and Payne at the stroke of eight, but she couldn't shake her grogginess this morning. She and Jane had been up late talking. Add to that the heavy French dinner with a large serving of wine, and she was surprised she wasn't late for work. *I'd better grab a cup of coffee and something to eat before I fall asleep at my desk.*

She walked into the lunchroom and dropped her spare change into the vending machine. The chocolate chip cookies looked good, or at least they looked better than the other selections. *I think I saw some of these same breakfast cakes here last week.* Of course she couldn't be sure they were the same ones, but they didn't appear tempting enough to take a chance.

As she bent to retrieve the cookies, someone shoved her from behind. It was a common enough occurrence. She had been bumped many times in the eight years she'd worked there, so Charlotte continued to retrieve her snack.

"I'm sorry," an oddly familiar, feminine voice said. "I didn't see you there."

Glancing up, Charlotte found herself looking at the out of work, redheaded actress she had seen a few days ago. "It's all right," she stammered.

Forgetting both her cookies and coffee, Charlotte made a quick exit from the lunchroom and ran to Ruth's office. She shook her finger in the direction of the lunchroom. "What's that redhead doing here?"

Ruth peered at Charlotte over the top of her wire rims. "Who?"

"The red-haired woman getting coffee in the lunchroom."

"Oh, that's Glenda West." Ruth turned toward her computer and typed in some information. "According to her personnel file, your boss hired her to work in the shipping office. She started two days ago."

Surprised, Charlotte said, "But I thought her name was... um, I mean, I wonder why John didn't tell me he hired someone. And why haven't I seen her here before this morning?"

Ruth swiveled her chair around to face Charlotte, her eyes narrowing in exasperation. "How often do you go to the shipping docks?"

"I see your point. I really should get away from my desk more." As she dallied in front of Ruth's desk, Charlotte contemplated whether to tell her what Glenda West's real name was. *But it might be better if I wait until I know more about this woman.* "Thanks for answering the question Ruth."

Walking toward the hall, she ducked in the lunchroom to retrieve her forgotten cookies and coffee. Then she meandered back to her desk, stopping occasionally to talk with her coworkers about John's upcoming nuptials and the new employee in the shipping department. No one knew much about either.

Finally at her desk, Charlotte sat in front of her computer and sipped coffee while she thought of her game plan. The best thing to do was to go down to the shipping docks to see what she could find out about this new hire. But first, she'd rifle through John's desk before he came in, just in case there was some gem of information she could dig up about why he'd hired this woman. He'd never done anything like this without talking to her first. Since he'd gotten engaged, everything had changed. He changed. It broke her heart that every conversation they had ended in harsh words.

John's office was as neat as usual, and there was really nothing she could garner without digging through his locked drawers. The only thing on his desk was the large calendar filled with various notes. In fact, every day's square was filled up with reminders for meetings with business associates, meetings with Susan, and any big deadlines that were coming up. Just the usual notes you would expect to see. On Friday's square, he had scribbled in something, but she wasn't sure what it said—sometimes John's handwriting was so bad, even he couldn't read it. On Saturday's square, he'd written "Susan at courthouse."

Finding nothing else useful, Charlotte was about to scurry back to her cubicle, when she recognized John's voice just outside his open door. She ducked behind it.

"Is everything in place for tomorrow night?" John asked.

A female voice that sounded vaguely familiar answered. "All set."

"Good." John hesitated, and then he said, "You know your part, and Susan knows exactly what she needs to do."

"Until tomorrow night then," the female voice confirmed. "I'll text you when we're ready."

Charlotte stiffened. After a short silence, John walked into his office and put his hand on the door to close it. Then he saw her. He flinched, and his eyes flashed. "What are you doing in here?"

His voice was harsh, and she swallowed hard. "I, um. I just came in to look for a pen."

The muscles in his jaw worked as he clenched it. Not waiting around to be reprimanded, she turned and marched out. On the way back to her cubicle, Charlotte checked the office. The only person walking around was the redhead who was now heading toward the back hallway. Why would he be talking to that woman in such a confidential manner?

Charlotte figured she didn't have anything to lose, so she stormed back into John's office. He was hunched over some official-looking documents. He glanced up and flipped the papers over.

"Who's the redhead?" Charlotte demanded.

John cleared his throat. "I hired Glenda to work for me in the shipping department."

"Work for you?" Charlotte huffed. "In what capacity?"

John squared his broad shoulders. "Not that it's any of your business, but I'm training her for Susan's job, so she can quit as soon as we're married." He tapped his pen on the desk, each tap of the pen sounding his irritation "Why are you getting so upset?"

"I'm not upset." Charlotte took her voice down a few decibels. "I only want to know why you didn't discuss it with me first."

"I don't need your approval. I can hire anyone I want."

"It's not only that." Charlotte wrung her hands, unsure if she should continue, "I couldn't help but overhear your conversation with her, and I want to know what kind of covert operation you have planned for tomorrow night on the shipping dock."

John laughed. "Covert operation?"

Charlotte breathed a sigh of indignation, hurt spreading into a timid smile as she realized what she had just said. *I'm spending too much time with Jane.*

John's laugh helped to relieve the tension that was stretched between them like a taut clothesline. He let out a long, slow breath and ran a tentative finger across his forehead.

"There's nothing covert about doing inventory," he said. "That's what's happening on the shipping dock tomorrow night."

Charlotte crossed her arms, the tension returning. She didn't know why, but she was positive he was lying to her. "We never do inventory on the freight dock. Why are we suddenly doing it now?"

"Some customers complained they were short on their deliveries." He shook his head in a gesture of exasperation. "You really have a crazy, overindulgent imagination. Now, go back to your desk, and finish the annual report."

His explanation sounds feasible, so why don't I believe him? The conversation he had with the redhead stuck in her craw. There was more to all this than he cared to admit. She kept her arms folded firmly in front of her and didn't move. *He's not going to dismiss me that easily.*

"You'd better get started." John's voice became serious. "If you want to keep your job, that report better be on my desk by the close of business tomorrow. Oh, and there's one more thing." He leaned back as Charlotte shifted her stance. "You should never wear a pink dress with feathers. It makes you look like a flamingo."

The restriction of being tied to her desk, working on the annual report all day, was more than she could take. She pushed her chair back and stared at the open door of John's office. When would she find time to snoop around the shipping area? She had to get down there to find out about this new hire and to check if Susan might have had any motive to murder Carlton Witherspoon.

She picked up the first few printed pages she'd already completed and flung them down on her desk. "Why doesn't he do his own damn report?" The anger in her voice made the words come out slightly louder than she intended.

"What did you say, Charlotte?" John's voice echoed through the office.

This guy must have superhuman hearing. Snatching up the telephone receiver, she placed her hand over the mouthpiece. "I'm on the phone."

As John stepped out of his office, she suddenly got an idea, and spoke into the buzz of the receiver.

"I don't understand your figures. I'll be there in a few minutes." She set the receiver down and swiveled her chair around to face him.

John stood squarely in front of her. "Where do you think you're going?"

"Down to shipping."

"I need you here to work on that report, not gallivanting all over the dock area."

Charlotte picked up a pen and a notepad from her desk. "But they're having a problem. I mean, I'm having a problem with the report."

Her eyes met his overly intense gaze as she stood.

"What kind of problem?" he asked.

She didn't falter, even though she was sure her knees would give out at any moment. "I, um, don't understand their figures. I want to check them out in person."

"Why go all the way down there," he lifted the telephone receiver and handed it to her, "When you can make a phone call?"

Taking the receiver, she gave him a withering look as she placed it back on its cradle. "I already did that."

John randomly rummaged through the papers on Charlotte's desk. "If you tell me what figures you're talking about, I'll have someone check them out for you."

With her eyes wide and her lips pressed tight against her teeth, Charlotte slammed her hand on his. And for a single, pulse-pounding moment, a tingle of excitement ran down her spine as his fingers tenderly trailed through hers.

"I'd prefer to do things my own way," she said. "*If* you don't mind."

John leaned over her desk. The faint lines at the corners of his troubled eyes were defined with tension. "But I do mind. I don't want you down there. You could get hurt."

She glared at him. Her tone was terse as all the frustration of being lied to by him bubbled to the surface. "My first job here was in the shipping department, so I'm familiar with the docks. I can take care of myself. Besides, if you want your precious report on time, you need to let me get it done—my way."

John's face hardened as he shoved his hands in his pockets. "Fine. Go down if you have to."

Damn right I will. She left her boss standing at her cubicle as she walked away. But she didn't have to look back at him to know he was watching her with his jaw clenched. Her knees shook, and she ignored the tears burning in her eyes at her false display of bravado.

Charlotte made her way down the long hallway and opened the door to the dock area. Crates of various shapes and sizes jammed every available space. They must have unloaded all ten trailers that were in the dockyard the night before.

She decided to hang around for a while and talk to some of the forklift drivers. Of all the drivers she knew, Josh Granger was the most talkative. Whenever she wanted to hear the latest gossip about the people at Longbourne and Payne, she could contact him, and he would tell her everything and then some.

Charlotte didn't spot Josh, but she did see Susan walking up from the staging area. She turned a sharp corner to avoid the girl and found herself behind two large crates, where the familiar aroma of coffee delighted her. She attempted to read the words printed on the crates when a god-like voice filled the surrounding air. "Can I help you?"

Charlotte's heart leapt to her throat as Susan's father appeared out of nowhere. Mr. Blanchard, long-time shipping manager who was so cruel to the employees who worked under him that it nearly gave her an ulcer, now towered over her, his skinny nose bent in two directions, as if he'd once been a prize-fighter. Two huge green eyeballs stared down at her. Perspiration trickled along the side of his face, ruddy from the summer heat. From the way his fat lips curved downward into a miserable frown, he was not happy to see her there.

"No, Mr. Blanchard." She tried to sound casual. "I was just going to the shipping office to get some figures."

"And why did you stop here?"

His voice had a note of suspicion that worried her. "Because the coffee smelled so good."

"You'd better be on your way. You should know the dock is a dangerous place to hang around."

She swallowed hard. "I'm going. But first, can I ask you a question?"

"What is it?" His lips twitched a quick smile.

Charlotte's insides twisted as she looked up at this great hulk of a man, remembering all the times he'd reported her for stupid, petty things. "Have you heard any details about the, um, upcoming nuptials?"

"Nuptials?" He sounded confused.

"Your daughter's wedding?"

The man wiped the sweat from his top lip with the back of a dirt-encrusted hand. "You mean about her marrying that dandy from the front office? What about it?"

Charlotte moved her gaze to the wall. The sight of him wiping his lips with a filthy hand disgusted her. "Do you know when the wedding is going to be?"

His eyes bulged with skepticism. "Why do you want to know?"

"I want to give them a gift."

Tim Blanchard caressed his unshaven chin. "Say, ain't you the one who's been giving my daughter grief about her engagement?"

"Grief?" She'd never said anything to Susan. But then, Susan was a great one for spreading rumors, especially about people she didn't like. Charlotte checked her watch. "No, that wasn't me," she answered quickly. "Oh, look at the time. I've got to be on my way. It was nice chatting with you."

She fled toward the shipping office while Blanchard watched, but as soon as he turned away, she ducked behind some tall boxes stacked three high near the aisle. *Whew, that was close.* She breathed a sigh of relief, but her heart still raced as the boxes in front of her rose upward at a fast pace, higher and higher until the forklift driver's face was visible.

"Hi, Charlotte. I haven't seen you in a while."

Finally, a friendly face. "I was looking for you, Josh," she said. "We haven't talked in a long time, and I was wondering about the latest gossip."

The forklift driver set his load on the floor near the overhead door, then he drove the jeep alongside Charlotte as she made her way along the dock area.

"There's always gossip around these days," he said, his eyes full of mischief. "I heard Longbourne's been arrested for killing Witherspoon. Never trusted that man—Longbourne that is, there's many that still think he killed his first wife."

"But that was ruled an accident."

"Accident my foot. He murdered his first wife, and he murdered Witherspoon. And I'll tell you something else. Blanchard's been acting real nervous ever since Witherspoon's murder. Kinda squirrely. I don't trust him, either. Some say he's nervous 'cause his daughter's engaged to your boss. Blanchard don't like him much."

"Have you heard a wedding date mentioned?"

"Naw, everything about that wedding is hush-hush. You'd think it was some kinda secret or something."

Oh good. A sense of temporary relief washed over her heart. "Any juicy gossip about the new hire?"

"You mean the good-lookin' redhead?"

Charlotte nodded, just like Josh to be hitting up the new girl.

"She's something, all right. I don't know what, though. She got close to Susan real fast. Supposed to be taking over her job, I hear. Looks like Susan's old man's got a crush on her too. She really plays up to him, and he treats her real nice. I can't believe she likes that buzzard-faced cretin. She must be up to somethin', and I got a feelin' it's no good."

Maybe she's just trying to get on Blanchard's good side. But I don't think he has one, so there has to be more to this new hire. That conversation the redhead had with John nagged at her.

"Thanks for the information." Charlotte smiled. "I'm going to the shipping office to see what I can dig up. You'd better get back to work before Blanchard catches us talking."

"Yeah, he can be a real bastard."

"You don't have to tell me."

The forklift driver headed back toward the dock area, and she slipped into the shipping office. The cool air inside the large square room was refreshing after being in the sweltering heat out on the dock. She glanced over the odd variety of old furniture, mostly castoffs from the front office that filled the empty spaces, giving the stark white room an eclectic feeling.

Susan's desk was the closest. While rummaging through the stacks of scattered papers, she picked up one of a dozen empty pop cans and tossed it into a nearby wastebasket, uncovering a small wedding picture in a silver frame. It was Susan's parents. She'd never met Susan's mother, but she recognized Mr. Blanchard. His wife looked a great deal younger, and a little on the thin, homely side, unlike her daughter. Charlotte heard through the office grapevine that Carolyn Blanchard had a nervous breakdown twenty-three years earlier, right after Susan was born, and hadn't been seen since.

She continued to search through the mess. "Aha! Here's a sticky note from John." It was only business. Another note from John. More business. "Where does she keep her personal stuff?" She slid a side drawer open. Files. She slid the drawer on the other side open, more files. *This is beginning to look hopeless.*

Charlotte sat down at a rickety wooden desk across from Susan's gray metal one. After checking the side drawers, she came to the conclusion there wasn't much there either. She heaved herself out of the chair to move to the desk behind her, but the loose button on her jacket caught on the curved wooden handle of the middle drawer. As she tugged at it, the button popped off and rolled under the desk. Charlotte dove after it, and when she tried to stand up again, she banged her head on the drawer. "This is not my day."

She slammed her hand against the bottom of the drawer. "Stupid!" The entire drawer collapsed and landed in her lap. "Oh, great! Blanchard will kill me if I've broken one of his desks. How am I going to explain this?"

Charlotte tried to fix the drawer, but something was preventing her from sliding it back in its slot. She felt around and discovered a slim notebook jammed in the side. When she pulled it out, the drawer slid back in easily.

The office door opened, ushering in the scuffle of heavy, steel-toed shoes.

"And another thing," Mr. Blanchard said, "I don't trust that guy you're engaged to."

"I'm marrying John, no matter what you say," Susan answered.

"I'm telling you, he's gonna be trouble."

Susan snorted. "Don't worry, Dad. Once we're married, he'll do whatever I say, or I'll make his life a living hell. I know just how to treat him so he'll toe the line."

Charlotte caught her breath. No matter what he'd done to her, John didn't deserve this. His life would be ruined if he married Susan. But how could she convince him he'd be making a terrible mistake without sounding like a jealous shrew?

While she wanted to stick around to hear more, they were bound to discover her soon. She slid the notebook into her pocket, cleared her throat, and slowly rose to her feet.

Their faces were filled with stunned anger. "What are you doing snooping around down here?" Extreme irritation was evident in Tim Blanchard's tone.

"I'm not snooping. I told you I was coming here to check your figures for the Annual Report."

Blanchard's voice became ugly, "Did you think you would find them under my friggin' desk?"

"I just bent over to pick up this pen." Charlotte produced one of the pens from the fallen desk drawer.

"The information is all in the files."

"I know," Charlotte said. "I've already been through the files and found the information I need. Now, if you'll excuse me," she side-stepped the cretin, who was blocking her path. "I've got to get back to the front office."

She walked toward the door, ignoring Susan's glare. She wanted to confront her about John in the worst way, but stopped herself before she said something she might regret. Instead, she slammed the office door with all the force her anger could muster.

Chapter Fourteen

Finally home from work, Charlotte turned on the window air-conditioner to get a cool breeze flowing through her stuffy apartment. "What a horrible day. I'm so glad it's over."

She flipped off her shoes just as the telephone rang. "Hello," she breathed into the receiver.

"Charlotte, dear, you're home. Good." Her mother's voice sounded cheerful this evening. "Why don't you come down for dinner? I'm making your favorite—fried chicken."

It wasn't her favorite, but she could never convince her mother of that. Not being in the mood to cook, or even argue the point, she said, "Great. I'll be right down."

As she walked through the front door of her parents' house, the smell of chicken frying brought back memories of being sixteen again and coming home from cheerleading practice. It was funny how a familiar smell could take her back to a time when life was so simple. Back then, her only worry was passing the next algebra test.

"Charlotte, is that you?" Mrs. Ross called to her from the kitchen.

"Yes, Mom."

"Go into the living room. We have a guest for dinner."

Charlotte walked into the large, open living room bedecked in French Provincial décor, and spotted the back of a young man in uniform. "Oh no." he groaned. "Not tonight."

Todd Shlagg stood in front of the baby grand piano looking at the numerous family pictures grouped on top. He turned around. "Hi, Char."

"Todd." Charlotte gave him a weak smile. "Jane told me you were on duty tonight. Why are you here?"

"Your mother invited me for dinner, and I couldn't refuse. You know how persuasive she can be."

"I know." Charlotte sank down on the edge of the sofa. "Then you're only on a dinner break?"

Todd nodded.

"Oh, good." Charlotte dropped her shoulders. "So you'll have an excuse to leave as soon as dinner's over."

"I beg your pardon?"

Charlotte put a hand to her lips to cover a smile. She gave Todd her best sympathetic look. "Sorry, I didn't mean to sound insulting. You know you're always welcome here. But do you have any idea why my mother invited you for dinner?"

"Because she thought I might be hungry?"

Charlotte sighed. "Well that, and she's trying to fix us up."

"You mean, you and me?"

" Of course I mean you and me."

Todd's voice boomed. "Are you sure?"

"Please, keep your voice down." Charlotte walked over to the piano and whispered in his ear. "I'm sure. I've been through this dozens of times."

Todd inched away from her and smiled. "It's not that I don't like you, Char, I do, but you know how it is with Jane and me. I've had this thing for her ever since we were sophomores in high school, when she rescued me from drowning in the country club swimming pool."

"Yes, I know." Charlotte held her hands up, palms facing Todd. "And trust me. I'm not interested in you."

Almost laughing at the incredulous look on Todd's face, Charlotte quickly said, "Sorry. Didn't mean to hurt your feelings again. Just eat your dinner, and hopefully we'll get through this meal with as little embarrassment as possible. If she tries to fix us up, turn things around."

Todd nodded knowingly. "I understand."

"Dinner's ready," Mrs. Ross called from the doorway.

Walking into the dining room with Todd, Charlotte waited as her mother placed a large, earthenware bowl filled with fried chicken on the table. Her husband came from the kitchen, carrying a matching bowl containing steaming ears of corn on the cob.

Mrs. Ross glanced at her daughter. "Will you get the potatoes, dear?"

Charlotte went to the kitchen, picked up the tureen of mashed potatoes and made her way back to the dining room. Her dad came up alongside her, holding the butter dish. "Dad," she whispered. "Why is mom doing this again?"

"Because she loves you and she wants you to be happy."

Mrs. Ross sat in the chair across from her husband as Charlotte set the bowl on the table and took the seat next to Todd.

"Don't you think Officer Shlagg looks handsome in his uniform, Charlotte?"

"Yes, you look, um, very official in your uniform. Mashed potatoes?"

"Sure." Todd helped himself to a large dollop from the tureen. "These look great, Mrs. Ross."

"Thank you." She smiled. "Isn't he sweet, Charlotte?"

"Yeah," Todd continued, "They're nice and lumpy. The kind you can really sink your teeth into. It's just the way they serve 'em at Shorty's Diner."

Mrs. Ross passed him the fried chicken. "Do you eat at Shorty's a lot?"

After grabbing two legs from the bowl, Todd answered, "A couple of times a week. They have great food."

Mrs. Ross looked at her daughter. "Charlotte eats there too. Don't you, dear?"

"Occasionally." Charlotte looked away so her mother couldn't see her eyes rolling.

"You know, you two have so much in common. You've both lived your entire lives in this town, and you attended the same schools. You have the same friends."

Todd took a bite of chicken and wiped his chin. "This chicken is just the way I like it."

Maggie Ross touched her hair randomly. "It is?"

"Yeah, real greasy. My mom never fries chicken when I come over for dinner. She bakes it. Says it's better for me, but I think it's too dry."

With a sudden blush to her cheeks, Mrs. Ross said, "My chicken is not *greasy,* young man. And if you think..."

"How's the murder investigation coming along, Todd?" Charlotte's dad interrupted in a voice loud enough to drown out his wife's comment. He shot a sharp, no-nonsense glare at her. She took a deep breath and settled back in her chair.

Todd swallowed a mouthful of food. "It's a work in progress, Mr. Ross."

"Find out anything new?"

"I can't discuss the investigation."

"Has anyone proven a relationship to Carlton Witherspoon, yet?" Charlotte asked.

Todd put his chicken leg down and wiped the grease from each finger with a napkin. "A lot of people put in fake claims at the lawyer's office, but he's yet to find any real proof of a relationship."

"Anyone in town might be related to Carlton Witherspoon." Mrs. Ross exchanged glances with her daughter. "Even that girlfriend of yours."

"Jane?" Todd and Charlotte asked simultaneously.

Mrs. Ross raised an eyebrow. "It's a well-known fact that Carlton was quite the playboy. Every young woman in town was after him."

How would her mother feel if that rumor was about her? "If every woman in town was after Carlton, does that include you?" Charlotte asked.

Mrs. Ross's face went red. "You know your father and I were high school sweethearts." She smiled at her husband. "Oscar is the only man I ever wanted."

Mr. Ross nodded his agreement.

"Speaking of relationships," Charlotte said, in a quick change of subject. "How well do you know the Blanchards?"

"Not what you would call well." Mrs. Ross plopped more potatoes on her plate. "Why do you ask?"

"I saw their wedding picture at the office today and was wondering about them."

"I remember when Carolyn worked for Mr. Witherspoon. They were seen around town quite a bit together. She seemed like a very nice young woman. She was engaged to Carlton for a while, but before anyone knew it, she turned around and married Tim Blanchard. No one could figure that out. It came as a complete surprise. Far be it from me to spread gossip, so I'm not going to say another word about it. Except that there were rumors at the time that Carlton paid Blanchard to take her off his hands."

"Really, Maggie," Mr. Ross said. "Nothing was ever proven."

Mrs. Ross sighed in feigned despair. "I didn't think Carolyn even knew Tim Blanchard, much less had dated him. And speaking of dating, I don't believe you have a date for the Country Club's annual Midsummer Night's Dance this Saturday." She smiled at Charlotte. "Do you, dear?"

Charlotte was amazed at how her mother segued from the Blanchards to the country club dance. But it wasn't the first time she was baffled by her mother's thought processes.

"No, I don't."

Mrs. Ross sent a predatory glance in Todd's direction. "Are you going to the dance?"

"As much as I'd like to go, I can't." Todd scooped a heaping pile of mashed potatoes and another piece of chicken onto his plate. "I'm on duty Saturday night."

Mrs. Ross addressed her husband. "Oscar, couldn't you talk to the Chief and get Todd the night off? After all, Joe is your friend and golf partner."

Mr. Ross winked at his daughter. "Sure, I'll have a talk with him later."

"Thanks, Mr. Ross," Todd said. "Now I can take Jane to the dance. She was kinda disappointed when I had to decline. I really appreciate this. If there's ever anything I can do for you, let me know."

Charlotte flashed a smug smile at her parents and took a big bite out of the ear of corn she had just buttered.

"I will," Mr. Ross told Todd, with a resolute glance at his wife.

Mrs. Ross stood up and asked if anyone wanted dessert, but before anyone could answer, the doorbell rang.

"I'll get it," Mr. Ross said, as his wife headed for the kitchen.

Todd turned to Charlotte. "How'd I do?"

"You were great. Thanks."

Matt Bridgewater burst into the dining room. "I was driving by and saw your cruiser parked in the driveway. The Chief's hopping mad. I just wanted to give you a heads up."

Todd rose to his feet. "About what?"

The old policeman inhaled deeply and let his breath out in one big whoosh. "The murder weapon is missing. The Chief thinks Jane took it. She's been spending a lot of time at the station lately, sticking her nose into things she shouldn't."

"So Jane's your only suspect?" Charlotte asked.

Matt shrugged.

Charlotte dropped her jaw and glanced at Todd. "Everyone knows security is pretty lax at the station house. Anyone could have strolled in and walked off with the dagger."

"What's going on?" Mrs. Ross came out of the kitchen carrying a brown rattan tray, holding four small bowls of cherry vanilla ice cream. "Oh, Matt. Would you like something to eat?"

"No thanks. I don't have time." Officer Bridgewater turned to walk out the door.

"I'd better have a talk with the Chief and straighten this whole thing out," Todd said. "Thanks for the great dinner, Mrs. Ross. Sorry I have to miss dessert."

Mrs. Ross put the tray down on the table and set a bowl of ice cream in front of her daughter. "Eat your ice cream before it melts, dear. It's cherry-vanilla, your favorite."

Charlotte usually enjoyed eating ice cream, but at that moment, she couldn't force down another bite. *What reason would Jane have to steal a crucial piece of evidence? Unless she wanted it as a souvenir of the crime or to replace the dagger that had been stolen.*

"I'm not in the mood for dessert tonight, Mom. I've got a headache. I think I'll go to my apartment and lie down."

"Well, all right." Her mother sounded crushed. "You can take your ice cream with you."

Charlotte shoved the bowl away. "No thanks."

"Oscar, just look at your daughter. She barely touched her dinner. An ear of corn, a couple of bites of chicken, and now she won't even eat dessert."

Charlotte's dad put a hand on her shoulder and whispered, "For my sake, take the ice cream."

She eyed her mother and, in voluntary defeat, picked up the bowl. "Okay, if it makes you happy, I'll take it."

When Charlotte reached her apartment, she put the bowl of ice cream into the freezer. *I'd better tell Jane what the police are thinking.* She pulled her cell phone out and punched in Jane's number. *If she gets arrested and finds out I didn't warn her, I'll be hearing about it for the rest of my life.*

Chapter Fifteen

At eight that evening, Charlotte rushed into the lobby of the Eldridge Inn and was met by Sophie Eldridge's lively hazel eyes. The few seconds it took to walk to the reception desk had Sophie's round, friendly face widening into a welcoming smile. "Hello, Charlotte."

"Hi, have you seen Jane today? I've been trying to call her for the past hour, but I only get her voicemail. I get no reply with a text either."

"I saw her walk out the door a few hours ago. Maybe she left without her phone." Sophie picked up a pen and began writing in a large, square book lying open on the desk.

Charlotte paced back and forth in front of Sophie. "Did she tell you where she was going?"

Sophie looked up and raised her eyebrows. "Jane never tells me anything. She barely acknowledges my existence."

Drumming her fingers impatiently against the side of the desk, Charlotte scanned the room and glanced out the front window.

"You seem stressed." Sophie sounded genuinely concerned. "What's the matter?"

Charlotte checked the door. "Nothing," she said, trying to play down the anxiety tightening her lungs.

Sophie came around the desk and put her husky arm around Charlotte's shoulder. "Why don't you come into the office with me and have a cup of coffee while you wait for Jane? You can keep me company. The desk is dead tonight, and I'm so bored, I'm about to fall asleep."

Sophie ushered an uneasy Charlotte into a small room off the lobby. In the middle of the room was an antique oak desk that had seen its share of abuse. Sitting on the desk was a large silver tray holding a white carafe and several cups from the Tea Room. Assorted pastries were arranged on a dinner plate next to the tray.

Charlotte sat down in one of the two brown suede chairs situated in front of the desk. Sophie selected a cream puff from the tray. "Have a pastry."

She didn't really have much of an appetite, but watching Sophie bite into a large, cream puff, the white cream pressing out of the sides, she changed her mind. "Well, I guess I can force myself to eat one mini éclair." She picked up the delicate pastry and bit into it.

"I can never resist the pastries from Auntie Jean's Bakery," Sophie said. "I think I'll have another." She poured more coffee into her cup, and selected a slice of cheesecake. "Now, what's all this about Jane?"

Charlotte opened her mouth to speak, but Sophie interrupted. "She's a strange one, writing mysteries and all. I haven't seen her first novel in the bookstore yet. When does it come out? Never mind, I suppose I'll see it soon. I may just go online and pre-order it. It's so exciting having our very own celebrity author. Everyone's dying to read it. She should write another one based on the Witherspoon murder."

"She might," Charlotte said vaguely, grateful to get a word in. "If she can solve, I mean, if the case ever gets solved."

"Oh, I think it will, eventually." Sophie poised a dainty finger in the air. "Ask her to interview *me* sometime. I could give her a lot of interesting background on Carlton Witherspoon."

Charlotte stiffened in her chair and leaned forward. She fought to keep the interest off her face but was sure it was evident. "Like what?"

Sophie closed her eyes and pressed a finger to her rosebud lips as if she was trying to choose the right words, or making up her mind about whether to tell anything at all. After a short silence, she said, "Did you know that Witherspoon was quite the playboy in his day?"

"So I've heard." Charlotte was unimpressed. It seemed as though everyone in town knew that about him.

"My own mother was once engaged to him."

"Wasn't he a little old for her?" Charlotte tried to keep the boredom out of her voice, but it was the same old information she had been privy to already.

Sophie cocked her head to one side. "The words, 'fabulously wealthy' have an attractive and hypnotic quality to them, and suddenly age doesn't matter. After a few months of being engaged, I suppose he got tired of my mother and dumped her for someone even younger, Carolyn Mays, who you know as Carolyn Blanchard, Susan's mother. She was his companion or his maid or something."

"I'm pretty sure she was his secretary." Charlotte had garnered that from his autobiography.

"From what I understand, my mother was devastated by the breakup and she married my father on the rebound. There were rumors at the time of my sister's birth that Vivie wasn't really an Eldridge. Sophie put a self-conscious hand over her mouth and spoke through her fingers. "Please don't tell her I told you. She'd be furious."

"She could be in for a fortune," Charlotte said. "If she can prove she's a blood relative."

Sophie took her hand from her mouth and waved Charlotte's words away. "She's got too much pride for that." She giggled. "But I may contact the lawyer in spite of her objections. Come to think of it, there could be a lot of little Carlton's running around town. I often thought Susan looked a lot like Carlton's mother. Not as beautiful, of course.

"Carolyn quit working for Carlton kind of abruptly and then, before anyone knew it, she was married to Blanchard with a baby on the way. I know there was a lot of talk, especially when she went funny and had her breakdown. You don't suppose…" Sophie's voice trailed off, eyes dancing in delight.

Charlotte had been focused on Sophie's collar since she came in, but she didn't know how to broach the subject, so she decided to jump in before Sophie began speaking again. "That's an interesting pin you're wearing." She strained to get a better look.

Sophie touched the collar of her yellow linen blouse. "It's an old pin my grandmother gave to Vivie. I saw it in her jewelry box. I've always thought it was charming, but I never had enough nerve to borrow it before. This morning I said, 'What the heck!' After all, what can she do to me? It's just a worthless piece of costume jewelry."

"It certainly is different. I'd like to see it, if you don't mind."

"Oh, sure." Sophie took the small pin from her collar. Charlotte stood up and leaned over the desk to get a closer look. "Interesting initials, S.O.T. Do you know what they stand for?"

Sophie blinked and turned her head as if the answer might be written on the wall. "I don't remember. Some sort of society my grandfather belonged to a long time ago."

Charlotte squinted. "What's in the middle of the letter 'O'?"

"It's supposed to be a poppy, but the years have worn it away."

"I see it now." Charlotte handed the pin back to Sophie just as Vivie walked into the room. She glanced at Charlotte and glared at her sister. "What's she doing in my office? You know this room is off-limits to everyone, but us."

Sophie's face drained of all color. She shook and appeared as if she was going to faint. "S-s-she... I..., w-w-we—" she stuttered.

Vivie had always been overly protective of her younger sister. But even more so after Sophie's husband had cleaned out their bank account and run off with one of the maids.

"Sophie was kind enough to ask me in for coffee." Charlotte checked her watch and stood. "I have to go now. It was nice to see you again, Vivie."

Vivie's glare knifed through Charlotte's back, as Sophie blurted, "Goodbye, Charlotte."

Charlotte closed the office door behind her as a loud argument between the sisters ensued. Did Vivie think she was trying to get too friendly with Sophie? Or that Sophie might spill some family secrets? Maybe she already had.

Charlotte went to the lobby, and she hastily scribbled, "Call me on my cell, it's important," on a piece of stationery. Then she went to Jane's room and slid it under the door. She shoved the pen back into her purse and was halfway down the hall when Jane's door opened.

"What's so important?"

Charlotte swung around. "Where have you *been*?" She walked into the room. "I've been trying to call you all evening."

"I just got back from a murder mystery revival at the Orpheum Theater," Jane explained as she closed the door. "It's their last one. They're closing their doors at the end of the week. A five-screen movie complex is opening in the new mall on Friday."

Jane sat down on the edge of the bed with a faraway look in her eyes. "We had some great times in that old movie house, didn't we?"

"Yeah, great times." Charlotte stared out the window. The Orpheum held a lot of memories for her. "I remember the wonderful smell of popcorn when you first walked into the lobby, making out in the balcony with my latest boyfriend, stuffing ourselves with overpriced candy, getting sick on the old hotdogs they served, pulling chewing gum off the bottom of our shoes." Charlotte closed her eyes and rubbed her temples. "Listen, Jane, I'd love to get nostalgic with you, but we've got more important things to talk about right now."

"Well, I've got something important, too."

"Me first." Charlotte held her hand up in protest and quickly described the announcement made at dinner and her discussion with Sophie.

"Sounds like you've had quite an evening. I'll get all the information I can about Carlton Witherspoon from Sophie tomorrow morning. If she's had a fight with her sister, she'll be willing to tell me everything." Jane tapped a finger on her cheek. "So, she likes pastries, does she? I think Auntie Jean's Bakery opens at six." Jane checked her phone.

"Please don't try to bribe her with sweets," Charlotte said. She grabbed Jane's phone and dropped it on the desk. "You'd better think about what you're going to tell the chief."

"I'm surprised Todd didn't try call me as soon as he left your parents' house. Oh well, I'll see him later. He'll tell me everything, then." Curiosity crept into her voice as she said, "I wonder why the chief thinks I stole that dagger. I had a good look at it, and it's not mine."

"You know Todd will do his best to defend you."

"What was he doing at your parents' house, anyway?"

"My mother invited him for dinner."

"Your mother? Oh, no." Humor twinkled in her eyes. "Not one of those *fix up* dinners?" She put her hands up to her cheeks and laughed. "You and Todd? How ridiculous."

"Isn't it?" Charlotte turned her smile into a frown. "Wait a minute. Why is it so ridiculous?"

Jane wiped the tears from her eyes. "You know Todd is my 'ace-in-the-hole.' Right now, I still have a lot of living to do, but I can always count on him to be here for me. He's such a comfort to have around. At least, until someone better comes along."

"So, every time you get your heart broken, you come home to Todd, and he gives your ego a giant boost."

Jane nodded. "Actually, a better description of Todd would be, a friend with many benefits."

"Then you really shouldn't lead him on. One of these days, he's going to get tired of playing your little game."

"Don't worry about Todd. We've been playing the same game for a long time, and he knows the score." She nudged Charlotte. "Now it's my turn to tell you my news. I spent the entire afternoon with Range Warton."

Charlotte gave her a pensive look, as past memories came flooding back. "The owner of the Orpheum Theater? Why would you want to spend time with that dirty old man?"

"Because he knows a lot. He said there are some really old records concerning this town down in his basement file cabinet."

Charlotte glared at Jane. "No!" she said. "Don't ask me to go down to the theater's basement with Range Warton to search through those files, because I won't do it."

"I know you have a problem with him."

"Damn right, I do. He's not cornering me in that basement again. The man tried to take advantage just because I was working for him."

"I know. And I still think you should have pressed charges at the time. But you don't have to worry." Jane sat down on the bed. "I was already in the basement, alone, and the only records I found down there were some old seventy-eight

RPMs. But..." She reached into her purse and pulled out three black business cards with a flourish of her wrist. "Look what else I found?"

"Did you ask him about them?"

"Yeah. But he couldn't tell me anymore than your dad told you. He thinks his cousin may have been part of the Triumvirate, because he died of a drug overdose around that time."

A loud knock on the room door made Charlotte jump. "Who can that be?"

Jane leaned in close to the door and asked in a faint voice, "Who is it?"

"Open the door. It's me."

"Todd," the two girls whispered simultaneously.

"He's too early," Jane said. "He's not supposed to be off duty until nine."

Uneasiness gripped Charlotte's stomach. "I don't want him to find out I came to warn you." She scanned the room for a place to hide. Jane grabbed her arm and pushed her in the direction of the bathroom. "Go in there. I'll see what he wants."

Charlotte pulled the bathroom door closed behind her and then opened it a crack to peek, as Jane let Todd in.

"You're early." Jane attempted to clutch his arm, but he avoided the maneuver. Positioning himself opposite her, he pressed his thin lips together in an attempt to appear stern. "I'm here on official business. You'll have to come down to the station house with me to answer some questions."

"Questions about what, sweetie?" Jane casually flipped his tie up. "Why are you being so formal?"

"Give me a break, Jane." His voice lost some intensity as he spoke. "Grab your purse, and let's go."

"I'm not going anywhere until you tell me what this is all about."

"It's not really official if we talk here." Todd tilted his body closer to hers. "But, if you're going to be stubborn about it." He cleared his throat. "Did you steal the murder weapon from the station house?"

Jane caught her breath in a coy way. "Do you honestly think I would do something like that?"

Todd turned away and walked to the window. "I don't know. You can be so exasperating."

"Well, this time, I'm innocent."

"You know I believe you. It's the Chief. He thinks you did it, and there's no convincing him otherwise." Todd turned back and gripped her shoulder. "You've got to come down to the station and talk to him."

Charlotte bit her lip and leaned against the bathroom wall, waiting for Jane's answer. She was hoping it wouldn't be an argumentative one. She'd often heard spats between them turn into romantic interludes, and she had to do something before she was stuck in the bathroom for several hours. She peeked out the bathroom door and caught Jane's glance. Then she pointed at the bedroom door and mouthed the word, "Go."

Jane swung Todd around and pushed him toward the door. "Oh, all right. I'll talk to him, but it'll have to be on my terms. I'll meet you there in ten minutes."

Chapter Sixteen

Early the next morning, Charlotte sat at her desk and stared at John's face while he stood in the doorway of his office, having a quiet conversation with his fiancée. *What could the two of them possibly have in common—the handsome, sophisticated man of my dreams and the trashy, witless girl with whom he claims to be in love?* Charlotte's eyes never left him as the couple casually walked past her desk, arm in arm.

Susan continued walking, but John stopped and turned around. He leaned over her desk and spoke in a confidential tone. "Susan told me all about your visit to the shipping office yesterday. Blanchard is extremely upset, to say the least. He thinks I sent you to dig up some dirt on him. What were you really doing down there?"

Do I want to tell him the truth? Absolutely not. "I don't know why he should be upset. I explained that I only went there to get some figures for the annual report. Which I got, and speaking of which, I'm falling behind on." She scooted her chair closer to her computer keyboard and began typing. "If you want this report done by the end of the day, you'll have to excuse me."

John leaned in closer, his warm breath fluttering her hair. He lingered there a moment longer than was comfortable. She held still and stared straight ahead as he took in a long, slow breath. "Just a friendly warning. Don't stick your nose in where it doesn't belong."

If this was his attempt at intimidation, it wasn't working. She quirked an eyebrow and wrinkled her nose at him.

With a jerk, he pulled himself away from the desk and strolled back to his office.

A breath of relief escaped Charlotte's lips as she continued typing. The report was taking more time to complete than it should have. Partly because she hated doing reports and partly because she couldn't keep her mind on her work. How could she concentrate on one thing, when so many others were fighting to occupy the same space?

Bits of conversation she'd had the previous day drifted in and out of her thoughts. Every time she saw John, her heart sank at what might be taking place tonight on the shipping dock, or worse, tomorrow morning at the courthouse. She needed to confess what she heard Susan say about him in the shipping office, but would he believe her, or would he think she was lying out of jealousy?

It was nearly five when she finally raised her eyes to check the office clock. How quickly time passed when most of it was spent daydreaming. As she typed the final words of the report, John poked his head out of his door, "Charlotte, can you come in here please?"

Sighing, she wandered in, defeated. Any fight she'd had earlier was gone.

"I want you to include some of the previous years' charts in the report, so we can compare the growth of the company from its first year to the present," he said.

"Old company charts?" Gloom overcame her.

"You know the ones I mean."

"Yes, I suppose I do, but why didn't you tell me sooner? I'm nearly finished."

John tapped an impatient finger on his desk. "I just remembered."

"It's past quitting time." Annoyance made her tone sharp, but it wasn't about the extra work.

His brow creased with irritation. "Putting in a little over-time isn't going to kill you. Get those charts, and add them to the report."

"Ohhh," Charlotte growled. Her nostrils flared and she clenched her fists as she stormed out of his office, John following close behind. "You're not leaving, are you?" She asked. "I thought you were doing inventory on the shipping dock tonight."

John's eyes gazed up and to the right. "Computer glitch. Had to make it another time. Tonight, I have a..." He turned his face toward the door, as if he couldn't look at her as he said the words, "a date."

Pain sliced through Charlotte's heart. He used to say the same thing moments before they met in the parking lot for a romantic evening together. She pushed her bottom lip out in a pout. "But I'll be here all alone."

He shrugged. "Sorry. I have to go." He pulled his car keys from his pants pocket and turned to leave, but took only a few steps before he stopped and turned back to her. "Charlotte?" His voice was soft.

She gazed into his eyes and held her breath in anticipation. "Yes?"

John opened his mouth to speak, but closed it again.

"Is there something you want to tell me?"

He hesitated a moment. "Um... no." Then he turned and walked out.

She huffed out her breath as he headed toward the front door, and then she grabbed the beige jacket hanging over the back of her chair. The office was cold in the summer with the air-conditioning blasting. She threw the jacket around her shoulders and scurried toward the back of the building.

The empty cubicles and silent offices echoed each footfall. She dreaded going into the old vault to look for those charts. Even though the vault door was always kept open, she couldn't stand the feeling of being in such an isolated, confined space.

When she had first started with the company, the vault was used to store the employee's paychecks and valuable company assets. These days, it was just a dank, dusty room where old records were kept in file drawers built into its thick, gray walls. Various obsolete and broken office machines and unused tables and chairs had been shoved into the corners, increasing its claustrophobic feeling.

As she approached the vault door, she checked over her shoulder. Although everyone in the office had left for the day, she still had the feeling someone was watching her. She turned. "John, is that you?"

Only silence answered, but she didn't believe it for a second. Her instincts told her someone was nearby, even if it wasn't her true love.

I should have told John how afraid I am of being in the vault alone, but then he'd think I'm just being a baby. After all, she'd been in this vault many times before.

Charlotte glanced around and tried to prop up her courage. "See, there's no one in here."

As soon as I find those charts, I'll be on my way. She made a mad dash toward the file drawers, but before she could reach them, the light went out. Charlotte drew her breath in and spun around to see the vault door closing. She ran toward it as the last sliver of light disappeared.

"Very funny, John! Aren't you ever going to grow up?" She switched the light on and searched for a door handle, but there was none on the inside of the vault door.

"Okay, you can open the door now and let me out. You've had your fun." She pounded on the door, lightly at first and then harder and harder until both hands hurt. Nothing happened. The door didn't swing open, and no one answered from the other side. Fear clawed at her throat, and she took a calming breath, urging her hands to stop shaking.

"John, open this door!" she screamed. "This isn't funny anymore."

Glancing around the vault, questions flitted across her mind, raising her anxiety with each one. How long would it take before someone noticed she was missing? Were there any vents in here? She searched the walls of the vault looking for a vent of some kind. Nothing. A glance around the floor proved the same thing. As far as she knew, the only oxygen that made it into the vault was through the, now closed, door.

How long would it be before she suffocated in here? The air seemed to thicken at the thought of how limited the supply was. She rapped her knuckles on the door of the vault once more, a sob escaping from her throat. There had to be some way out before all the air was used up. Her throat began to close as panic tightened the pit of her stomach.

Chapter Seventeen

Charlotte stared at the bleak gray walls and the clutter taking over the vault. *Was the room getting smaller?* No, it had to be her imagination. She'd never been claustrophobic before.

"Hello," she shouted at the door. "Is anyone out there?"

Why was she yelling? The vault was soundproof. No one could hear her. She paced the perimeter of the room and checked every inch of the wall for an air vent again. It was hopeless.

A thought lightened her spirit. This might be a joke. John might come back and let her out soon. But then a dark thought replaced it. She remembered the warning note in Jane's hand. If it wasn't John, then whoever locked her in could come back to make sure she never made it out. Alive.

She pulled an olive-green office chair from the pile of discarded furniture, and plopped down as she let out a labored breath. Either the air was getting thinner, or she was hyperventilating. She dropped her head between her knees and focused on slow, calming breaths.

Tiny beads of perspiration formed on her forehead and under her arms. She lifted her head and waved her hand in front of it to cool her heated face. No air conditioning. She pulled her jacket off and tossed it over an outdated fax machine. A small black notebook fell out of the pocket. Scooping it up, she tried to remember where she had gotten it. Suddenly, it clicked. This was the one she'd found in Blanchard's desk in the shipping office. She'd forgotten all about it.

Since there was nothing to do but wait, she flipped it open. Numbers filled the pages of the small book, except for the last page, which was blank. But what did the numbers mean? She took another look. Staring at the first line, she concluded it had to be a bill of lading number, with a UPC Code, a date, and a time. But these bill numbers didn't match up with the numbers used in their shipping office. Of course, they may have had new bill numbers printed after she left the department. This might be information about the missing items from the shorted shipments John had told her about yesterday.

She shoved the book in her pants pocket. A low growl emanated from her stomach. She checked her watch. Six o'clock. Had she only been in here an hour? It seemed longer.

Her mouth was dry, like she'd been chewing cotton balls. Why didn't she bring water with her? Hungry, hot, and thirsty— what a way to spend the night.

Gazing around the vault, Charlotte headed toward the back wall. She rummaged through the files, one by one, tossing papers out. If there wasn't anything to eat, at least she could find enough reading material to keep her mind off of food until she could fall asleep. Or until the air ran out. But Charlotte didn't want to think about *that* anymore.

A slight shake of her shoulder, and Charlotte awoke with a start. She squinted and put a hand up to her eyes. *Where am I?*

"Miss Ross? Why are you sleeping in a chair in the vault with the door closed?"

Charlotte glanced up to see the wrinkled face of an old man wearing a khaki security guard's uniform. "Oh, Dave. I've never been so glad to see anyone in my life!" She jumped up and dashed out through the open door, taking a deep breath. *Fresh air!*

The elderly guard followed her into the office and asked again, "Why were you sleeping in the vault?"

"Someone closed the door on me."

The guard scratched his graying head. "But the vault door is never closed. Company policy, I think." He talked slowly as though he was trying to remember. "When I got to work this morning and saw your car in the parking lot, I figured I'd come in to see what you were doing here. But I couldn't find you anywhere. Then I noticed the vault door was closed, so I opened it. Never expected to find you in there."

"I'm so glad you came in to check on me." Relief and desperation colored Charlotte's words. "Otherwise, I might've been locked in the vault for the entire weekend."

The old man smiled. "Just doin' my job, ma'am."

"Well, as far as I'm concerned, you're a hero. I'll see that you're rewarded." She checked her watch. It was after nine. "But right now, I just want to go home."

Charlotte ran to her desk and grabbed her purse, then she bolted out the front door and into her car. At the first stoplight, she rolled down her windows and took a deep breath of the warm, morning air. "I've got to pull myself together and figure out who locked me in that vault."

She turned right on Main Street, passing the courthouse, and remembered that John and Susan were supposed to be there this morning, possibly getting their marriage license. A gut feeling made her drive into the parking lot next door to the building. At the end of the first row, she spotted the dented fender on John's silver Corvette and pulled in alongside his car. Being locked in the vault suddenly seemed unimportant, at least for the moment. She had to talk some sense into John before he filed for a marriage license. He couldn't possibly know what Susan had planned for him.

Charlotte took the six courthouse steps two at a time. The front door was opened for her by a six-foot-tall, buxom brunette bailiff in dress uniform.

"Have you seen John Trent this morning?" Her voice came out sounding anxious.

"John Trent?" The bailiff said. "I don't think I know him."

Charlotte was sure every woman in town knew John. "Tall, chestnut hair, warm brown eyes, face like a Greek God." The bailiff's blank expression urged her to add, "He came in with a trashy-looking young woman."

The bailiff transferred a quick, dark gaze to her. "Oh yes, I remember." She sighed and pointed to a corridor of doors. "They went into the first room down the hall. But before you go after them, you'll have to go through security."

"Thanks." Charlotte took a minute to adjust her wrinkled clothes and walked through the security doorway, holding her breath. She didn't set off the alarms. With the way things were going these days, she'd expected just that.

She let out a breath of relief and rushed toward the hallway, stopping at the room the bailiff had indicated. Opening her compact mirror, she took a look at her face. Her makeup was faded, and she had large, dark circles under her eyes. She looked haunted, and her mess of tangled hair didn't help the look. Charlotte ran her fingers through her hair, using the time to pull her thoughts together.

She had a plan. She would calmly go into the room, find John, and have a quiet talk with him, pointing out how he'd have to suffer the devastating consequences if he married Susan, a woman so obviously unsuited to him.

Charlotte took a deep breath, made another attempt at smoothing her wrinkled clothing, and assumed a dignified stance. She opened the door quietly and walked into a courtroom full of people, some standing and others seated on the benches at the back of the small room. When she spotted John and Susan poised in front of the judge's bench, a tendril of panic tightened her stomach. *What's going on?* They couldn't possibly be getting married already. All the blood in her body rushed to her face as she ran up the short, middle aisle.

"Stop!" her voice rang out. A trembling hand flew to her lips. She didn't mean to say that.

"Are you addressing the court, young lady?" Annoyance colored the judge's tone and his round face.

Charlotte tentatively glanced around. Every eye in the room was on her. But with her heart stuck firmly in her throat, she couldn't speak, so she shook her head, no.

"Then why are you stopping the proceedings?"

"Huh?" Charlotte whispered and mustered a weak smile.

"Are you a witness?" the judge asked.

"Why are you here?" John hissed.

Charlotte glanced at her boss. His lips were pressed together in a stern look that told her there'd better be a darn good reason for what she was doing. And there was, but she couldn't tell him. Not in front of everyone.

"I'm a little confused as to what's going on here," she said.

"I was in a car accident," John said. "But it wasn't my fault. Susan was in the car with me at the time. She's my witness."

"She's your witness in an accident case?" Charlotte's head throbbed as she recalled the dent in his fender. "Sorry. I thought..." Her mouth suddenly went so dry she could barely spit the words out. "I thought the two of you were..."

John looked at her with interest. "We were what?"

"Yes, I'm interested to hear that, too," the judge insisted.

She put a hand to her forehead. The room had become unbearably hot and a deep pulse of pain was pounding in her temples. The murmuring from the crowd grew louder, and someone snickered. The heat of embarrassment crashed against her face. She was making a complete fool of herself, and while it wasn't new to her, it was still mortifying. Unlike all the other times, this was the first time she had no idea how to get out of it with her dignity still intact. "I've got a splitting headache," she said. "If you'll excuse me, I'm leaving now."

She turned and headed toward the door. The judge pounded his gavel on the bench several times and demanded the court to come to order. "Not so fast," the judge commanded. "Come back here and explain yourself."

Charlotte let out a long, heavy breath and inched her way back toward the judge's bench. Why couldn't there be a trap door in the floor to conveniently drop through? She tried to come up with a reasonable excuse for being there, but there wasn't one. This was going to look bad for her no matter what she said.

The room fell silent. John and Susan stared at her with interest. When she finally reached the judge's bench, she looked up to see his angry face glaring down at her. "The court is waiting for an explanation." His voice, loud and strong, echoed through the courtroom, sending tremors of fear through her. There had to be a rational way out of this.

An elderly woman opened the courtroom door and walked in. Everyone turned to see who it was, giving Charlotte a few extra seconds to come up with an idea. There was only one thing left to do.

She closed her eyes, made her body go limp, and dropped to the floor.

Chapter Eighteen

"That was a stupid stunt. Stupid, stupid, stupid! What was I thinking?"

She couldn't stop admonishing herself as she gobbled down an Egg McMuffin on the drive home. She shouldn't have gone there. Now she looked like an idiot in John's eyes, pretending to faint right in front of him. She probably looked like a nut case to everyone in the courtroom.

Charlotte turned into her driveway. Jane strolled toward her car, stopping in front of it. She placed both hands firmly on her hips. "I've been waiting for you all morning. Where in the world have you been?" Jane's worried expression conveyed how much she really cared, something Charlotte needed right now. "I tried calling you last night, but you didn't answer."

"I've got a lot to tell you." Charlotte glanced at her parents' house as she got out. "But not here. Come up to my apartment before my mother sees us."

Charlotte opened her front door and froze.

"What the heck happened here?" Jane asked. "Looks like a tornado hit this place."

Charlotte's heart nearly exploded. "I'm gone for one night and my apartment gets ransacked."

"What could the person possibly be looking for?"

"Well, whoever it was didn't get any money. I never keep money in my apartment."

"You don't suppose they were looking for the manuscript, do you?"

Charlotte went around the room assessing everything she owned. The television, stereo, and her computer were in place, so was her DVD player, iPod and all of her DVDs. She opened the desk drawer to check for the manuscript. It was still inside. She picked it up and placed it on the desk before turning toward her bedroom doorway.

Her bedroom was in the same disarray as the rest of the apartment. Her clothes and other things were out of the drawers, and everything in the closet had been tossed out on the floor. But from a quick glance, nothing seemed to be missing.

"It doesn't look like anything's been stolen," she said finally. Despite the reassurance that everything was accounted for, Charlotte couldn't help the feeling washing over her—violated and scared that whoever did this might come back.

"This is pretty intimidating." Jane echoed her thoughts. "I remember how scared I was the day my apartment in the city was burglarized, and it didn't look half as bad as this."

Charlotte stamped her foot. "This is the last straw! The ultimate frosting on a horribly unappetizing cake." She pulled her cell phone from her purse. "I've had it. I'm calling the police."

"Wait." Jane scrambled for her phone. "Don't dial the station. I'll contact Todd on his cell. At least we can count on him to be discreet."

She dialed Todd's number. "Hey, it's me," Jane said. "Remember when I told you I had a gut feeling something was wrong? Come over to Charlotte's apartment right away. It's important."

Charlotte grabbed the phone from Jane's hand and spoke into it. "Come around the back, and don't let my parents see you. I don't want to alarm them."

She hung up, went to the kitchen, and pushed the debris from two chairs. Then she tossed some ice cubes into a couple of tall glasses, handed one to Jane, and set one on the table for herself. She filled each glass from a two-liter bottle of cola and gulped hers down. The sudden rush of caffeine seemed to steady her nerves as she sank down into the chair. "Now I'll tell you what happened to me."

As she gave Jane the details about being locked in the vault, a loud knock on the door made Charlotte leap out of her chair. She pressed a hand to her chest to keep her heart from jumping out, and exhaled raggedly.

"Take it easy," Jane said. "It's probably Todd." She opened the door to let the officer in. "That was quick."

"I was around the corner when you called." Todd stepped inside, his eyes appraising the trashed apartment. "Whew! What a mess. What the heck are you mixed up in, Charlotte?"

"Nothing." She looked earnestly into his eyes. "I don't know why anyone would want to ransack my apartment."

The officer pulled a pen and a small pad from his shirt pocket and began taking notes. "Was anything stolen?"

"I don't think so." Charlotte raised her hands in frustration. "It looks like everything's still here."

Jane walked up to Todd and put her arms around his neck. "Can you investigate this without filling out a report, sweetie?"

"I don't think so. After all, a crime did take place here."

Jane gave Todd a menacing look and let go of him. "What good are you if you can't help us?"

Todd dropped his hands to his sides. "Are you asking me to be derelict in my duties as a police officer?"

"No, of course not," Jane replied. "But isn't there anything you can do for poor Charlotte, a dear friend of yours whom you've known practically your entire life? I'm sure if she was in your place, she would do as much as she could to help you."

Todd must have noticed the pathetic expression on Charlotte's face. "All right." He shook a finger at her. "I probably shouldn't do this, but since you're such an old friend, I'll check the place out, take some pictures, and see if I can get fingerprints. I won't fill out a report." He looked pointedly at Jane. "For now."

"Thanks, Todd." Charlotte walked over to the sofa and put the cushions back on. "I don't really want to stay here tonight." She shuddered. "What if the person comes back?"

"Why don't you stay with me at the Inn," Jane said. And tomorrow morning, Todd can check things out as you and I straighten up the place."

"Wait a minute," Todd said. "Tonight is the Midsummer Night's Dance at the Country Club." He reached into his shirt pocket and handed his ticket to Charlotte. "Here, you take it. Go with Jane and relax a little. Take your mind off of everything. I might have to work late, anyway. But I can meet you both there later. Say around nine."

One thing Charlotte learned at a young age is that every bad experience could be comforted by a large banana split. It was her go-to and had been for years. So it was no surprise that she and Jane found themselves at the Olde Soda Fountain on Main Street, a large banana split nestled in front of her as the 50s decor of the restaurant soothed her nerves.

"I wonder who wanted me out of the way while they searched my apartment," she said between mouthfuls of the rich ice cream.

Jane sat across the booth from her and sipped a glass of ice water. "You know, it might have only been a coincidence you were locked in the vault the same night your apartment was ransacked."

"I don't think so." Charlotte shook her head emphatically. "It must have been someone who works at Longbourne and Payne, someone who knew I would be working late. Probably the same person who closed the vault door on me. But what were they looking for? It certainly wasn't the manuscript. Maybe it was the missing pages."

Jane tilted her head. "There were pages missing?"

"Yeah. All the information about the Triumvirate was missing."

"Interesting turn of events. If someone wants them that badly, there must be something incriminating in them. Who knew you'd be working late?"

Charlotte glanced down at her ice cream. "There was only John. But he might have told Susan. It seems like he tells her everything these days."

"Why would John want those missing manuscript pages?"

"I don't know. There doesn't seem to be any connection here."

"Well, then maybe it was Susan who locked you in the vault." Jane took a sip of water, her finger tracing the water ring left by the glass. "At least we know she dislikes you enough to lock you away. But again, why would she want to search your apartment?"

"Maybe she told that horrible father of hers I was annoying her, and he just wanted to teach me a lesson." Charlotte shuddered. "Imagine him accusing me of snooping around the shipping office."

Jane fished a chunk of banana out of Charlotte's bowl, but hesitated before eating it. "Is it okay if I take this?"

Charlotte nodded. "Help yourself."

Jane plopped it in her mouth. "What were you doing in the shipping office, anyway?"

"Snooping. I wanted to get some information about the new redhead that John hired to take Susan's place and possibly something to link Susan to Carlton's murder." Charlotte spooned another mouthful of ice cream. "But I never expected to overhear Susan's plans for John once they were married. She's horrible. I've got to warn him about her before his life is ruined."

"Is he all you ever think about?" Jane licked chocolate sauce from her lips.

Charlotte stared up at the Casablanca-style ceiling fan above her head. The feathered air felt cool on her warm face. She couldn't admit to Jane she was completely crushed over John's impending marriage, and it was becoming increasingly difficult for her to concentrate on anything else. Her thoughts came down with the cool breeze, and she countered with, "Is this murder case all *you* ever think about?"

"Yes," Jane said without hesitation. "And I'm spending a lot of my mental energy on it, but that's different." She softened her tone as she reached across the table and patted Charlotte's hand. "If you're so concerned about John, why don't you just tell him what you overheard Susan say?"

Charlotte crossed her arms, pulling her hand free of Jane's comfort. "I can't talk to him anymore. Every conversation we have ends in an argument. It breaks my heart to think he's going to marry that witch. I love him too much to see him mess up his life."

Chapter Nineteen

That evening, after she and Jane had changed for the dance, Charlotte pulled her car out of the Inn's parking lot and merged with the few cars that constituted Saturday night traffic. "I've got to make a quick stop at the office," she told Jane. "I left my favorite lipstick in my desk drawer."

Jane checked her face in the side-view mirror. "Is it important?"

Charlotte pressed her foot to the floor. "It is to me. That lipstick gives me confidence. It'll only take a few minutes." She sped up to pass the car in front of her and smoothly merged back into traffic.

"If they close the bar before I get a drink, I'm going to make you open it and make me one yourself." Jane's slight smile gave lie to the threat in her words.

"Do they ever close the bar at the country club?" Charlotte made a left turn into the company parking lot and pulled into her usual space. "Wait in the car. I'll only be a minute."

Charlotte opened the front door with her key and went inside. The office was dark and silent, but as she neared the light switch she noticed a dark figure lurking beside her desk. Flicking on the lights, Charlotte gasped. "What are you doing there?"

Tim Blanchard turned, his face taut, lips pulled back into a snarl. He pounded a fist on her desk. Then he shook it at her. "Where is it?" he roared.

She took a step back before she steeled her spine and stared at him with contempt. She swallowed down her fear, but her throat felt tight around it. "Where's what?" she managed, proud that her voice didn't shake in terror.

"I've had enough of your innocent act." He shoved his work-worn hand out in front of him, palm up. "Hand it over."

"Hand what over? I don't know what you're talking about." *Has he finally gone off the deep end?* Charlotte's heart raced as she glanced from side to side. *Where's the guard this evening?*

"Give me back the book you took from my desk drawer when you were snooping around the shipping office yesterday afternoon!"

Charlotte's eyes widened. In a show of bravado she didn't really feel, she placed her fists on her hips. "I did not snoop! And I don't know what book you mean."

"Don't lie to me." His voiced boomed. "You were the only other person in the shipping office besides my daughter and me."

Something in the way he wrung his hands gave Charlotte the feeling he'd rather be wringing her neck. "I didn't take anything from your office."

"You took it all right, and I want it back." He spoke through clenched teeth, pushing out the blue veins on his forehead.

She strengthened what was left of her meager resolve. "What are you going to do, shake an imaginary book out of me?"

He took a giant step toward her. "Don't tempt me, lady. You're playing a deadly game, stealing that book from me, and I'll do whatever I have to do to get it back."

As Mr. Blanchard took a second step toward her, Jane appeared in the doorway. "Charlotte, what's taking you so long?" Her voice broke the tension like a string being severed.

Relief washed over Charlotte. Jane's appearance gave her a modicum of courage. She shook an accusing finger at her aggressor. "If you touch me, I'll sue you for everything you have or ever will have. Jane's my witness."

Tim flew past Charlotte and headed toward the front door, but before he reached the reception area, he turned around. "I know you have my book, you petty thief, and I'm giving you fair warning. I want my property back, or *you're* the one who'll pay."

Charlotte spun around. A sinking feeling made the words slip out before she could think to stop them. "It was you," she hissed. "You're the one who locked me in the vault last night so you could ransack my apartment. But you didn't find what you were looking for, did you?"

Tim shook his head with a vengeance and growled, "This isn't over!" He glared at Jane as he bolted out the front door.

"What was that about?" Jane asked.

"He makes me so angry." Charlotte's hands shook, but she wasn't sure if it was in anger or fear. "If he would have asked me nicely for that book, I'd have given it back to him."

"What book?"

Charlotte opened her purse and pulled out the slim volume with a plain, black cover. She flung it at Jane.

"This one."

Jane caught the leather-bound notebook in both hands and paged through it. "It's only a bunch of numbers."

"I know, but those figures must be important. He's frantic to get them back." She searched the desk drawer for her lipstick.

"Where did you get it?"

"It fell out of his desk when I hit the drawer with my head. I shoved most of the other things back in, but he and Susan came into the office before I could get the book in. Instead of dropping it, I panicked and put it in my pocket. I was going to put it back last night before I left, but I got locked in the vault."

Jane shoved the book in Charlotte's direction. "Why don't you put it back now?"

"I can't. If I do, he'll know I took it. I'd sooner be locked up in prison than let him know I have it."

"That's kind of drastic, isn't it?"

Charlotte finally located her lipstick and looked up. "It's the principle of the thing."

Jane nodded in agreement. "What do you suppose the numbers mean?"

Charlotte took a closer look. "They look like they might be tracking numbers for shipments, along with the dates and times they were shipped."

Jane flipped through the pages slowly, and Charlotte could see the gears working overtime in her head. "If they're shipment tracking numbers, why is he hiding them in his desk? Unless he's tracking something illegal." Jane gave her a sideways glance. "But what?"

Charlotte shrugged. "They could be the missing products from our shipments, and Blanchard doesn't want anyone to know what he's doing until he fingers the culprit. John said they were coming up short."

"Or." Jane hesitated and looked thoughtfully at the door Tim had exited through. "Maybe he's the one doing the stealing." She ran to the copier. "Before we leave, I'm going to make a copy of the pages in this book."

Chapter Twenty

Cocktail hour at the country club was in full swing. The main dining room was alive with the chatter of enthusiastic meetings between old friends and new. Soft lights emanating from the large crystal chandeliers were upstaged by numerous, star shaped candles strategically placed around the darkened room.

Charlotte glanced around. "See if you can find our table."

"Let's stop next to one of the candles," Jane said. "I can't read the number on our tickets." She leaned in close to a candle flame and squinted. "It looks like thirteen."

Charlotte pointed. "I think it's over there, to your left. The table closest to the dance floor."

A shrill voice pierced the din like the point of a sharp knife. "Yoo-hoo! Over here, Charlotte. We're over here. No, you're going the wrong way, dear. We're over here!"

Charlotte felt the eyes of everyone in the room on her. She spun around and headed in the direction of table thirteen.

"Your mother's got a voice like a witch with a bullhorn," Jane said, lagging behind.

"That doesn't begin to describe it." Charlotte turned around, but Jane had disappeared into the crowd, so she trudged the final steps alone.

"It's so nice to see you, dear," Mrs. Ross said. "I didn't think you were coming to the dance." She contemplated her daughter's appearance and spoke with a note of concern in her voice. "How are you feeling? I heard you fainted at the courthouse this morning."

Charlotte rubbed her forehead, the beginnings of a head-ache forming behind her eyes. "What did they do, broadcast it on the six o'clock news?"

"Of course not." Maggie Ross motioned her daughter to lean in closer. "The bailiff called me."

"The gossip hotline, huh?"

Mrs. Ross pushed back in her chair. "There's no need to be nasty, Charlotte. I merely asked you how you were feeling."

Charlotte sighed before she touched her mother's shoulder in a soothing manner. "I'm sorry, Mom. It's been a long day. I'm feeling much better now."

Mrs. Ross sniffled, but her voice seemed unaffected by any hurt feelings. "By the way." Her mother looked up, concern turning to curiosity. "What were you doing at the courthouse?"

"Oh, not much." Charlotte spoke unemotionally. "I was trying to save someone from making the mistake of a lifetime."

"You and your lofty ideals." Mrs. Ross stood and picked a piece of imaginary lint from the bodice of Charlotte's black silk evening dress. "This is very nice, but it's too low-cut." She pulled the top of the dress up by the thin shoulder straps. "Do you want to wear my shawl?"

Charlotte pushed her mother's hands away. "No, I'm perfectly fine."

Mrs. Ross's head jerked around as if she was looking for someone. "Where's Todd? I knew he'd change his mind and take you to the dance instead of his criminal girlfriend. Everyone knows she's suspected of stealing the weapon that killed poor Carlton."

Charlotte glanced up at the ceiling and slowly counted to ten. "Could you talk a little louder, Mother? I don't think the people in the parking lot heard you."

Mrs. Ross sat down and pulled her chair closer to the table. "Don't be silly, dear. They can't hear me in the parking lot."

Charlotte sighed. "Todd couldn't make it tonight, but he was nice enough to give me his ticket, so *I* brought his criminal girlfriend."

As if on cue, Jane stepped out from behind Charlotte. "Hello, Mrs. Ross."

"Oh, Jane!" Charlotte's mother squealed, and Charlotte had no doubt that it wasn't a squeal of joy. "I didn't recognize you. What have you done to yourself?"

"I've had a complete makeover." Jane spun around so Mrs. Ross could get the full effect.

"It's about time," Mrs. Ross said. "You really needed one."

Jane glared at Charlotte and opened her mouth, but Charlotte shook her head, signaling that an argument would be pointless.

"You never change, Mrs. Ross." Jane almost sounded pleasant.

"For heaven's sake," Charlotte said. "If we're going to talk to my mother, let's sit down." As the ladies took their seats, Charlotte leaned over and quietly asked, "Where's Dad?"

"He's around somewhere."

Charlotte chuckled. "You don't seem to be the least bit concerned. I know you usually keep him on pretty short leash."

"You know your dad. He's a big-time schmoozer. He finds it vital to his business interests to work the room every chance he gets." Mrs. Ross checked the bar. "Look, he's over there talking to someone. I don't know her, but she looks interesting." Her facial expression became stern. "Yes, interesting. I think I'll take a walk over and introduce myself. Your father and I will be back in time for dinner."

Jumping to her feet, Mrs. Ross pushed her way through the crowd toward her husband.

"Isn't she the actress who works in your shipping office?" Jane asked.

Charlotte turned to check the bar.

"Wait," Jane touched Charlotte's chin. "Don't turn around. You'll never guess who's sitting two tables behind us."

Charlotte flipped Jane's hand away. "If we're going to play twenty questions, at least give me a hint."

Jane hummed a few bars of the Wedding March.

Charlotte closed her eyes as her heart hit the floor. "Not the future bride and groom."

"Including the father of the bride." Jane peeked behind her friend's head and jerked back. "And he's staring straight at you."

"Great." Charlotte pinched the bridge of her nose. "That's all I need, those blood-shot eyes burning a hole in the back of my head. Is Mrs. Blanchard here, too?"

"I don't think so, but the girl with the red hair just sat down at their table." Jane rubbed her hands together. "Looks like the gang's all here. Now, aren't you glad you bought a new dress?"

"Get serious." Charlotte massaged her temples. "I've got to think of a way to get the black book back to Blanchard. Otherwise, he won't leave me alone until he gets some kind of confession out of me. If that book has something illegal in it, and he knows I have it, I'm in big trouble. What did you do with the copy you made?"

"I put it in your glove compartment."

Charlotte moistened her lips. "I suppose it's safe enough in there."

"Unless he decides to search your car."

"If he gets the book back, he won't have to do anymore searching."

Jane tapped the red linen tablecloth with her long nails. "Have you come up with a plan yet?"

"I can't think clearly when John's in the same room. Look at me. I'm sweating, and my hands are shaking." Charlotte extended a hand directly in front of her, toppling her crystal water glass. "See what I mean?"

Jane shook her head and grabbed two napkins. Throwing them onto the water, she sopped up the liquid. The linens absorbed as much water as they could hold. Charlotte grabbed another napkin from the plate next to hers and mopped up the last of the water. "This has given me an idea."

Jane smiled. "What are you going to do, go over there and spill water all over Blanchard?"

"No." Charlotte looked smugly at her friend. "You are. And it's not Mr. Blanchard, it's Susan."

Jane's eyes widened. "What?"

Charlotte leaned forward in her chair and lowered her voice. "I want you to walk up to their table, pretend to trip on something, then accidently spill your drink in Susan's lap. You don't have to spill a lot, just enough to make her jump up. Be loud and noisy so you're sure to draw a crowd. While everyone's making a fuss, I'll sneak up behind her chair like I'm concerned.

Charlotte continued to lay out her plans. "Then I'll grab her purse, drop the book inside, and place it back where it was. Simple."

"Sounds easy enough, but won't it look suspicious?"

"I'll be careful." Charlotte leaned back in her chair. "Then Blanchard will have his property back, and he'll leave me alone."

"If you think it'll work, I'll give it a try." Jane said. "I never liked Susan. Spilling something icy in her lap will be my pleasure."

Realizing she had forgotten to get a drink, Charlotte's gaze wandered in the direction of the bar. "Brace yourself. My parents are coming to the table. I think dinner is about to be served."

Charlotte swallowed a sip of coffee and glanced at her parents, who hadn't said a word to each other or anyone else during the entire meal. She finally broke the silence. "I have to admit, the food here is essentially decent."

There was never a meal where her mother let an opportunity go by to criticize the amount of food she ate, but tonight, not a word had been said. Mrs. Ross stared at her plate while toying with her mashed potatoes but never managed to put any into her mouth. Her father stared into the flower arrangement while he polished off his prime rib dinner. Charlotte smiled at each one in turn, and they smiled back.

She leaned toward her co-conspirator." Are you ready?"

"Definitely."

"Excuse us," Charlotte said. "We're going to the bar."

Each parent nodded as the ladies got up and slid their chairs back under the table. Since they'd already had wine with dinner, Charlotte waited for the big question. 'Don't you think you've had enough to drink this evening?' She'd usually heard it from one or both of her parents whenever they went out to dinner together. This time, however, neither said a word.

"It's a little cool in here," Jane said as she rubbed her hands across her bare arms.

"Frigid, is more like it. There's nothing's colder than the silent treatment."

At the bar, Charlotte turned and glanced back at their table, concern etching her heart. Her parents were now sitting with their backs to each other. This was not a good sign. At times like these, she was glad she wasn't still living at home.

"When you get your drink," Charlotte told Jane. "Walk toward our table by way of the Blanchard table. After that, you know what to do."

"It'll be my pleasure." A mischievous smile spread across Jane's lips.

Charlotte walked back to their table and sat where she could get a good view of Jane's movements. A few moments later, Jane bumped Susan's chair. Liquid splashed from her glass.

"Oops, I'm *so* sorry."

Susan Blanchard shot up like a bullet, nearly knocking over her chair. "You clumsy bitch!" She snatched up a linen napkin and speared Jane with a rage-filled glare.

"I said I was sorry. What else can I say?" Jane picked up another napkin and made a pretense of helping her.

Tim's large eyeballs bulged out at her. "She did that to Susan deliberately."

"I certainly did not." Jane turned to the next table and addressed the guests seated there. "Did it look like I did that deliberately?"

Six people mumbled their opinions.

"Really, Tim," John said. "Give the girl a break. It's crowded in here tonight, and accidents do happen."

From the way Tim was glaring at Jane, Charlotte recalled the meaning of the phrase, 'If looks could kill.'

She stood and walked over to the table, positioning herself behind the waitress who was checking out the damage to Susan's skirt. Susan's purse was lying on floor. Charlotte stooped down and put her hand out to pick it up, but the waitress dropped to her knees and grabbed it.

"Here." She handed the purse to Susan. "This was on the floor."

Charlotte got to her feet and moved away before Susan could see her.

"Don't you know who this is?" Tim said to John, loud enough for the entire room to hear. "She's your secretary's friend."

John turned his handsome face toward Jane, his eyes sparkling in the candlelight. "I remember you. You worked at Longbourne and Payne."

"Yeah, she was in Human Resources," Susan said, still blotting her skirt.

John cocked his head. "You left about the time I started with the company. As I remember, you were supposed to go back to college, but you ended up doing something else. Writing a novel, wasn't it?" He took a solicitous account of her facial features. "But you looked different then."

"I've had a makeover."

"I don't trust her," Blanchard shouted. "I know she and that secretary of yours are up to something."

The redhead glanced at John. "You know what Freud said. 'There are no accidents.'"

"Don't be ridiculous," Jane scoffed. "Sometimes an accident is just an accident." She turned and sauntered away.

Susan walked to the kitchen with the waitress. No doubt to get her skirt dried.

Charlotte went back to their table.

"Did you do it?" Jane asked, when she arrived.

"No."

"What happened to your plan?"

"Everything went wrong." Charlotte bit down on her bottom lip, frustration causing her to chew on it. "Why do these things always come off so cleverly in the movies, but never work in real life? Now, I'll have to come up with some other way to get the book back to him. I've got to get rid of it this evening, or I won't be able to sleep tonight."

Charlotte was sure the creases in her forehead were setting like concrete. "You're usually the one with all the great ideas, Jane." This time, she'd pawn her problem off on her overly imaginative friend. "Can't you come up with something?"

"I'll find a way."

Jane's voice was a little too confident for Charlotte's taste. *I might have just made a terrible mistake.*

Chapter Twenty One

With her elbows on the table and her face cupped in her hands, Charlotte watched John and Susan on the dance floor. He held her in a tight embrace, and she rubbed her hand across his neck in a loving caress.

"Look at them. They're absolutely nauseating—dancing and laughing as if they were the only two people in the world. I can't believe she's wearing that gaudy silver dress. It couldn't get any shorter or tighter." Charlotte leaned back in her chair and folded her arms in front of her. "How can he stand to be seen in public with someone who looks so trashy?"

"You've got to get over your jealousy of Susan," Jane said. "It's not her fault. Any woman would fall for John's clean-cut good looks given half the chance."

Jane was right, but it didn't diminish the pain in her heart every time she glanced at the dance floor.

"Todd should be here pretty soon." Jane sounded like she wasn't happy with her alternative.

"He can't get here soon enough." Charlotte tore her gaze away from the dance floor. "By the way, do you know what happened to my parents? Weren't they sitting at this table the last time we saw them?"

"I don't know where your mom went, but I saw your dad when I was at the bar."

Charlotte glanced in that direction. "Was he talking to the redhead?"

"No." Jane motioned to the table behind Charlotte. "She's sitting at her own table and appears to be very chummy with you-know-who of the bulging eyes and nasty snarl. I wonder what she's up to."

Charlotte resisted the urge to turn around. "The impression I got when I was snooping around on the shipping dock is that she's trying to get close to him for some reason."

"What reason?" Jane's question was accompanied by a look of astonishment.

"I wish I knew."

Jane glanced over Charlotte's shoulder. "Todd's here."

Charlotte turned, and in her peripheral vision she spied someone with him. "Oh, no," she groaned, searching for an escape route.

"This is just *not* your night." Jane's voice sounded sympathetic, but laughter danced in her eyes.

Charlotte felt herself slipping under the table, but she couldn't stop.

"Come out from under there, you coward."

Charlotte looked up with the edge of the tablecloth draped over her head. "Pretend I'm not here."

Jane snickered. "You can't spend the entire evening on the floor."

"Sure I can." Charlotte pulled her dress over her knees. "It's comfortable down here."

"This is no time to act silly." Jane smiled vaguely at a passing waitress who stared at her, as she appeared to be having a conversation with no one.

Charlotte pulled her head back in. "No, Jane, really, I can't."

"He's not that bad." Jane tried to sound reassuring, but she had to know she wasn't being the least bit successful. "He's good-looking, in an odd sort of way. Maybe he'll make John jealous."

Charlotte shook her head. "Tell him I had to leave because I suddenly came down with a severe case of rigor mortis."

"After Todd went to all the trouble of fixing you two up, the least you can do is stick it out for one evening. Now, get up here." Jane hooked her hand under the table and caught Charlotte's arm.

"I won't forget this." Charlotte dusted off the bottom of her skirt before resettling herself at the table.

The two police officers sauntered toward them in all their testosterone-soaked manliness. Charlotte's top lip curled in silent revulsion.

"We nearly missed you," Todd said. "Luckily, we ran into Charlotte's mom. She told us where you were sitting."

"Another thing I have to thank my mother for," Charlotte muttered with a forced smile. "How did the two of you get in without tickets?"

"We can get in anywhere." Billy Price slid into the chair next to Charlotte. "Our badges are the only tickets we need."

He leaned in close. "Hi, Babe." His hot breath smelled of stale coffee, and heated her open neckline.

Fighting the urge to turn her head away, Charlotte gave him a cool smile.

Jane patted the seat to her right. "Sit down next to me, Todd. We have a lot to talk about."

Todd pushed the chair closer to Jane and slid into it. "Do we have to do any talking tonight?" he asked in a suggestive tone.

"Well," Jane said, putting a finger on Todd's bottom lip. "It's either talk now or talk later, if you get my meaning."

"All right." Todd assumed a formal demeanor. "What do you want to talk about?"

"First of all, Charlotte is sure Tim Blanchard's the one who broke into her apartment. She thinks he was looking for a book Charlotte accidently took from his office."

"What kind of book?"

"It's a book of numbers," Charlotte said. "We don't know what they are, but they must have some special meaning to him." She signaled with her eyes toward the table where Blanchard sat. "Otherwise, he wouldn't be so anxious to get it back. He threatened me and demanded I return it. He was furious, and he looked like he would have killed me for it."

"I don't think so, babe." Billy spoke in a low, sleek voice, the very one he used to impress women, but it had never worked with her. His glassy, green eyes glanced down the front of her bodice as he spoke. "Blanchard has a bad rep in this town as a mean character, but I don't think he would resort to murder."

Charlotte put a hand across her chest to block Billy's view. "You didn't see the evil in those enormous bulging eyes when he confronted me."

"You're imagining things." Billy's hot hand caressed Charlotte's shoulder.

"Somehow, I don't find that comforting." Charlotte dropped her shoulder, and Billy's hand fell away. "As a police officer, you should know anyone is capable of murder if given enough cause."

"A book ain't enough cause to murder anyone, not even you, babe." Billy leaned forward in his chair. "Now Witherspoon's murder is different. Personally, I think that old butler did it."

Jane turned her curious gaze toward Officer Price. "And how did you come to that conclusion?"

"As I see it," Billy said, "The butler claims the old man was alive when he left in the morning at eight, but he was dead when he came back to the house and found him in the afternoon at one. Crofts has a shaky alibi. He had plenty of time to do the old guy in. And no one else was seen entering or leaving the house."

Charlotte glanced at Jane. "You have to admit, that sounds logical. But what reason would the butler have to kill his employer?"

"That butler don't need no reason to commit murder." Billy gestured toward his temple with a short, thick finger. "He belongs in a nut house."

"Just because the butler is old and a little eccentric," Charlotte said, "doesn't necessarily make him crazy."

"True enough." Billy leaned back in his chair in a lazy sprawl. "But that doesn't mean he ain't."

Todd shook his head as if he couldn't believe the conversation that just took place. "The key words here are, 'no one else was seen.' Just because no one was seen doesn't mean no one else was there. Jane said she heard someone upstairs."

Jane nodded. "I did. And those streets around Treadwell Square are deserted. That house is partially hidden by trees. No one saw *me* enter or leave, either."

Todd scanned the room. "Actually, the murderer could be anyone here."

Charlotte and Jane both glanced at Blanchard's table.

Billy picked up on Charlotte's frightened expression. "Don't worry, babe." He placed his arm down firmly on the back of her chair. "I'm here to protect you for the entire night."

"Swell." The pulse at Charlotte's temple pounded a throbbing beat. She gritted her teeth and peered into Billy's shifty green eyes. "And stop calling me babe."

"You got spunk, babe, I mean Charlotte." He clipped her lightly on the chin with his knuckle. "I love girls with spunk."

Terrific. That's just what I don't need. She turned to face him and tried to smile, but her lips twisted into a disgusted grin.

"Speaking of a murderer being in this very room," Jane said. "I noticed that the Longbourne's aren't here tonight."

"I don't think Jim Longbourne has enough guts to show his face in public after he was arrested," Todd said.

"Maybe *he* don't wanna show his face anywhere," Billy said. "But his wife ain't afraid to show hers."

The conversation suddenly went silent. Jane glanced at Todd. "Is this true?"

Todd checked the area around him and motioned the ladies to lean in close.

"Every Saturday night, Alyssa Longbourne gets all dressed up in one of those tight fitting, low-cut dresses, a fur coat, and as much jewelry as she can—you know the really expensive stuff. Then she sends for her car. After she leaves the house, Longbourne calls the police station to see who's off duty, and one of us follows her around until she staggers home, usually around two a.m. The next morning, we report her activities to Longbourne, and he gives us a generous tip."

Charlotte teetered on the edge of her chair. Another inch, and she would be on the floor, which is where she wanted to be in the first place. "Why isn't one of you following her tonight?"

Todd shrugged. "Longbourne didn't call the police station this evening."

"I'm surprised he lets her get away with bar hopping alone," Jane said.

"What's he gonna to say?"

"I see your point," Charlotte agreed. "Now can we get back to my problem? I think that once I get the book back to Blanchard, he'll leave me alone. But I don't want him to know I'm the one who took it, so I can't exactly walk up to him and hand it over."

Billy leaned in close to Charlotte's face. The warmth of his breath brushed her cheek. "Why don't you give me the book?" Billy put a solicitous hand out. "I'll get it back to him, and he'll never know who took it."

"No," Charlotte said. "But thanks anyway." She dreaded having to be grateful to Billy Price for anything.

The evening dragged on as the ladies watched their dates devour a late dinner, one course at a time. When dessert was served, Billy took a bite of pastry, whipped cream squirting out of the sides of his mouth. Charlotte couldn't help comparing him to John and wishing for the life she could have had. She'd imagined herself married to John for such a long time, she couldn't see him married to anyone else. After all, he deserved a nice girl like her.

Thinking about John being married to Susan caused tears to well in Charlotte's eyes. Jealousy gave way to feelings of desperation as John hurtled blindly toward marriage vows that would take him out of her life forever.

"You gonna eat that pastry or not?" Billy shoved his plundering voice right into the middle of Charlotte's worries. She sighed in exasperation as she stirred cream into her coffee while refusing the last helping of dessert.

"I see your mother heading this way." Jane hung on to the sides of her chair as if the impact of Mrs. Ross's visit would send her flying through the roof. "You'd better get ready."

Mrs. Ross excused her way through the crowd of people and made a beeline for their table. When she finally reached them, she motioned for Charlotte to stand up and then she whispered into her daughter's ear. "I need your car keys. I want to go home now."

"What about Daddy?"

Mrs. Ross lowered her gaze. "I'm never speaking to him again."

"I see." Charlotte seized her opportunity to escape. "I'll drive you home."

"Don't be silly. You stay here with your friends and have a good time. I'll drive myself. Besides, I want to be alone to clear the cobwebs before I confront your father. You understand."

Charlotte knew only too well that when her mother got jealous, usually over something her father didn't do, it was always a long, drawn-out battle. She eventually forgave him, even though he rarely did anything requiring forgiveness.

"But how will Jane and I get home?"

Mrs. Ross smiled at Todd. "Will you be kind enough to drive my daughter... and her friend, home tonight, Officer Shlagg?"

Todd touched Charlotte's shoulder. "Sure, I'll be glad to."

"See? I told you." Mrs. Ross put a hand to her forehead. "Now give me your keys, please. I've got such a splitting headache, it's beginning to pour out of my ears."

"All right." Charlotte reluctantly dug through her purse and gave her mother the keys.

She would now be at the mercy of her companions. As much as she liked Jane, she was never quite sure what the woman really had on her mind. This evening, she had a strange feeling Jane had plans she'd somehow neglected to tell her about. Or maybe the two police officers had a plan they were keeping to themselves until they were ready to spring it on their unsuspecting victims.

A sudden burst of thunder shook the foundation of the building. With the festivities in full swing and the band playing so loudly, no one at their table appeared to notice the noise, except Charlotte. She glanced up, cautious eyes scanning the ceiling.

Billy slipped his arm around her shoulder. "What's wrong?"

"Was that thunder?" She pulled away from his grasp.

"I didn't hear anything," he said.

Jane leaned toward her and whispered, "Your boss just stood up. It looks like he's getting ready to come over here."

Charlotte's heart jerked. She turned her head to glance at his table. John was staring at her with an intense glint in his eyes.

Susan gripped John's arm, stopping him before he took a step forward. With a tight frown on her lips, she shot to her feet and whispered in his ear. A moment later, she grinned and took his hand, leading him to the dance floor.

Charlotte let out a long, slow breath. Her tender heart had endured enough of John and Susan for one evening. It couldn't take them a moment longer. "Let's get out of here," she said, her knees shaking. "It's getting late and, and I'd hate to be caught in a thunderstorm tonight."

Billy checked his watch. "It ain't even ten o'clock, babe. The evening is just getting started."

"No, Charlotte's right." Jane stood and grabbed her purse. "Let's get out of here. We really shouldn't get these evening dresses wet. Besides, the music they're playing is getting on my nerves. One thing you can always count on here, if they're not playing elevator music, they're playing old-timers' music."

Charlotte couldn't believe how quickly Jane had agreed with her decision to leave. Now she was really worried.

Chapter Twenty Two

The air was thick with the smell of impending rain as Charlotte and her companions strolled toward the squad car in the parking lot. In the distance, flashes of light played in the clouds. A violent storm would be on them soon. Jane snuggled closer to Todd as they crossed the parking lot, her face radiant with a huge smile. This was exactly the kind of night Jane liked, dark and stormy—an atmosphere custom-made for a thriller.

Charlotte slipped into the backseat of the squad car. "I can't wait to get back to your room at the Inn." She was relieved to find Jane in the backseat with her, instead of Billy. Having to fight him off for the rest of the evening would have been tantamount to torture.

"We're not going back to the inn. We're going to Blanchard's house," Jane said, as if it were as common a destination as going to the supermarket.

"Blanchard's house?" The headache she was fighting all day came screaming back into her temples. "For heaven's sake, *why?*"

"I've been thinking. If the tracking numbers in his little black book are shipments of illegal goods, where would Blanchard hide them? Not on the shipping dock, too many nosey people around." Jane held up her finger as though she was making a deduction. "So where else? The most obvious place is at home."

Todd glanced at her in the rearview mirror. "We can't just break in and search his house. We need probable cause."

"What about the black book?"

Todd sighed and shook his head. "Your suspicions about what's in that book aren't enough. What we need is factual evidence."

Jane tapped her chin, her eyes clouded from thought. "Suppose we go to his house on the pretense of visiting his wife to see why she didn't go to the dance? And if we happen to find anything incriminating, so be it."

Charlotte had a feeling something was up when Jane agreed to leave the dance. It all clicked into place now. "And you wouldn't be the slightest bit nosey about Mrs. Blanchard, would you?"

Jane crossed her legs and straightened her skirt. "If no one has seen Carolyn Blanchard in years, then yes, I'd like to find out why. Wouldn't you?"

Charlotte nodded, although she was a little skeptical about going there. "I guess so."

Todd turned his head toward the back seat. "You two keep Mrs. Blanchard busy while Billy and I have a look around. If we spot anything that looks suspicious, we'll come back with a search warrant."

As they stood on the front porch of the Blanchard's white brick bungalow, arguing over who should be the one to knock on the door, the rain began. It came as a swift, torrential downpour, so strong it flooded the front sidewalk and the street in front of the house within a few minutes.

The front door opened a crack. "What's all the ruckus out here?" someone asked in a voice so quiet the words could barely be heard over the raindrops splashing against the sidewalk.

Charlotte stepped closer to the door. "Carolyn Blanchard?"

"Yes, I'm Mrs. Blanchard," the soft voice confirmed, "But who are you?"

Charlotte peered through the crack, but the darkness from the storm and the dim light from inside didn't give her a view of the speaker. Mrs. Blanchard was still nothing more than a rumor and a voice.

"We're good friends of your daughter, Susan. We were worried when you didn't come to the country club dance this evening, so we came by to see if you were all right."

"Well, if you're friends of Susan's..." Carolyn Blanchard cracked the door open a little wider and peered at them with a look of caution in her pale green eyes. "You'd better come in the house. It's raining out, you know."

She opened the door, and Charlotte took in the sight of Mrs. Blanchard. She was a middle-aged woman with a slim build, but she seemed small and unassuming in her blue and white pinstriped housedress. Her straight, mousy-brown hair was neatly pulled back into a bun at the back of her head. Worried eyes peered over the top of a pair of black-rimmed reading glasses and darted from face to face as though she was afraid to look at anyone for too long. "You'll have to excuse my appearance," she said. "I wasn't expecting company."

Todd gave her his best reassuring smile. "You look just fine."

"Thank you, young man." She moved her glasses to the top of her head. "If you'll all take a seat in the living room, I'll get you some refreshments."

"Please don't bother, Mrs. Blanchard," Charlotte said. "We don't need anything."

Mrs. Blanchard smiled, but it was a timid smile that held little warmth, almost as though she had forgotten how to smile. "I'll bring in some coffee, then."

"Coffee's fine," everyone agreed.

Mrs. Blanchard disappeared into the kitchen.

"She looks all right to me," Charlotte whispered to Jane as they stepped into the lavishly furnished living room, the sounds from the kitchen confirming that Mrs. Blanchard was busy making coffee. "She's wearing nice clothes, and she lives in this beautiful house. It doesn't make sense." Charlotte surveyed the living room and finally settled herself into one of the burgundy velvet easy chairs.

Jane picked up a Chinese porcelain figurine and checked the bottom. "How can Blanchard afford all this expensive stuff?"

"He makes a good living as the shipping manager." Charlotte shrugged, not sure what else to say.

"I don't know." Jane put the figurine back on the shelf. "Do you really think a shipping manager makes enough for this kind of house. I mean, look at this stuff," she gestured to the room as a whole, "These aren't bargain basement knock-offs."

Jane took a seat on the white sectional sofa next to Todd. "This whole setup looks a little suspicious to me. Let's ask Mrs. Blanchard a few questions. She might let something slip as long as she doesn't know why we're really here."

The sounds of shuffling in the hallway alerted them that Mrs. Blanchard was returning. Charlotte pasted a pleasant smile on her face. Mrs. Blanchard toddled into the living room, balancing a large wooden tray.

"Well now, along with the coffee, I brought some of my homemade muffins for you young people to enjoy."

"Thank you, Mrs. Blanchard," Charlotte said as their hostess handed her a dessert plate with a large, warm muffin in the center.

"We were wondering why you didn't go to the dance tonight." Jane set her plate in her lap.

Mrs. Blanchard stiffened as her eyes flitted on each of them. "I'm not really much for dancing."

"There's still plenty of time for you to go and mingle with your friends," Charlotte offered. She shuddered when she sipped the bitter coffee. It was clear that making coffee was not among Mrs. Blanchard's skills. "Your husband and daughter are there."

"Yes, I know they are." She glanced from side to side and back again. "I would really love to go, but I can't."

"Why not?" Jane urged, sensing a secret that Carolyn Blanchard might disclose. "Are you waiting for something? A special delivery maybe?"

Charlotte gave Jane a questioning glance, but Jane ignored it, her attention narrowed on their hostess.

Mrs. Blanchard placed the empty tray on the glass-topped coffee table, her hands light and delicate as she did. She looked down at her housedress. "No, I'm not expecting any deliveries. But I'm afraid I don't have anything appropriate to wear."

"Oh," Jane sounded disappointed.

"This muffin is delicious," Billy said. "What kind is it?"

"It contains my secret ingredient." Carolyn placed a finger to her lips. "It's poppy seed," she whispered. "But don't tell anyone. I don't want *them* to know."

Todd placed his plate on the end table and leaned forward, his eyes sparkling with interest. "Them?"

Mrs. Blanchard nodded vehemently. A stray tendril of hair slipped from her tight bun as her gaze darted around the room. "It's the only thing that can protect you from them."

Everyone looked around. They appeared to be the only ones in the room. Jane's voice asked anxiously, "From whom?"

"You know… from *them*." Carolyn Blanchard hissed out the last word and pointed an accusing finger at the living room drapes. "And it works like a charm," she said happily. "They haven't bothered me for months. That is, not until tonight."

She peered at Jane with one eye squinted. "And that worries me, because they can read your thoughts if you don't take the proper precautions." She opened the living room closet door to reveal two-dozen hats neatly stacked on top of each other. She grabbed the top hat and carefully arranged it on her head. "There. That's better."

Todd jumped up from the sofa and raced over to check the drapes, but no one was there. He asked in a cautious voice, "Is that why all your hats are made of aluminum foil?"

"Yes," the older woman said. She took on a sinister air. "I almost never leave the house anymore. My husband had some special things built into this house to protect me from them. They've been fooled for a long time, but now I'm afraid they're back."

She pressed her hands firmly against her cheeks and edged toward the window. "I'm sure I saw one of them outside a little while ago when I opened the door to let you in, but don't worry, this hat makes my brain invisible to them. They can't get me if they can't read my thoughts."

Todd nodded slowly, his eyes filled with worry. He turned toward Charlotte and Jane and mouthed, "Let's get out of here."

Billy grinned openly as he watched the agitated Mrs. Blanchard pace near the window. He came up behind Todd, and the two inched their way toward the front door.

Charlotte couldn't help but pity the mentally unstable woman with the angst-ridden eyes. While the monsters that she imagined were all in her mind, it was clear that her fear was genuine.

"It's been a real experience visiting with you, Mrs. Blanchard." She placed her plate on the glass coffee table and shot to her feet. "But, we really have to go now."

"No one is going anywhere!" Carolyn jumped in front of them. "You can't leave. Don't you understand?" With her eyes wide and her mouth twisted into a clown-faced frown, she pointed toward the door. "They're out there waiting to whisk you away and do horrible, unspeakable things to you."

"Really, Mrs. Blanchard, we're not afraid of them." Charlotte tried to edge past, her heart racing. "Besides, they're not after us."

"I can't let you go." Carolyn flung herself against the front door, blocking them from leaving. "Now that you're here, you'll have to stay." She turned the key in the lock, slipped it out, and squeezed it in the palm of her hand. "I'm doing this for your own good."

Todd glanced out the front window as a pair of headlights neared the house. "Lanchardbay," he said, motioning toward the window.

"I've got an idea." Jane's voice was soothing. "How about if we each wear one of your aluminum hats? Then we can sneak out the back door. That way our brains will be invisible, and they won't be able to read our thoughts."

Mrs. Blanchard nodded, her gaze darting back to the door. "I think that will work, but you have to hurry, or they'll get suspicious."

Jane smiled softly and patted Mrs. Blanchard's shoulder. Then everyone snatched a hat from the front closet and shot out the back door in single file as a key turned in the front lock.

One by one, they jumped from the back porch into a puddle of water below before running across the grass alongside the house until they reached the squad car parked around the corner. Billy revved up the engine in an effort to speed away, but the tires only spun around, throwing water into the air.

"Slow down," Todd said, his voice stern. "Or we'll never get out of here." The wheels continued to spin in the mud, and Todd sighed. "Get out, I'll drive."

Todd jumped out of the passenger's side and switched places with Billy. Within a few seconds, he slowly maneuvered the car out of the mud, and they were safely on their way.

Charlotte crushed her aluminum hat into a large ball and threw it at the floor of the car. It landed next to Jane's as they sped down the road. "Don't you ever put me in a situation like that again," she growled at Jane.

"How could we know the old bat was out of her skull?" A grin spread across Billy's lips. He winked at Charlotte, laughter playing in his eyes.

"Don't call her an old bat," Jane said. "It sounds degrading. But she is a little crazy, isn't she?"

Billy shoved his arm over the top of the seat and glanced at her. "No criminal activity going on there that I could see. It looked to me like Mrs. Blanchard just forgot to take her medication."

Jane gave a one shoulder shrug. "You're probably right."

Todd eyed them in the rear-view mirror. "Okay ladies, where to now?"

"Let's go to the shipping dock and see what we can find there," Jane said. "You still have the keys to the dock door, don't you, Charlotte?"

"You three go. I'm exhausted," Charlotte huffed. After that debacle at Blanchard's house, the only place she wanted to go was to bed. "Take me home."

Billy gave her a lewd wink, his eyes roaming over her cleavage. "You can drop us off at Charlotte's apartment."

Charlotte leaned her head back. "No, Billy. I meant I want to go home, alone."

"Don't I even get a goodnight kiss?" Billy licked his lips in anticipation.

She sat up bolt straight, her seatbelt holding her in place. "No!"

"I think we'd better drop this party pooper off," Todd said. "And then we can do more investigating on our own."

Charlotte smiled. She'd finally gotten her point across. "I don't think you need to come to my place tomorrow morning, Todd. I'm sure it was Blanchard who broke into my apartment, searching for that little black book of his. But I'm not pressing charges."

Jane glanced at her. "Whatever happened to that book? Do you still have it?"

"No," Charlotte said. "Remember when Mrs. Blanchard handed us the plates with the muffins on them? I slipped the book under my plate when I put it down on the coffee table. So now, I'm rid of it for good." A dark thought raced across her mind, and she caught her breath. "What if Mrs. Blanchard tells her husband we were there tonight?"

Todd smirked. "Do you think he'd believe her?"

Charlotte leaned back confidently in her seat. "I wouldn't. But there *are* four empty plates and coffee cups. Not to mention the muddy footprints outside the back door." She sighed deeply. "What if Blanchard figures out what happened?"

"Don't worry," Billy said. "We didn't do anything wrong."

A loud boom pierced the night air, and the car gave a violent shudder.

"What was that?" Charlotte asked.

"Flat tire," Todd said, jerking the steering wheel to regain control. He slowed the car, expertly steering it onto the side of the road before it stopped.

Charlotte dragged her hands over her face. "Things like this always happen to me when it's late and I'm tired."

"Stop complaining, babe," Billy said. "You don't have to change it."

Charlotte shot him a nasty smirk.

Jane rolled the window down and glimpsed the rolling clouds. "At least it isn't raining anymore."

Todd opened the driver's side door. "You two stay in the car while we change the tire."

Charlotte decided she'd check out the water damage to her new three-inch, sling-back pumps while she waited.

The officers stood next to the driver's side and stared at the flat. "I'll get the jack from the trunk," Billy said.

Charlotte leaned back in the seat, closing her eyes while she waited. It had been a miserable, stressful day, and all she wanted to do was go home, take a nice relaxing bath, and go to sleep.

Jane fidgeted in her seat. "I can't stand just sitting here. I'm going to see how they're doing."

Just as she opened the back door, Todd opened the driver's side door. He picked up the handset and called in something in code to the station.

Jane stopped and stared at Todd. Then she closed the back door again. "Charlotte, you'll never guess what they found."

"I don't want to know. If they can't fix the tire, I'll call a taxi."

"But you can't go." Jane's voice sounded urgent.

Charlotte didn't care. Her nerves were still on edge from that visit to the Blanchard's, and whatever was going on right now didn't interest her. She'd had enough of Jane's schemes, and murder, and crazy people. "Oh, yes I can. Watch me."

Opening the car door, she stepped onto the pavement and took a deep breath. The humid night air clung to her throat, making it difficult to breathe. She leaned against the squad car, gazing down at the black pavement stretched out before her. A light, moist breeze ruffled her hair as she took a quick survey of the area. She wasn't sure where she was. The new construction was disorienting, but she couldn't be far from town, clusters of lights twinkled in the distance. Stepping away from the car, she headed toward the trunk for a flashlight so she wouldn't be stumbling around in the dark.

"Oh, my God!" Charlotte's hand flew to her mouth as she shrank back, but she couldn't tear her eyes away. The dim trunk light gave Alyssa Longbourne's face a pale green cast. Her limp body lay oddly twisted, fading into the shadows. Dark blood welled around the handle of the dagger in her chest.

The scene was surreal, as if it had been staged, and she was looking at it through someone else's eyes. Charlotte couldn't move. Her feet were rooted to the spot by some horrible fascination, but an unexpected sound shocked her back to the moment. She shuddered as a piercing shriek escaped her throat.

Chapter Twenty Three

A warm hand touched Charlotte's clammy shoulder, and she nearly jumped out of her skin. Jerking back, she slipped out from under the hand, her blank eyes focusing on the face in front of her. "Alyssa Longbourne's in the trunk!"

"I tried to tell you Billy found Alyssa's dead body in there," Jane said. "You wouldn't listen."

Charlotte couldn't believe how calm Jane was when she felt as though she would fall apart. It was horrible seeing a dead body, and that was something she would never get used to.

Dead body.

Something pricked at her mind as she tried to remember what she had heard before she was startled by Jane. She glanced toward the trunk. "But she's not dead!"

Jane's eyes widened. "What?"

"She's still alive. I heard a gurgling sound."

"Really?" Jane leaned into the trunk and carefully placed two fingers on Alyssa's throat. "You're right. I can feel a faint pulse." Removing her hand, she typed a message into her cell phone.

After a few moments, Todd said. "Ambulance is on the way. Should be here in a few minutes." He shook his head.

"I should have checked Alyssa's pulse instead of letting Billy do it."

Charlotte closed her eyes as nausea set in. "I can't look anymore." She walked to the side of the road as Jane leaned into the trunk again.

"Alyssa," Jane murmured soothingly. "Everything is going to be okay. Help is on the way, so you hang in there."

Charlotte gasped at the heavy air. Lights danced in her vision, and she felt like she was going to collapse on the ground. Alyssa was in that trunk, and while she might not be able to hear anyone, she must be hurting and terrified. Bile slid up Charlotte's throat, choking her even more than her emotions. "I think I may be sick."

"Don't think about what you saw," Billy's deep voice comforted her. "Just keep breathing from your diaphragm. I'll walk you around, and in a few minutes, the feeling will pass."

Charlotte glanced up at him. *Who knew Billy had a compassionate side?*

He parted his lips to show a brilliant white smile. "I've been through this, too..." *Maybe he's not so bad after all.* "Babe."

What was it about the term of endearment that just irritated every nerve ending? Telling him off would be a pleasure, but after what happened, it seemed unimportant. She opened her mouth to tell him that, and to thank him for his advice, but the shrill sound of sirens silenced her.

The ambulance stopped right behind the squad car, and two paramedics jumped out. After a few moments, the other police officers arrived. The brilliant flash of a camera cut through the darkness like lightning, and Charlotte shuddered at the indignities Alyssa was suffering.

The Chief, in the center of the chaos, directed everyone—the perfect example of efficiency, which was surprising considering it usually didn't seem like he was at the top of his game. The police searched the vehicle, while the paramedics carefully pulled Alyssa from the trunk and trundled her onto the gurney. As they placed her into the ambulance, Charlotte raced forward. "Wait, can I go with her?"

Everyone paused and stared at her, including the Chief. Heat spread to her face. "I don't want her to be alone," she said quietly.

Jane peered at her from behind Todd. "I'd like to go, too."

The Chief gave a firm nod of his head. "The ladies will just be in the way here. Let them ride with Alyssa," he said to the ambulance driver before turning to face them. "You two wait at the hospital. We need to question you."

With that, he turned back to the trunk as Jane and Charlotte climbed into the ambulance.

The lights in the hospital emergency room were muted for the evening hours, but that didn't stop the quiet hum of excitement from invading the stillness. As soon as they walked inside, a systematic chaos took place. Alyssa was rushed into a different room while an orderly directed them into the waiting room before following the chaos that Alyssa's still form brought in its wake.

Jane and Charlotte settled into the leather chairs and stared blankly at the muted television playing in the corner. For once, Jane didn't have anything to say, and Charlotte wondered if she was concerned or simply plotting her next, "Who done it." As the seconds slid into minutes, Charlotte could barely contain her worry and paced the hard tile floor. Jane's eyes followed her movement, but she still said nothing.

"What do you think is happening in there?" Charlotte finally asked.

As if on cue, Nurse Nan Truhart entered through the doors of the waiting room.

"I thought you'd like to know they're prepping Alyssa for emergency surgery. Doc Wilson is performing it himself. They texted him at the dance, and he came right over. He's changing now."

"Do you think she's going to pull through?" Charlotte asked. As much as she had disliked the new Mrs. Longbourne, she would never have wished this on her.

Nan's eyes widened with uncertainty. "Only God knows that. And he's not talking. All we can do is wait and pray."

For as long as Charlotte could remember, Nanette Truhart had been a nurse. The woman never seemed to change. Her faded yellow hair was styled the same way it had always been, a short, smooth bob with finger waves that clung close to her long, narrow face. That style had gone out of fashion decades ago, along with her thinly penciled-in, arched eyebrows. The nurse's care-worn face had the appearance of an elderly matron. But then, she had always looked old even when she was younger.

Todd came through the doors, and nodded slowly at them. "The Chief asked me to come down and collect Jane for questioning."

Jane stood and gathered her things as Charlotte asked, "Does he want me to come down, too?"

"Not yet. You can stay with Alyssa in case she needs anything, or until we can locate Mr. Longbourne. Matt Bridgewater is on his way here to guard the patient if she makes it through surgery. I'll be by later to pick you up."

Charlotte nodded as Jane gave her a quick hug, before she walked out the door with Todd.

Nurse Nan went to her desk and pick up a clipboard with attached paperwork on it. She returned to the waiting area. "I've got to fill out these admittance forms for Alyssa. Most of it's done, but there are a few things I still need. Since no one can find her husband, would you know of any other relatives?"

In the short time she'd known Alyssa, the subject of Alyssa's family hadn't come up. "Sorry, he's the only one I know. You should ask your daughter. After all, Ruth is Jim Longbourne's administrative assistant. I'm sure she knows everything about his new wife."

"Yes, I'll call her." Nurse Nan paused mid-turn. "How has Ruth been anyway? I haven't really spoken to her in weeks."

"Don't you see her when she does volunteer work at the clinic?"

The nurse tapped an impatient pen on the clipboard. "She hasn't volunteered at the clinic in ages. I wish she would start again. Did you know she trained to be a nurse?"

"No, I didn't."

"After Ruth finished nursing school, she was a great help to me until Jim Longbourne tempted her with that high-paying office job."

"But I ran into Ruth at the clinic last week, and I assumed she was volunteering. Anyway, she said she was meeting you."

"I don't know who she was meeting, but it certainly wasn't me. The woman has entirely too much free time on her hands. I hope Jim hasn't involved her in this ghastly murder business. You know, Charlotte, murder doesn't just concern the victim and the guilty, it affects the innocent, too. Jim has some nasty character flaws. One being that he wasn't always a faithful husband. Bessie put up with him, but she didn't trust him. And neither do I, especially after her death."

"I remember when the accident happened," Charlotte said, walking slowly back to Nurse Nan's station with her. "Mrs. Longbourne's death came as a shock to everyone."

"Accident?" The nurse scoffed. "My dear, I don't think it was a regrettable accident."

"Are you insinuating she was murdered?"

The nurse shrugged. "Who can say for sure? A piece of string could have been tied across the top of the basement stairs and carefully removed afterward. Or maybe a gentle nudge could have sent her tumbling down. There are many ways to make a fall look like an accident."

"I can't believe anyone would kill a dear person like Bessie Longbourne."

The nurse's beady gray eyes moved from side to side and back again to meet Charlotte's. "There would be no way to prove it, of course." She leaned closer. "There's only suspicion."

So she thinks Jim murdered his first wife. How interesting.

"My daughter needs to find a nice man to marry and get out of that office before Jim does something..." A look of horror flitted across her face for an instant. "I mean," she composed herself, "Before something happens to her, too."

"I wouldn't worry if I were you." Charlotte tried to sound reassuring. "Ruth's got a level head on her shoulders."

The nurse was silent for a moment as her eyes examined Charlotte's face.

"You're looking a little pale. I heard you fainted at the courthouse. It sounds to me like you might have hypoglycemia. You should get that checked out."

"Thanks. I will."

The nurse glanced at her watch. "I really must go now, but I'll keep you up to date on Alyssa's condition."

With that, Nurse Nan walked back to her station, leaving Charlotte standing in the middle of the waiting room. She went to her seat and took up her silent vigil once again. With Jane gone, it seemed lonelier than before, and her mind wandered. Why did Ruth's story about being at the clinic differ from her mother's? One of them was lying. *But why would either of them lie to me?*

Weary from the long night she hadn't anticipated, Charlotte could barely keep her eyes open as the sun peeked over the horizon. She turned the key in the lock of her apartment and walked in. Everything in the living room was back in place. Even the carpet appeared to have been vacuumed. A loud, rustling noise in the bedroom made her freeze.

"Where have you been all this time?" Her mother's voice echoed through the apartment. Mrs. Ross's freshly washed face and red rimmed eyes peered questioningly at her daughter from the bedroom doorway.

"Oh, Mother! You nearly scared me to death. What are you doing here at," she checked the kitchen clock, "Six ten on a Sunday morning?"

"If you must know, I spent the night in your bedroom. I'm still not talking to your father. But when I woke up this morning and found that you hadn't come home, I got worried. I was just about to call your cell."

Charlotte collapsed on the sofa. "You can't imagine what happened to me last night." She stifled a yawn as she slipped her ruined pumps from her feet and attempted to ignore the heaviness that invaded her body.

Her mother sat down next to her and shook her index finger at her daughter. "I think you'd better tell me all about it."

Her mother's finger was well-known to Charlotte, having pointed out every one of her character flaws, her short-comings, and her weaknesses over the past twenty-nine years.

Charlotte massaged her sore feet and slumped down deep into the lumpy folds of the sofa cushion. "I'm exhausted right now. I'll tell you about it later."

Mrs. Ross paced the floor in front of the sofa. "I'd rather you tell me now, or I'll worry over it all day."

Sighing in resignation, Charlotte closed her eyes. "All right, but I'm only giving you the highlights. You can watch the details on television later."

The night came flooding back to her—the flat tire, finding Alyssa's bent and broken body in the trunk. The silence of the hospital as she waited, her body tense from worry for the news that Alyssa was going to make it.

She finally wove the story for her mother, taking in the startled look that flitted across her mother's face. But she left out some of the details—her confrontation with Tim Blanchard, the trip to the Blanchard's house, and her ransacked apartment. Her mother would be concerned enough.

By the end of the story, Charlotte was so physically, mentally, and emotionally exhausted that she could barely keep her eyes open. "And Doc Wilson did some pretty impressive emergency surgery on Alyssa. I have to give the old guy credit. He's still a skillful surgeon, even at his age."

"Don't talk about him as if he's an antiquity." Her mother huffed. "The man's only sixty-two."

Charlotte stretched her arms above her head. "Doc Wilson said Alyssa's in a medical induced coma right now. He doesn't know when they'll be able to take her out of it. And that's about all there is." Charlotte's voice trailed off as she stifled another yawn. "If you'll excuse me, I'm going to bed."

She stood up and attempted to shake the weariness from her shoulders as she hobbled toward the bedroom, but stopped short of reaching the door. "Oh, a couple of other things, Mom. Thanks for cleaning up my apartment. And don't forget to lock the door after you leave." She didn't want any-one sneaking in on her.

"You're welcome." Mrs. Ross called from the kitchen. "But I don't understand how you can live in such a pigsty. I thought I raised you better than that."

Charlotte was too weary to explain, so she just shrugged.

"And what makes you think I'm leaving? I might stay for the rest of the day."

"Stay as long as you want."

Part of her wanted her mom to stay—to have someone there to watch over her while she slept. The other part of her, however, knew her mother. There was no doubt she couldn't wait to bolt down the stairs and start gossiping with the neigh-bors who were always eager to hear blazing hot news.

Sunday morning had started out sunny and warm, but by the time Charlotte woke up late in the afternoon, the sky was overcast. She shivered as she made her way to the bathroom. There was a definite chill in the air, unusual for an afternoon in July. Since no one had called or made an effort to contact her, she assumed everything was status quo, so she took a shower and changed into her pajamas.

She'd been so tired when she got back to her apartment that morning, she'd fallen asleep in the evening dress she'd worn the night before. Even though she had slept for nine hours straight, exhaustion still clung to her.

After throwing together a quick supper of scrambled eggs and toast, she sat on the sofa, feet up, with a fresh cup of coffee. She grabbed her remote control and turned on the television, switching the station to the local news channel.

There they were, the four of them and the police chief, giving interviews as a group and individually. Photos of Mr. Longbourne, along with those of his two wives, were up on the screen. The details of the first Mrs. Longbourne's death were dredged up and reexamined with new speculation that maybe it hadn't been an accident. Along with those insights came the news that Jim Longbourne was still missing and was wanted for questioning about the attack on Alyssa Longbourne as well as the murder of Carlton Witherspoon.

Charlotte closed her eyes and leaned her head against the sofa cushion. *Will this nightmare ever end?*

Chapter Twenty Four

"I'm glad to see you decided to come to work this morning." John hung his gray sports coat on the back of his desk chair.

Charlotte's heart jumped at the sound of his voice, but it settled back into its usual place, slightly askew, whenever he was near.

"Morning," she said in a startled voice as she crossed his office. "I didn't see you come in."

"Do you have something for me?" He leaned forward in his chair and put his hand out toward her.

"No, I'm looking for a tissue. I've got a paper cut."

"Help yourself." He handed her the full box from his desk. "After a weekend like you had, I thought you might want to take a few days off to rest." He grinned to express his pleasure with her. "You're a real heroine, rescuing Alyssa Longbourne like that."

Charlotte wrapped a tissue around her finger. "Thanks, but I don't need any more rest. I slept my entire Sunday away."

He smiled and typed something into his computer. "Then you haven't checked the town's social media pages yet?" He waited for a screen to come up and clicked his mouse. "Come here and take a look. I found these candid photos from the Midsummer Night's dance, yesterday." His voice took on a sarcastic tone. "I think you'll find some of them amusing."

Charlotte came around to his side of the desk, a sense of dread building in her, and glanced at the computer screen. She caught her breath at the photos of her and Billy Price seated at the dinner table. One where he had his arm around her shoulder, just before she shrugged it off. Another of him peering down the front of her dress, just before she put her hand up to block his view.

"You're right." Charlotte sighed deeply. "I do find them amusing." *And seriously disturbing.*

"Why are you getting involved with a sleeze-bag like Billy Price? I'm sure you know that he's got a bad reputation with women."

Charlotte walked to the front of his desk, stress making her irritable. "Did you get your information about him from your fiancée? She lived with Billy for nearly two years, until a couple of months ago, when he kicked her out. Or didn't she tell you about that?"

He raised his index finger and wiggled it at her. "I never thought you were the catty type. And you've got it wrong. He didn't kick her out. She moved out when she discovered he was playing around."

Charlotte folded her arms across her chest. "Well, you're wrong about me, too. I'm not dating that guy."

"Then why were you with him at the dance on Saturday night?"

"I wasn't with him. He came in and sat down at my table."

John jutted his chin out in sarcasm. "Oh, it was a random act, huh?"

"That's right."

"The two of you looked awfully chummy to me."

A streak of red flashed across her eyes as anger wrenched her insides. "Why should you care?" She could barely control her breathing. "You spent the entire evening dancing and laughing with that... that sad excuse for a fiancée."

"That's my business!"

Her blood boiled just beneath her skin. "And this is *my* business."

"Well, Charlotte, *your business* is all over the Internet."

"Aarrgghhh!" Charlotte felt her face turn scarlet.

She dashed out of his office. As she reached the hall, she glanced around and saw him standing in his doorway with a Cheshire-cat grin on his smug face.

She somehow made it to Ruth's office and dropped herself into the chair next to her desk. She took a deep breath and let it out in a big whoosh. "I've really had it with John." She pounded her fist on the desk. "I can't work for him anymore. He makes me so mad."

"Why don't you quit?" Ruth appeared only mildly interested in Charlotte's intentions as she paged through the morning edition of *The Gazette*.

Charlotte slumped down. "I can't right now. I need the money. But I'm not sticking around after he marries Susan."

"According to this article in the paper, it appears your friend, Jane, is assisting the police in solving Carlton's murder. Frankly, I've always considered her capabilities as a detective to be greatly exaggerated. If she's so clever, why can't she tell me where Jim is?"

"If she knew, she would have told the police." Charlotte pursed her lips and glanced at the paper in Ruth's hands. "We thought *you* might know where he is."

"Me?" Ruth appeared genuinely surprised. "How would I know?"

"You're his executive administrative assistant."

Ruth put the newspaper down. "Do you know where John is every minute?"

"I don't think I want to know, these days. But you've made your point."

"I wish I did know where Jim was," Ruth sighed as she tapped out a long sequence on her desk with her short, scarlet nails. The top of Ruth's old oak desk appeared as though it had endured quite a bit of nail-tapping over the years. "It makes me nervous to know he's out there, somewhere."

"You? Nervous? Miss 'I-never-lose-my-composure' is nervous?"

Ruth adjusted her wire-rimmed glasses and narrowed her eyes. "That's right." Her sharp voice made Charlotte straighten up in her seat. "If you don't mind, I have a lot of important calls to make. You know, the lawyer's office, the insurance agency, and the like. I'll be quite busy on the phone for several hours." Ruth scooped up the newspaper pages and shoved them into her wastebasket. "By the way, would you happen to know what room they put Alyssa in after surgery?"

"Sorry, I can't help you there." Charlotte shrugged. She'd promised the police that she wouldn't discuss anything about Alyssa's recovery. The killer might come back to finish the job.

"I really need to know." There was a demanding tone in Ruth's voice. " She tapped her fingers on the desk again. "I'd like to send her a card to let her know we're all pulling for her speedy recovery. And send her some flowers from the staff, of course. According to the newspaper, you were at the hospital with her, and afterward, you were with the police all night. Surely, you must know something. I would hate to think of her all alone without a caring hand to help her."

Charlotte found it hard to believe Ruth was genuinely concerned about the wellbeing of Alyssa Longbourne, despite all her claims to the opposite. "No, honestly, I don't know. And even if I did, I couldn't tell you. Have you tried asking your mother?"

Ruth's face turned to stone. She evidently had. Her cold, gray eyes bored into Charlotte's over the top rim of her spectacles. Without saying another word, she stood up, went into Jim's office, and slammed the door behind her.

Charlotte pondered their exchange. She could understand why Ruth was nervous about Longbourne being on the loose, but she didn't understand why those phone calls couldn't be made from her own desk. And all that concern about Alyssa. It's not like Ruth had any love for her.

From inside Jim's office, drawers opened and slammed shut. Charlotte leaned against the door to listen. It sounded like Ruth was frantically searching the files. Shrugging her shoulders at the closed door, Charlotte returned to her desk.

The morning dragged on as Charlotte mechanically performed her office duties. She kept an eye on her phone for the lights to go on, signaling that Ruth was making phone calls from Jim's office, but they never did. That was odd, but then, there were too many things that didn't make sense about this whole situation.

Where was Jim Longbourne, and why would he attack his new wife? And for that matter, why would he want to kill Carlton Witherspoon? Even if the rumors were true that Witherspoon was selling the company out from under him, there must have been another way to handle it. What did that Triumvirate card have to do with all of this? *There has to be a link somewhere, but I can't figure out what it is.*

Things were closing in too fast. She'd never been nervous about being at work until Ruth mentioned Jim Longbourne being "out there" somewhere. Charlotte stared at each of her co-workers with contempt. Someone had to know something. Why wasn't anyone stepping forward?

At twelve o'clock, she sat in the lunch room eating the chicken salad sandwich she'd brought from home, when Ruth appeared around the corner with a file folder clutched in her hands. She ran from the building and raced to her car in the parking lot.

Charlotte finished her sandwich and nibbled on a chocolate brownie for dessert. *What's going on with Ruth these days?* Eventually, her curiosity got the better of her and she left to get the key to Jim Longbourne's office.

She opened the door, and her breath caught in her throat. His desk and file cabinet drawers were wide open. Stacks of papers were scattered across the desk, and files lay strewn on the floor from one end of the room to the other, as if someone had been searching through them.

Charlotte walked in and tiptoed around the mess. Taking a quick glance at the papers on his desk, she didn't see anything important, but then again, she didn't know what Ruth considered to be important. Careful not to disturb too much, she left the office, locking the door behind her.

She went back to her desk to find Officer Todd Shlagg, in his street clothes, standing at her cubicle.

"What are you doing here?"

He crossed his arms and leaned against Charlotte's cubicle wall. "Jane sent me over to pick up Carlton's manuscript. We're gonna go over it. She thinks there might be a clue to his murder in there."

"Well, I don't have it with me. It's at home. Tell her she can pick it up later."

He nodded and turned to leave just as Ruth returned to the office. Her face went pale before she rushed up to Todd, "Have you found Jim Longbourne?"

"Not yet." Todd gazed at the floor and shuffled his feet.

Ruth's eyes slanted as a cat's eyes would moments before it pounced on its victim, the color returning to her face in a deep flush. "Then why are you standing around here when you should be out searching for him?"

"It's my day off," he said, still looking down before he brought angry eyes up to glare at Ruth. "I'm entitled, you know, even during a murder investigation."

Ruth huffed and stared up at him.

Todd's face held a guilty look as he spun around and walked toward the front door.

Charlotte mopped the perspiration from her forehead with a tissue. She wasn't good at confrontations, and she needed to confront Ruth about her suspicious behavior this morning.

"You told me you needed to go into Jim's office to make some important phone calls, but you never used the phone. I didn't see either of the lights go on, so I got a little worried. Later, when you went out to lunch, I got the key. I know I shouldn't have gone in there, but I did. When I opened the door, his file drawers had been riffled through. Papers were everywhere."

"The reason the phone wasn't lit up was because I used my cell to make those calls." Ruth pinched the bridge of her nose. "And Jim's office was perfect when I left it. For all I know, you riffled through the files yourself."

Charlotte's nervousness at accusing Ruth turned into determination. "I don't have any reason to search through Longbourne's files." *I've already found the confirmation that the company was being sold.*

"Then someone is trying to make me look bad," Ruth whimpered.

"Who?" Charlotte couldn't imagine why anyone would want to do that.

Ruth quickly pulled herself together. "No one." She cleared her throat. "Forget I mentioned it. Now, if you'll excuse me, I have work to do." Ruth gave her a frosty glare before she walked back to her desk.

"Hmmm," Charlotte said, a little despondent. *Is it my imagination, or is there a lot more to this than meets the eye?*

John appeared at Charlotte's cubicle. The frown on his lips and the intense look in his eyes made her wonder if she'd done something wrong.

"Was that guy another boyfriend?"

"No," Charlotte groaned in exasperation. "He's only a friend."

"Attend to your personal life on your own time," John said. "This happens to be a business, not your private playground." He stormed off.

She'd heard that irritated tone in his voice before—when he was jealous. But why would he be jealous of Todd? Does he still care? Hope fluttered in her chest, delicate as a butterfly's wings until her rational mind took over. Why would he be jealous if he was marrying someone else? *Let it go, Charlotte.* She was beginning to wonder if he ever had feelings for her, even though he'd always hinted at them. He exerted his charm and swept her off her feet so easily and so naturally, she'd fallen for him without a second thought.

He may be engaged to Susan, but he's not married to her yet. There could still be a chance for me.

Chapter Twenty Five

Five o'clock couldn't come soon enough. At a quarter before the hour, Charlotte turned off her computer in anticipation of leaving a few minutes early. Calling in sick the next day had seriously crossed her mind, but she didn't want to give John the satisfaction of thinking he caused her to show any kind of weakness.

At the stroke of five, the front door was nearly within Charlotte's reach when Ruth walked up to her. She grabbed her arm and whispered in her ear. "I have to talk to you, but not in front of them." Ruth pointed to a group of co-workers preparing to leave the building. "Come back into the hall with me."

As she followed Ruth into the hall that separated the lunchroom from the front office, Charlotte braced herself for the worst, convinced Ruth was going to let her have it for what she'd said earlier.

But instead, Ruth seemed edgy. She ran trembling fingers through her short, dark hair and fumbled to pull a slim cigarette from her handbag. "If I don't find out where Jim is, I think I'll lose my mind." She paced the hall in front of Charlotte. "He's been leaving me threatening messages, telling me to keep my mouth shut, or he says I'll end up like Alyssa." She produced a folded paper and handed it to Charlotte. "Look at this."

Charlotte read the typed message out aloud.

"Don't talk to the authorities, or you'll be in the morgue."

Ruth snatched the paper from Charlotte's hand and shoved it in her purse. She took a long drag from the unlit cigarette. "He must have gone into his office right after I left for lunch today. Probably searching for something he left behind. I'm sure of it."

Charlotte focused on Ruth's shaking hand as she rolled the unlit cigarette between her fingers. Something seemed off about all of this. "If he was here, I would have seen him come in and leave."

Ruth waved the unlit cigarette in the direction of Longbourne's office. "He's got a secret entrance. He uses it when he doesn't want anyone to know he's here."

"What was he looking for?"

"Anything that might incriminate him," Ruth said. "I noticed the cache of money he always keeps locked in his desk drawer is gone. The point is, if he could sneak in here without anyone knowing, he could easily kill me."

The desperate note in Ruth's voice touched Charlotte. "Why tell me all of this? Why didn't you tell Officer Shlagg when he was here this afternoon?"

Ruth stopped pacing. "That stumblebum?"

Charlotte remembered the first time she'd ever seen Todd. He was a tall, scrawny sixth-grader with a bad complexion, flicking peas off his lunch plate in the school cafeteria. Although he'd filled out physically, and his complexion had cleared up, she could never quite get that image of him out of her mind.

"I'm sure Todd can protect you from Jim," she said in a voice brimming with uncertainty.

"Nobody can protect me." Ruth placed a trembling hand on Charlotte's shoulder. "I really don't want to be alone tonight. Do you mind if I stay with you?"

Panic set in as Charlotte raised her eyebrows. "With me? Why?"

"I can't think of a place where I'd feel safer."

Given time, Charlotte was sure she could come up with at least a dozen safer places for Ruth to stay.

"You can tell me what's going on when you come home from the office. No one needs to know."

Charlotte's heart sank under the weight of this huge imposition. "Somehow, I don't think this is going to work."

"Don't be silly." Ruth puffed on the unlit cigarette and let out imaginary smoke in one long breath. "It'll only be for a night. Or two maybe. You won't even know I'm there." Ruth opened her purse, dropped the cigarette inside, and then closed it with a loud snap. "Don't look at me like that. I just quit smoking, and I don't intend to start again, but I'm so nervous I have to do something."

"I understand." Charlotte hoped this was the only weird thing she'd have to put up with for however long Ruth decided to stay. "I guess you can stay with me—that is if you don't think there's somewhere else that might be safer."

"Great." Ruth smiled in relief. "I'll go home, pack a few things in my overnight bag, and be at your door as soon as it gets dark. I don't want anyone to see me arrive. Is there a back entrance?"

"Yes, the staircase from the garden is relatively private."

Ruth nodded. "See you later." She walked out the door and headed toward her black Chrysler Town Car.

This whole situation didn't sit right with Charlotte. And the suspicion grew that she might have been railroaded into doing something she was going to regret. *There isn't much to eat at my place except leftovers and junk food. Maybe I should go to the supermarket. Then I'll have to change the bed linens. But then again, maybe not.*

Why should she be put out? If Ruth wanted to stay with her, she'd have to eat what was in the fridge and sleep on the sofa.

At five forty-five, Charlotte pulled her Mustang into the driveway with a large take-out order from Shorty's Diner. Her mother stood in a defensive posture at the bottom of the staircase leading up to her apartment.

What does that woman want now?

She placed her sweater over the front seat, concealing the paper bag. Her mother didn't approve of take-out food, and she was in no mood to get into an argument about it.

Mrs. Ross stalked over to the driver's window. "I'm glad you're home, dear. I have something to tell you." Charlotte opened the car door and stepped onto the pavement as her mother blurted out, "I've decided to leave your father."

"Again?" Charlotte slammed the door. "Is this the same decision to leave Father you've made ten times in the past thirty years?"

"No, this is different." Mrs. Ross pointed to three pieces of luggage near the front door. "This time, I'm really going."

Every time her parents had a major disagreement, her mother packed. "And where are you going this time?"

"This time, I'm moving in with you."

Charlotte's stomach churned. Hunger and anxiety were not a good mix.

Mrs. Ross pulled a tissue from her sleeve and dabbed at her nose. "If your father wants to talk to me, he knows where to find me. I left him a note."

"You can't move in with me." Charlotte inched her way toward the luggage.

"And why not? I can live wherever I want, and right now, I prefer to live with you."

Charlotte's mind raced to come up with a plausible excuse. "Well, you can't live with me."

Mrs. Ross wiped a tear from her eye, her voice trembling on a sob. "Give me one good reason."

"You just can't." Charlotte wasn't good at coming up with last-minute excuses, and her mother was a hard person to convince. She stared at Charlotte with annoyance flashing in her eyes.

"That's not a reason."

"Okay, then, um. I didn't want to tell you this, but Jane is moving in with me this evening."

The look of distress on her mother's face was replaced by one of annoyance. "Why do you want *her* living with you?"

Charlotte decided to elaborate on the best lie she could come up with at the moment. "She's run out of money and has to move out of the Eldridge Inn." She took a few steps closer to the luggage. "What could I say? I can't let her sleep in the street, can I?"

Mrs. Ross waved her tissue in the air. "The street is where she belongs. You're much too good for her."

"Don't be that way, Mom. Jane's not a bad person, and she's certainly not a criminal. At least, she's never been convicted of any crime." Charlotte was nearly within reach of one of the bags. "I think you should move back into the house and give Dad another chance."

A few more steps and she'd be able to reach the worn, black handle. "Please, do it for my sake. I can't stand to see the two of you at odds with each other. You know you're only hurting me when you argue like this. Now go and make peace with Daddy. You want me to be happy, don't you?" She let a whimper enter her voice as she gave her mom the best puppy dog eyes she could.

Mrs. Ross slipped the tissue into her sleeve and stepped closer to the luggage. "You know I do, dear, but that's beside the point."

"Okay, then look at it this way. Thirty years is a long time to invest in a marriage."

"Yes, it's a year more than your lifetime." Mrs. Ross's lips curled into a look of distain. "Much too long to be living with the same man. That's probably why he gets on my nerves so much."

"Please, go into the house, Mom." Charlotte opened the front door of her parents' home. "The neighbors are watching us."

"If you're so worried about the neighbors, let's go up to your apartment and have a nice, long talk."

If I have to have a long talk with my mother right now, I'll go insane. Even though the feeling of dread was slowly eating away at her insides, she put on a pleasant face and, in a kindly voice, continued pleading with her mother. "I would love to, Mom, but Jane will be here any minute, and you know how she is. She'll probably be glad that you left Dad."

A look of distaste filled Mrs. Ross's face, and Charlotte knew she had her. It was strange how much her mom hated Jane, and there was no way she'd want to make Jane happy. Catching her moment of weakness, Charlotte said, "If you like, I'll help you carry your bags back inside."

She grabbed her mother's overnight case and propelled it through the open door into the living room. It hit the floor and made a three-point landing near the piano.

"Why don't you give your marriage one more try," Charlotte pleaded. She shoved the larger of the two suitcases through the open door as her mom hesitated behind her. "And if, after a week or so, you decide to call it quits, you and I will have a long talk, and I'll help you move out. I promise."

"And we'll talk without that dreadful girl around," her mother asked hopefully.

"Definitely, if, and I mean *if*, after a couple of weeks, you and Dad can't work it out, I'll send Jane back to the inn, and you and I will have a long heart to heart." *Like that's ever going to happen.*

"That sounds fair." Mrs. Ross sniffed as she picked up the handle on the last suitcase. She wheeled it through the front doorway mumbling, "I've put up with your father's shenani-gans this long. I suppose another week or two won't hurt."

Charlotte leaned against the house and wiped the sweat from her upper lip. "Thank you, Mother. You don't know how much better you've made me feel."

Closing the front door, she dashed to her car, grabbed the paper bag, and leapt up the stairs to her apartment two at a time. When she reached the top landing, the cell in her purse was ringing. After opening the door, she slipped the phone out, breathing a heavy "Hello" into the phone as she tried to catch her breath.

"Charlotte, are you busy this evening?" Jane asked.

"Busy? Ah, yes. I'm trying to talk some sense into my mother." She winced at how easy it was getting to lie.

"Did you succeed this time?"

"For the moment."

"The reason I called is because I have a problem."

Another problem? I don't have time for any more prob-lems. Ruth will be here any minute. And since when did every-one's problems become mine? Charlotte stared up at the ceiling and counted to ten, trying to calm the irritation tighten-ing her shoulders.

"Hello, are you there?"

"Yes, I'm here." Charlotte sighed. "What kind of problem do you have now?"

"I don't want to discuss it over the phone. I'll come over to your place around seven."

"You can't." She blurted it out before she could stop herself.

"Why not?"

"Well, um, because my mother's moving in with me tonight."

"Why is she moving in with you?"

"She and my dad had a fight, and she needs a little breathing room."

"How long is she going to stay?"

"For as long as it takes, I guess. But I can't really say." Charlotte squeezed her eyes tight. The hole she was digging for herself nearly overwhelmed her.

"Well, if I can't come over, why don't you come to *my* room?"

"I can't. My mother wants to talk, and I have to stick around and listen. It could take hours. You know my mother and her little talks. Why don't you call me tomorrow, and we can make some other arrangements to meet."

"Why can't we make arrangements to meet now?"

"Because I don't know what my mother's plans are."

"You're going to have to be much firmer with your mother. You can't let her take advantage of you all the time."

"I know," Charlotte answered. *I need to be a lot firmer with everyone.* Her eyes focused on the paper bag on the counter. "I'll call you when I know anything for sure."

She ended the call and set the phone down. Then she grabbed the bag with her dinner inside and ripped it open, but she wasn't sure if she could eat a bite with her stomach churning. Maybe drinking a glass of wine would help. After a few sips, it did, and she managed to clean her entire plate.

An hour had passed since darkness engulfed the small town, and there was still no sign of Ruth. Charlotte hated waiting when she wasn't sure if someone would show up. *What if Ruth is being followed by Jim? She's probably running around town trying to lose him. That might be why she's so late. Or maybe Jim caught up with her. Ruth might be dead.*

What a horrible possibility. The poor thing may be lying in a ditch somewhere. Shivers ran down Charlotte's spine. Of course, if the woman was already dead, there wouldn't be anything she could do except to call the police. Picking up her phone, she paced around her small apartment. *But if Ruth's just running late...*

Growling in frustration, she tossed the phone on the couch and flopped down beside it. *I'll give her a little more time. And then I'll panic.* She picked up the newest arrival from the Mystery Lovers' Book Club, *Murder in a Small Town*, shuddering at the coincidence. She turned to chapter one anyway and tried to focus on the words.

Her eyes grew heavy as she read through the first paragraphs, and before she realized it, she'd dozed off.

Tap, tap, tap, tap. Charlotte was startled awake. *Did I hear something, or did I dream it?*

Tap, tap, tap, tap. There it was again. Charlotte stumbled to the front door, tripping over the novel, that had hit the floor when she stepped off the sofa. "Who is it?"

"It's me, Ruth." The voice was hushed and nervous.

Charlotte swung the door open. Ruth walked in, pulling two large, black suitcases behind her.

"Where have you been? I was getting worried."

Ruth set the suitcases in the middle of the living room. "I told you I wasn't coming until after dark."

"It got dark three hours ago. Why did you wait so long?"

Ruth set her purse on the sofa and slipped off her white pumps. "I was having dinner at the Torchlight Steakhouse when I ran into some old friends I hadn't seen for years. We had so much to catch up on, I simply forgot the time."

"You were having dinner out?" Charlotte's mouth dropped in irritation. "Weren't you afraid Longbourne might see you there?"

Ruth sat down on the sofa and ran her hands over the lumps in the seat cushions. "He wouldn't do anything to me in a public place. I knew I would be safer there than I would have been at home all alone."

Ruth got up and grabbed the handles on her suitcases. Charlotte's gaze followed her. Those were awfully big suitcases for just a night or two. Just how long was she planning to stay? "Where are you taking those?"

"To your bedroom." Ruth motioned toward the sofa with disdain. "You don't expect me to sleep on that lumpy old thing, do you?"

Charlotte sighed. "Of course not. I wouldn't think of asking you to sleep on that lumpy old thing. I'll take it. I'm used to the lumps."

"By the way," Ruth said when she reached the bedroom door, "Would you make me a cup of herbal tea while I change into my pajamas?"

"Sorry." Charlotte shrugged. "I don't have any."

"Here." Ruth rummaged in her purse before tossing a bright yellow box in Charlotte's direction. "I brought some with me. It's the only tea I drink. Make yourself a cup, too. It'll soothe your nerves and help you sleep."

Charlotte, always the good hostess, went into the kitchen, poured two cups of filtered water into a glass pot and turned on the gas. While waiting for the water to boil, she checked the ingredients on the box label but she didn't recognize any of the items listed since most of the printing was in Chinese. *This must be an exotic blend. Ruth's such a snob when it comes to things like this. It's probably something she had mixed especially for her by an herbalist.*

After a few moments, the water came to a boil. Charlotte put a teabag in each of the cups on the table and poured in the hot water as Ruth crossed the living room.

"It didn't take you long to change," she said. "Cute pajamas."

"Thanks." Ruth took a seat at the kitchen table. "A gift from, ah, from a friend. Is the tea ready yet?" She fingered the silky fabric of her pajamas as she watched Charlotte.

"I think so." Charlotte walked over to the refrigerator and opened the door. "Do you take cream, sugar, or both?"

"Neither. It tastes better straight." Ruth lifted the tea bag out of her cup, squeezed it against her spoon, and placed them both in the saucer. "Now we can have a nice little chat."

A chat? Charlotte had never considered Ruth the chatty type.

Ruth took a sip of tea and leaned back in her chair. "What do you think of the tea?"

Charlotte sniffed the exotic bouquet before taking an experimental sip. *It smells terrible.* "It's delicious," she said in a gesture of kindness.

"Good, I'm glad you like it. Now what's this about you being worried?"

Charlotte pushed the teacup aside. "It's not safe for you to be out on the street. When you didn't arrive at the first sign of darkness, I thought Jim had caught up with you, and well, you know what happened to his wife."

Ruth smiled. "It was kind of you to worry about me, but I would tend to worry more about your friend, Jane. From what I read in the newspapers, she's apparently up to her neck in all this. I wouldn't be surprised if she turned out to be Jim's accomplice."

"What are you saying?" Charlotte added several degrees of warmth to her cool demeanor.

"Look at the facts. Jane breezed back into town on the night before Carlton Witherspoon was murdered."

"That was a coincidence." Charlotte picked up her tea cup and walked over to the kitchen sink. When Ruth took a sip from her own cup, Charlotte dumped her tea down the drain.

"It could have been," Ruth said. "But then again, it could have been planned to look like one. Jane's clever, and she's chummy with the police, no doubt to find out what they know and how the investigation is progressing, so she can report back to Jim. I'll bet she managed to get into the Witherspoon mansion to check the crime scene so she could see if she left anything behind."

"Well, yes, she did," Charlotte said. She was sorry the moment she said it.

"I thought as much. Do you think it was also a coincidence her dagger was used as the murder weapon?"

Charlotte's movement transitioned from a confident stance to an indecisive one. *It wasn't the same dagger Jane brought back from England with her, but it was very similar.* She stiffened. "How did you know about the dagger?"

Ruth toyed with her spoon. "It was only a guess. But you just confirmed it."

"You're forgetting one thing." Charlotte set her empty cup in the sink. "Jane doesn't have a motive."

"Doesn't she?" Ruth met Charlotte's reproachful look and replied firmly. "How about money? It's always been an excellent motive for murder."

"I don't think Jane would put herself in the kind of jeopardy you're talking about over mere money. And you're forgetting another thing." Charlotte sat down opposite Ruth. "Jane had no reason to want Alyssa out of the way, But even if she did, which is unlikely, Jane didn't have time to attack her on Saturday night and stuff her into the trunk of the squad car. She was with me most of the afternoon, and then we attended the country club dance together."

Ruth leaned over the table. "Suppose Alyssa had suspicions and confronted her husband with them. He might have attacked her earlier and made arrangements with Jane to let him shove her body into the trunk of the squad car while everyone was at the dance. She could have passed him a set of keys."

"Impossible." Charlotte leaned back in her chair and folded her arms. "I know Jane. She wouldn't do that."

"Does anyone really know what anyone else is thinking? I've read a few mystery novels myself, and the person who is most eager to help the police solve the crime is usually the perpetrator."

Uneasiness washed over Charlotte as her throat tightened. She glanced out the window. She'd been discovering all kinds of things she didn't know about Jane since she came back to town.

Ruth let out a sigh of pure satisfaction. "Since she's so close to the police, it wouldn't have been difficult for her to let Jim get access to a squad car."

Charlotte placed her hands over her face. "It's too incredible to be true."

"You're so gullible, Charlotte." Ruth chuckled before her tone became hard and cold. "You'd better wise up. Being your friend doesn't automatically make her innocent."

Everything Charlotte knew and believed suddenly shifted and settled itself into a pattern, like the pieces in a kaleidoscope. But one of the pieces didn't quite fit, and that piece irritated her beyond comprehension.

"I see you finished your tea." Ruth pursed her rosebud lips.

"Yes, it was so good, I drank it right down."

Ruth yawned. "Did it make you sleepy?"

"Very," Charlotte said. "I think I'll go to bed now."

"Have a good night," Ruth said before retiring to Charlotte's bedroom.

Charlotte changed into her night clothes and grabbed the extra pillow from the hall closet. She dropped her body onto the lumpy sofa, although in truth, she wasn't a bit sleepy. After turning off the living room lamp, she stared into the darkness, her mind racing in a turmoil of mixed emotions as Ruth's words played over and over in her mind.

Chapter Twenty Six

Charlotte stood near her cubicle early the next morning, trying to decide whether she needed a cup of strong coffee to buck up her courage or a cup of chamomile tea to calm her nerves. John sidled up to her from behind and brought his face close to hers, dangerously close, so close she could smell his clean, fresh breath.

"Can you give me a lift home today?" He asked in a soft voice.

Suddenly, her fears disappeared, and her focus was only on John's presence. She toyed with the idea of throwing all caution aside as she leaned into him and brought her moist lips toward his soft cheek. But she suppressed the impulse to steal a quick kiss from the seductive mouth of her unsuspecting ex-lover. If anyone in the office had caught even a glimpse of her attempting to kiss John, the repercussions would be disastrous. She turned to face him with adoring eyes, searching his for a hint of warmth, and sighed. "Why do you ask?"

"My car needs to be in the repair shop for one more day."

She brought her fingertips up to brush his cheek and then down to straighten his shirt collar. An unconscious habit she had acquired over the time they'd dated. "Why didn't you get a rental?"

"I didn't think I'd need a car for only one day. I got a lift here, and I was counting on Susan to drive me home. But she had to take the day off. Her mother's ill."

"Have you met her mother?"

"Yes. She's a lovely woman."

She must have taken her medication that day.

His dark eyes searched hers. "So, do you mind?"

Charlotte wanted to spend time alone with him in the worst way, and without hesitation, she answered, "I'll be happy to give you a lift."

This would be the perfect opportunity to have a private talk with him about her suspicions. He'd be a captive audience.

"Thanks."

Their gazes connected, and she caught a glimmer of something there. Warmth? Tenderness? Affection? It was definitely more than mere gratitude.

He smiled and touched her shoulder, his fingers branding her skin through her blouse, before he walked back to his office.

It had been a long time since she felt the thrill of his touch. She relived that gentle feeling a hundred times during the next half-hour, and her mind couldn't forget the look in his eyes. The harsh ring of the telephone shocked her back to reality.

She picked up the receiver and sighed, "John Trent's office."

"Morning, Charlotte."

"Oh, it's you, Jane." She sat up bolt-straight in her chair.

"How about meeting me for lunch?"

I can't face Jane until I get things sorted out. "Sorry, I'm busy."

"Dinner?"

"No, I can't. I told you, I'm having trouble with my mother."

"I have to talk to you. It's important."

I've got to put her off until I can discuss things with John. I really need an unbiased perspective on this. "Can't you tell me over the phone?"

"Why are you avoiding me?" Jane's tone was tight, frustration coloring her words.

Charlotte swung her chair around to face the computer and lowered her voice. "I'm not avoiding you. I'm, um, really busy right now."

"I'm worried about you. But at least you're not alone when you're at home."

"I'm anything but alone." Charlotte wrapped the phone cord around her fingers as she focused on slowing her breathing.

"Please be careful."

The words hung in the air, and Charlotte gasped. "What do you mean?"

"Not a thing. I just want you to be careful."

"All right, I will. Bye." Charlotte set the receiver down and wondered if her new suspicions about Jane were justified? Was Jane warning her or simply worried about her?

The afternoon hours passed quickly as Charlotte busied herself getting the files ready for the company's yearly audit. But should she even bother? Would there still be a company when all of this was over?

Just as the clock struck five, John stepped out of his office. He leaned over her desk. "Are you ready to leave?"

"I'm ready." She turned off her computer, grabbed her purse and walked out the door in front of him.

Charlotte careened her Mustang out of the company parking lot and onto the street in a flurry of exhaust fumes and skid marks. John's hand gripped the door handle as she sped through a yellow traffic signal.

"You seem distressed," he said.

"I have so much to talk to you about. I don't know where to start."

He relaxed his grip. "Start at the beginning."

"All right, I will." Charlotte bit her bottom lip and glanced at John before setting her gaze back on the road. "It all started last Friday when you told me to go to the vault to get those old documents. I was locked in that claustrophobic place all night. I could have suffocated if the guard hadn't spotted my car in the parking lot on Saturday morning."

John caught his breath. "How did you get locked in the vault?" His concern sounded genuine.

"Someone closed the door on me. There's no handle on the inside to open it. If you ask me, I think Tim Blanchard did it."

John rubbed his chin and hesitated before asking, "Why do you think it was him?"

Charlotte didn't want to tell John about the black book she'd found when she was snooping in Blanchard's desk, so she said, "Because of my little visit to the shipping office earlier in the week."

"I wish you would have told me about this sooner."

"I would have, but I can't talk to you anymore. We used to have long talks all the time." The unsaid words hung in the air between them.

He turned to glance out the window. "I remember," he said in a soft voice, before clearing his throat. "Now getting back to the subject at hand, do you have a piece of paper so I can write all this down?"

"Try the glove compartment."

John twisted the knob, and the small door opened. Several pages of copy paper fell to the floor. He checked each page. "What's this?"

Charlotte silently cursed herself for her stupidity. She had completely forgotten about Jane shoving the copies of Blanchard's little black book in there for safekeeping. "It's just copies of something I found it in the shipping office. Jane thought it might be important."

The light turned green, and Charlotte rammed her foot on the gas pedal.

John slipped the papers inside his jacket. "Go on. I'm listening."

Charlotte sighed. "I thought you were writing."

John checked his pockets. "I don't have a pen with me. Do you have one I could use?"

"There's one in my purse."

He grabbed Charlotte's shoulder bag, opened it, and rummaged through the jumbled contents before closing it again. "Never mind., I'll remember."

"Now I forgot what I was saying." She searched her memory, but whatever she was going to say was lost.

Tapping the steering wheel, she glared out the front windshield as she gathered her thoughts. "I'm really furious with Jane for getting me involved in this murder case. I'm up to my neck in this mess, and now I've heard something disturbing about Jane that makes her look like an accomplice. I'm worried and more than a little frightened."

Charlotte's voice cracked. "The people who seemed innocent now appear to be guilty and vice-versa. I'm so mixed up. I don't know who to trust."

The car skidded up and over the curb in front of John's condo. Charlotte switched off the engine. "I need your help."

John pulled his necktie loose and unbuttoned the top button of his shirt collar, as if he was uncomfortable with her request. She couldn't resist the urge to look at the bare skin peeking out behind the open button.

With a hint of compassion in his eyes he said, "If there was anything I could do to help you get out of the mess you're in, you know I would, but my hands are tied. Surely you can see that."

The warm tone of his voice encouraged Charlotte to bring up the other subject she wanted to discuss with him. If she didn't do it now, she might never get another chance. "I know Susan would be upset."

She couldn't help the tears that crept into her eyes. He couldn't know what he was getting himself into with that woman. "Oh John, are you sure you're doing the right thing marrying her?" She sighed. "I've heard talk."

"I never took you for a person who listened to gossip."

Shaking her head, she muttered, "I usually don't, but this was right from..."

"Then drop it," he interrupted, adamant. "And don't bring it up again. The subject of my engagement is off limits."

She wasn't often at her wit's end, but this was the exception. He'd never change his mind. It was hopeless. Snatching the white linen handkerchief from the breast pocket of his suit coat, she wiped her eyes and blew her nose into it.

He glanced at her with a pained expression. "That's supposed to be a decorative handkerchief, not a functional one."

"Oh, sorry." She hastily shoved the wet hanky back into his pocket.

He gave it a quick, disgusted glance. "As I was about to say, before you changed the subject, you're an intelligent woman. I have every confidence in you. If you don't know who to trust, just trust your own instincts, and things will turn out all right. You'll see."

Charlotte leaned back in her seat. "I hope so."

The corners of his lips curved into a smile. "If you feel that distraught, take the day off tomorrow and relax."

His actions and his cavalier attitude about her problem sent alarm bells ringing through her head.

"Why, what's happening tomorrow?"

"Nothing, Charlotte. Nothing's happening."

His capricious tone made her even more suspicious. She knew in her gut, the very one he had just told her to trust, that something wasn't right.

"There must be some reason why you don't want me at the office tomorrow. Come on, tell me. What's going on?"

"Nothing's going on." John's usually calm and steady voice was loud and stern.

"Then why did you put those papers from my glove compartment inside your jacket?" She reached in and pulled the papers out. "You thought I didn't notice. They're important, aren't they? You know something about them. Is it something illegal? Are they bill of lading numbers from the missing shipments? You can confide in me."

John stared at her as he cleared his throat. He took a deep breath and snatched the papers from Charlotte's hand. "You're getting paranoid. I merely put these papers in my jacket to get them off the floor. All right, you don't have to take the day off tomorrow. I was just trying to be..."

"Dismissive?"

"Considerate." He glanced at his watch. "I really have to go. I'm late for an appointment."

As he opened the car door, Charlotte shouted at him, "An appointment with whom?"

"If you must know, it's with my barber." He slammed the door so hard, it nearly sent her car flying across his neighbor's driveway.

She put her hands over her face in disgust. "Well, that got me absolutely nowhere."

Chapter Twenty Seven

A little after six, Charlotte stretched as she slid the door of her apartment open. Setting a white, grease-stained bag on the kitchen table, she slung her purse on a chair. "I brought home some hamburgers from Shorty's Diner." She plugged her nostrils. "What's that smell?"

"We're having couscous and bulgur salad with falafel burgers in pita bread for dinner tonight." Ruth stood near the stove wearing a long, white apron over her navy tee shirt and jeans. She waved her spatula around like an apprentice to a famous chef. "It's my specialty."

"Sounds, um, wonderful." Charlotte tried to sound enthusiastic as she walked over to the stove to get a better look at what was frying in her best, copper-bottomed skillet. "You shouldn't have gone to all this trouble."

"No trouble at all. I brought some ingredients with me last night, and the others I got out of your fridge."

"Well, it looks appetizing," Charlotte lied.

"Go ahead, give it a try." Ruth shoved a plateful of bulgur salad at Charlotte with a proud flourish. "It's great. You'll love it."

Charlotte grabbed the plate and gently placed it on the kitchen table. "I don't think so," she said in defense of her appetite. "I'm not used to eating this kind of food. I brought these burgers from Shorty's, and I'd hate to waste them."

"Well, what about all of this? I'm not going to throw it in the garbage." Ruth sounded as if she would burst into tears at any moment.

Charlotte set the greasy bag on the top shelf in the refrigerator. *I really have to start standing up for myself.*

"Sit down, Charlotte, and I'll bring you a nice cup of tea to go with your meal."

Oh great, some of that awful tea to go with this unusual food.

Ruth set herself and the teacups down simultaneously. She devoured her food quickly, with the relish of a woman who hadn't eaten in days.

Charlotte took a small bite and chewed it with panache. *Different.*

"It's good, isn't it?" Ruth asked between bites.

Charlotte smiled. "I've never tasted anything quite like it." Parts of the salad were tolerable, so she ate the tomatoes and the cucumbers. *There must be millions of people in the world who love this kind of food, I'm just not one of them.*

"You haven't touched your tea," Ruth said as she began clearing the dishes from the table. "I made it especially for you because you enjoyed it so much last night."

"I'm getting to it." There had to be a quick way to dispose of the liquid in her cup without Ruth noticing.

Ruth lifted a suspicious eyebrow. "Finish your tea while I wash the dishes."

"That's awfully nice of you." Charlotte stood, her eyes searching the room. The sink was her only option. "So, what did you do today?" she asked as Ruth headed in that direction.

"I watched the news for most of the day." Ruth rinsed out a plate and placed it on the drain board. "But I didn't see any breakthroughs in the Longbourne case. Did you talk to your friend, Jane?"

Charlotte sat down at the table again, the teacup in front of her. "As a matter of fact, she called me."

Ruth wiped her hands on the dish towel and walked over to where Charlotte sat. She placed a hand on the back of her chair. "I don't know what you told her, but she showed up here this afternoon."

"Did you let her in?"

"No, your mother did."

Charlotte dragged her hands over her face. "That woman is so unpredictable." She wasn't sure if she meant Jane or her mother. Probably both if she really thought about it. "What did you do?"

Ruth slid her glasses off and rubbed her eyes. "I hid in the closet while she looked around. By the way, you have the neatest closet I've ever seen."

"Thanks." *Did Ruth make it a habit to check out people's closets?*

Ruth placed her glasses on the table and climbed into the chair across from Charlotte. "You'd better drink up before your tea gets cold."

Charlotte took a sip from the cup to show her good faith. She held the warm liquid in her mouth as long as she could stand the bitter taste until she had to swallow. After recovering from the shock of the tea hitting her stomach, Charlotte shuddered and opened her eyes. "You know, Ruth, with your glasses off, you look like someone I've seen before."

Ruth's lips curved into a crooked smile. "I look a lot like my mom."

Charlotte stared at her intently. "Nurse Nan? I don't think so. It's something about your eyes."

Ruth slid her glasses on and went to the back door to lock it, which gave Charlotte a chance to pick up her teacup and make her way to the sink where she flung the tea down the drain. Ruth turned around, and their eyes met as Charlotte placed the empty cup to her lips, pretending to finish off the contents. She set the cup in the sink as it suddenly came to her. The resemblance between Ruth's face and the one in the picture she'd seen at the Witherspoon mansion was undeniable. It was extraordinary how much information could flash through a person's mind in just a few seconds. Could Ruth be Carlton Witherspoon's missing child?

Charlotte stretched. "What do you know about your real parents?"

"I looked them up once. I know who my mother was, but according to my birth certificate, my dad is anybody's guess. Funny. I haven't thought about them in years." Ruth's eyes blazed with intensity. "Oh, by the way," she asked, "Did you stop by my apartment to pick up my mail?"

"Yes, I did." Charlotte continued to stare at Ruth.

"I hope you didn't let anyone see you."

Charlotte retrieved several envelopes from her purse and handed them to Ruth. "Don't worry. I took great pains to make sure."

Ruth glanced though her mail. "Would you hand me a knife to use as a letter opener?"

"Sure." Charlotte selected a steak knife from her silverware drawer and placed it in Ruth's open hand.

"No, not this one." Ruth walked over to the counter, where a small butcher-block held a variety of kitchen knives, and selected a sharp-edged carving knife.

As Ruth sliced into her envelopes, Charlotte said, "You know, it's funny, but from the way you're holding that knife you'd think it was a..."

Ruth looked up, letting the envelope slip out of her hand and waft down to the table. Her smile had a gleeful slyness, and a strange, unpleasant contortion to it. "It was a what?" She held the knife taut, the steel blade pointing directly at Charlotte.

"A dagger." As she said the words, a curious sense of danger overcame her. The weakness in her knees made her drop into the nearest chair. "I feel kind of light-headed and dizzy." She placed her cool hand on her heated forehead.

"You might be having an anxiety attack." Ruth's voice had a calmness Charlotte had never heard before. "Or it could be the tea working."

The feeling was intensifying. "Why would the tea make me feel this way?"

Ruth smiled. "Because it was laced with opium."

That explains it. It's a good thing I only took one swallow. "Really, Ruth, I know you said the tea would relax me, but don't you think lacing it with opium is going a smidgen too far?"

She struggled to stand up, managing to brace herself on the edge of the table and shuffle away from the point of the blade.

"Where do you think you're going?" Ruth's voice filled the air with sinister humor.

"To my bedroom to rest." Charlotte stumbled through the living room. The front door was only a few steps away. The doorknob beckoned. All she needed to do was turn it and run, but she'd never make it down the stairs without collapsing, and Ruth was only a few steps behind, still holding that knife.

Charlotte finally reached the bedroom door. She walked in.

"Jane!"

Her friend lying lifelessly on the bed made no sense. Charlotte swung around, her eyes catching the gleam of the sharp metal blade in Ruth's hand. "Is she dead?"

Ruth smirked. "Not dead, just out cold. But she'll recover, unlike you."

Charlotte slowly backed away, trying to appear calm, even though her heart beat so rapidly, she felt as if she would pass out at any moment. "What do you mean?"

Ruth toyed with the knife in her hand. "I mean, you and your snoopy friend were getting a little too close for comfort." There was a note of pent-up anger in her voice. "I had to think of something to stop you before you ruined everything.

I tried to warn Jane against continuing her investigation, but you know how tenacious she is. Now she'll wake up with this bloody knife in her hand, and the police are going to find your dead body on the floor beside her. She'll never be able to talk her way out of this one."

Charlotte's gaze searched the room for an escape route, but Ruth was blocking the only exit. Since there was nowhere to go, the only thing left to do was get answers to all the questions that had been plaguing her. "Why did you kill Carlton?"

"Actually, I didn't. Well, not really. He'd been depressed for months over a cancer diagnosis, and he asked my mother to help him commit suicide, but she refused. When she confided to me that she thought he might attempt it himself, I told her I would see if I could help. And after a lot of thought, I did."

Ruth took a menacing step forward as she talked, forcing Charlotte to step back. "He would have ended up dead, either way, and I had to pay Jim back for dumping me after nearly twenty years as his mistress, and running off to marry that ditzy girl. What better way than to frame him for Carlton's murder?"

"But how?"

"I've been slipping a little opium into Jim's afternoon coffee."

"I wondered why he was acting so nervous."

"He played right into my hands. As soon as I knew he was addicted, I convinced him he killed Carlton. I've been keeping him in a drug-induced stupor in a basement room at the clinic. It's so much easier to control him that way."

The jovial tone in Ruth's voice sent shivers down Charlotte's spine as she glanced at the door behind Ruth.

"Actually, it was simpler than I thought it would be," Ruth said. "He's trusted me for twenty years. I've never given him away, no matter what he's done."

"What has he done?"

"More evil than you'll ever know."

That was an unexpectedly short answer. Charlotte was near the bedroom window. It would be easy to open it and jump out, if there wasn't a two-story drop to the concrete below. There had to be some other way to escape. She needed time to think, so she kept talking. "I'm a little confused." She leaned against the bedpost, still unsteady on her feet. "I didn't know you were in love with Jim Longbourne."

Ruth took a few more steps toward her. "I was for what seemed like forever. But love and hate—they're two sides of the same coin. Hate is love twisted inside out. You could be in love with someone for years, and then you wake up one morning and realize it's all been one-sided. That's when your love turns to contempt and hatred. You want to strike out and hurt the person who's caused you to feel like less than nothing."

Ruth pounded her fist on the dresser, making the delicate perfume bottles lined up in front of the mirror tremble. "How could he have betrayed me?" Her gray eyes turned to stone as she stared at Charlotte.

Stunned at Ruth's answer, she had to ask, "And poor Bessie Longbourne. Did you kill her too?"

"I *had* to." Ruth's eyes narrowed into a crazed look. "She was in the way. Jim promised to divorce her and marry me, but he never did." She sneered in disgust. "With his wife out of the picture, I was sure Jim and I would be happy at last." She grunted. "I thought our chance had finally come, but he told me he needed some time away, to find himself and come back to me a better man. The idiot that I am, I let him take that trip alone."

She shrieked in outrage. "It was the biggest mistake of my life, because while he was gone, he married someone else." Ruth kicked the dresser viciously, rattling the perfume bottles again and making Charlotte flinch. "I hated Alyssa. But then something clicked inside my head, and I finally recognized it wasn't her at all. It was *him*. He must've been seeing Alyssa on the sly—cheating on his mistress. It was his choice not to marry me. She probably didn't even know about us."

"You're right." Charlotte attempted to talk her way out of becoming the next murder victim. "I understand what you're going through, what you've been going through. I'm having the same problem with John Trent. I know I can help you."

"You want to help me?" Ruth laughed maniacally. "Yeah, right into a prison cell. It's no use trying to talk me out of it. There's no other way."

Ruth started toward her.

Charlotte stumbled back a few steps. It was becoming harder for her to breathe as she inched her way backward. The point of that knife was getting uncomfortably close. "You're forgetting about Todd. He'll probably be here at any moment. He gets worried when he can't find Jane." Charlotte felt like she was clutching at a straw to paddle with while her canoe was going over a waterfall.

"He's out on a wild goose chase," Ruth said. "The idiot is looking for Jim in the next county."

"So you've thought of everything." Charlotte made a lunge for the bed. With a trembling hand, she slapped Jane across the face. "Wake up," she screamed as she shook her violently. "Wake up!"

Ruth came up behind Charlotte, the knife blade gleaming in the reflection of the mirror. With all her strength, Charlotte sprang off the bed and flung herself on Ruth. She knocked her down and grabbed her wrist in an attempt to wrestle the knife away, but Ruth hung onto it with the desperation of a mad woman.

Charlotte clawed her fingers into Ruth's wrist and struggled to keep the knife from slicing into her flesh, but she could feel herself weakening. Her assailant must have felt it too, because she thrashed even harder. Charlotte cried out for help, even though she had no hope of help coming.

With everything in her, she wrenched Ruth's wrist back, and the knife dropped to the floor.

A sense of relief filled Charlotte as she flung the knife under her dresser, but the next minute Ruth's hands were fastened around her throat, squeezing the life out of her.

Gasping for air, tears sprang to Charlotte's eyes, and she gave out one last choked cry.

Chapter Twenty Eight

As Ruth's fingers closed around Charlotte's neck, Jane leapt off the bed and caught Ruth around the throat, pulling her off Charlotte and knocking her back. Ruth grabbed Jane's wrists in an attempt to shake free of her, but Jane held fast.

The explosive gunshot and the sharp crack of wood splintering seemed to go unnoticed by the two women as they struggled for dominance on the floor.

Todd rushed in with his gun drawn.

"I've got her, Todd." Jane sounded triumphant.

"I can see that," Todd said in an amused tone. "But you can let her go now. I'll take it from here."

Jane bristled as she rose to her feet. "What took you so long?"

"We were at the clinic. Nan Truhart found Jim Longbourne wandering around in a state of shock, so she locked him inside her office and called us."

Todd grabbed Ruth and pushed her face down on the carpet. He pulled her hands behind her back. "You have the right to remain silent…"

Jane sat on the edge of the bed, her hands shaking as Todd read Ruth her rights. John Trent burst through the bedroom door and rushed to Charlotte's side, where he knelt down. "Are you okay?"

She nodded. "I'm fine," she whispered, her voice hoarse as she gently massaged her neck.

The concern in his voice soothed her frazzled nerves, but her curiosity wouldn't be quieted. "What are you doing here?" she managed to croak.

John smiled. "It's a long story." He checked his watch. "Tell you about it another time. Right now, I've got to go." And with those words, he ran out the door, leaving Charlotte to wonder if he had really been there, or was he just something she imagined.

Charlotte was happy to be driving Jane back to her room at the Inn after a long night at the police station. Dawn was slipping over the horizon as the car sped through the deserted streets. The horrific events of the previous evening were finally over. She checked her face in her car's rearview mirror. With everything that happened, she was sure she'd aged at least ten years.

"Did you have to hit me so hard?" Jane touched the tender, black and blue mark on her left cheekbone.

"I had to wake you up."

"You couldn't come up with another way to do it?"

Charlotte glanced at her friend. "Your face doesn't look too bad. Not as bad as these black and blue marks on my neck."

"They're hardly noticeable." Jane rolled the car window down and took a deep breath of the fresh morning air.

"I can still feel that woman's hands around my throat." Charlotte grimaced as she touched her neck. "And I didn't see it coming."

"It's my fault. I was sure everyone was after Carlton's manuscript. Boy, was I wrong. And I didn't recognize the potential danger in someone as innocuous as Ruth. That negligence on my part is what put you in jeopardy." Jane stared at the landscape. "Todd let it slip that they suspected a woman all along."

"Then why did the Chief arrest Jim Longbourne?"

"Red herring. They thought if she felt confident that she wasn't a suspect, then she'd show her hand. Which, of course, she did."

"But why suspect a woman?"

"Because of the stab wounds. Todd said there wasn't enough force for a man to have done it. Also, the angle was wrong. It had to come from either a short man or a woman. That throws a light on why the Chief suspected me of killing Carlton." Jane rolled the car window up and turned on the air conditioning. "Ruth's fatal mistake was making a five minute call from Jim Longbourne's office to his cell. The police had a trace on his phone. That's when things started to fall into place. And when I ran into your mother, and she told me that I had moved in with you, a little voice in my head said, 'Okay, what's wrong with this scenario?'"

Charlotte took the first turn off of Main Street to get out of early morning traffic. "I'm glad you decided to investigate." She let out a deep sigh. "Otherwise, I'd be in the morgue right now."

"Don't even think that way," Jane replied in a cheerful tone. "Anyway, I accomplished what I set out to do."

Charlotte pulled her silver-blue Mustang in front of the Eldridge Inn and turned off the engine. "So, my friend, what are your plans now?"

"I'm thinking about writing a novel about an old millionaire's murder, using some of the information from Carlton's autobiography. I don't know what happened to those missing pages, but from everything I've learned, I'm pretty sure I can fill in the rest of the story. My publisher's going to be so pleased when I tell him."

"Then you're going to stick around?"

"That depends on a lot of things. I'm undecided at the moment." Jane opened the car door and stepped out. "Why don't you come in for breakfast?" She glanced at her watch, "The Tea Room should be open."

"I think I will." Charlotte slid out of the driver's seat. "I couldn't go to sleep now anyway. I'm as wound up as the spring on my grandmother's old alarm clock."

The usual early morning crowd was gathered in the small restaurant, sipping coffee and ordering takeout, before heading off to work. But this particular morning, an element of electricity sparked the air. The constant buzzing of voices charged the room with excitement.

They grabbed the last available table and seated themselves. A waitress scampered up to them.

"You poor things. Have a rough night? I'll get coffee for you right away. You look like you can use a pick-me-up."

Charlotte never thought of how bad they must look. But that aside, she narrowed her brows as the waitress scurried away. "What did she mean by that? Do you suppose she knows already?"

"News travels fast in this town, but it doesn't travel *that* fast."

The speedy waitress set two cups down on the table and poured the coffee from a pot she carried. "Can I get you anything else? The breakfast special this morning is a mushroom omelet."

"We'll have two orders, with extra toast for me. And lots of butter," Jane said. "I'm so hungry, I'm skipping my usual diet plate." She glanced at the waitress. "By the way, what's all the excitement about?"

"You mean you don't know what happened last night? It's all over town."

"That depends," Charlotte said glancing at Jane. "A lot of things happened last night."

The eager waitress went to the counter and picked up a remote control. She clicked on the twelve inch, flat-screen television that hung near the ceiling in a corner of the room.

"See for yourself."

The room went quiet as the patrons turned to watch a Pepsi commercial. Then a recent photo of John Trent and one of the redhead who worked in the shipping office, appeared together on the screen as the newscaster's voice said, "If you're just joining us, last night, FBI agents Brett Stalworth and Catherine Effingham arrested Ezra Blanchard, better known as Tim Blanchard, at Longbourne and Payne Freight Consolidation, where he worked as the shipping manager."

Jane turned to glance at Charlotte, shock written all over her face, as a photo of the company appeared. "Your boss and that redheaded actress are FBI agents?"

Charlotte barely heard the remark and could only watch, stunned, as the newscaster continued, "Blanchard and his associates were caught in a drug deal, which would have netted them close to fifty million dollars."

Tears crept into Charlotte's tired eyes. "I don't believe it."

"Believe what? That Blanchard's been dealing drugs out of Longbourne and Payne? I can. I had a feeling those numbers in his little black book had something to do with contraband." Jane crossed her arms.

"I don't care about Blanchard or the drugs. I'm talking about John Trent. He's been lying to me all this time."

"So he twisted the truth around a little. If he was working undercover, he wouldn't be permitted to tell anybody." A glint of intrigue flashed into Jane's eyes. "I think this makes him all the more fascinating."

Intense heat rose to Charlotte's face as her insides twisted. "If there's one thing I won't tolerate from any man, it's lying. I'm going to have it out with that son-of-a..."

She flung her napkin on the table and stormed out to her car, leaving Jane sitting alone waiting for two orders of mushroom omelet.

Charlotte didn't know how she arrived at Longbourne and Payne. With her heart so full of anger, she didn't remember driving there, but she was now standing face-to-face with her former boss.

"You look awful," John said. There was a definite sternness to his voice. "You shouldn't have come to the office today."

An angry flash of red shot across her eyes. "I look awful? Do you have any idea what I went through last night? You can't tell me what to do anymore. You're not my boss. Come to think of it, you never were. This has all been one big sham, John... Brett. Whoever you are." She couldn't stop the tears that fell in huge drops.

Her former boss walked around his desk and handed Charlotte a tissue. His voice took on a sympathetic tone. "As you've probably heard on the news, my real name is Brett Stalworth. But you can call me whatever you like."

"Don't tempt me," she said between sobs. "You have no idea what I'd like to call you right now."

He lifted Charlotte's chin, his fingers warm against her skin, and gazed into her eyes. "I know what you went through last night. And I was relieved to see that you were okay. But I didn't think you were in any real danger."

Charlotte remained incensed. "Not in any danger? I could have been killed. I might have died."

Her knees buckled as the words tumbled out. She stumbled a few steps but was caught by her former boss before she touched the floor. He held her close. His strong arms were like a protective cocoon against the horror she'd experienced, and for those few moments, they comforted her.

Then he eased her into his desk chair. Charlotte rubbed her hands over her eyes. Her anger was gone, but the emptiness and fatigue lingered. She sighed in resignation. "I'm tired and very confused."

"You look like you could use something to eat. Come with me." His reassuring hand enveloped hers in warmth and strength. "I'll take you out for breakfast."

"But what about the office?"

He looked around his former workplace. "It's been shut down until the investigation is complete."

Charlotte stepped into Brett's spacious living room and plopped down on the leather sofa situated against the back wall, sinking her feet into the taupe Bokara carpet. "I thought you were taking me out for breakfast?"

"I wanted to take you somewhere private so we could talk. There are too many nosy people out there right now. No matter where we went, we'd have been mobbed. I'm not much of a cook. But I can scramble you some eggs."

"Anything." Her stomach growled, but her nerves were so tight, she didn't think she could keep much down. Anything he made would be fine. She glanced around. "You never did have enough furniture for this condo."

"I wasn't planning to stay here very long," Brett shouted from the kitchen. "This sting operation was supposed to go down several months ago."

She pried herself off the sofa and walked to the kitchen as he poured each of them a cup of re-warmed coffee.

Charlotte slipped into a chair. "I'm assuming that this 'sting operation' has been going on since the first day we met."

"You're right. It all began when your former boss came to the FBI office in Virginia. He'd found out some drug dealing was going on at Longbourne and Payne, and he was worried that the people who were involved might find out about his suspicions."

Charlotte lifted the coffee cup to her lips and took a sip. "That's probably the reason his health was suffering."

"We suggested he take an early retirement so we could put one of our own people in his place, namely me."

"I remember the day you started." Charlotte placed her cup on the table. "You actually had me convinced you were the new vice-president."

Brett's soft eyes narrowed. "While I do have a business degree, the actual day-to-day work was being done by your former boss, from an off-site location. You realize why I had to lie, don't you?"

"I do now." She eased back in her chair. "But why didn't you take me into your confidence?"

"I didn't know you, and I had no idea who was involved."

Charlotte nodded. She could understand that.

Brett set her plate of eggs on the table. "Do you remember when you came to the office on the Monday morning after the murder and flashed that black business card with the Triumvirate logo on it?"

"Yes."

"The card was supplied by Carlton Witherspoon."

Charlotte scooped up some egg with her fork, but hesitated before putting it in her mouth. "You mean dear old Carlton was a drug supplier?"

"He was. If you rubbed the back of the card with some lemon juice, a coded message would appear, giving the date, the time and the place for Blanchard to pick up his stash of opium, which he split up into smaller packets. Carlton's butler, Crofts, finally admitted that he delivered those business cards to Blanchard."

Things were falling into place. "I get it now," Charlotte said. "Then Blanchard shipped out the opium, along with a 'special' bill of lading."

"Exactly. My partner, Catherine, and I searched Longbourne and Payne for his codebook. She was the one who found it in Blanchard's desk, but she had to replace the book before he discovered it was missing. When she went back to get it, the book was gone, and we were frantic."

Charlotte had to smile. "It was the one I took."

Brett nodded. "When I saw a copy of it fall out of your glove compartment, I knew I had to get that information to my partner, pronto. There was going to be one last big drug move, and it had to be soon. A few days before Witherspoon died, he sold his controlling shares in Longbourne and Payne to a large conglomerate. The new company was planning to take over next week."

Charlotte ate up the last of her eggs. Everything that happened seemed unreal. She was still having a hard time believing it. "I should have listened to my dad. He told me getting involved with anything that had to do with that black business card would bring me nothing but trouble."

Brett crossed the length of the table to where Charlotte sat and stood behind her. "You're still tense. You need to relax."

His voice sounded soothing as his sensitive hands massaged her shoulders and worked their way up the back of her neck. Whatever he was doing felt sinfully good. Charlotte closed her eyes and let out a sigh of intense pleasure. Tiny goose bumps stippled her skin where his hands worked their magic, but when they slowly wandered toward the front of her blouse, she stiffened and clasped her hands over his. "You shouldn't be touching me like that while you're engaged to Susan."

"Oh, yeah, Susan." He took his hands from Charlotte's shoulders and dropped down in the chair next to her. "Susan was the person who first came to your former boss with her suspicions about her father being involved in the drug dealing. Our engagement was just part of the scenario."

"Then you're not really engaged?" The pain that had plagued Charlotte's heart since she'd first heard the announcement disappeared.

Brett reached into his shirt pocket and pulled out the engagement ring. "Susan returned this to me this morning."

Charlotte imagined the glint of its enormous diamonds sparkling around the third finger of her left hand, but her heart fell when he slipped it back into his pocket.

"I have to get it back to the jewelers today," he said. "It's only on loan."

She sighed as resignation washed over her. "Too bad you have to return such a fabulous piece of jewelry. I'm sure Susan didn't want to give it back. She's in love with you, you know."

Brett narrowed his brows in a look that told her he was considering what she'd said. "I don't think so. Susan knew the arrangement when she agreed to help me with the assignment. But she did seem unduly upset when she returned the ring to me. She's actually a very sweet girl despite the trashy performance she puts on."

Charlotte's curiosity was piqued. "Did the two of you get very close? I mean, did you...?"

He hesitated as he searched for the right words. "If you're referring to what I think you are, we had to act out certain things to make our relationship believable. If her dad thought for one moment that it wasn't genuine, our cover would have been blown."

With all the lies he's already told, why couldn't he have lied to me about that? Charlotte eyed him with the perspective of a stranger. After all, she'd never *really* known him. From now on, she was playing it cool.

"Your whole charade was entirely convincing. Perhaps Susan thought you had the same feelings for her that she had for you."

"I told you, it had to look that way." His dark eyes took on a soft glow as he stared deeply into hers. "But there was one thing I didn't take into consideration at the time all this started."

She huffed out a breath of indifference. "And what might that be?"

"That I might fall in love with you."

Charlotte's heart stopped before it began pounding against her chest from the massive amount of adrenaline that flooded her bloodstream. A nervous flutter tickled her insides. "I suppose you fall in love with all the administrative assistants you've worked with as an undercover FBI agent."

Brett smiled and shook his head. "Only you."

He brushed the loose strands of hair from Charlotte's forehead. "We were getting much too close. So close that I didn't want this assignment to end, but I knew it would, and soon. I had to find a way to put some distance between us before my feelings for you began to cloud my judgment. That's when I thought of the engagement to Susan. I know I should have ended our relationship before I got Susan to agree to all this, and I'm sorry for that. It's just that I didn't want you involved in this drug sting."

The sincerity in his eyes warmed Charlotte's heart. He tilted his body closer to hers. Her adrenaline pumped faster. "It wasn't easy for me," he said. "You were so adorable and your antics were so endearing. You can't imagine how difficult it was to be near you at the office and not tell you how I felt."

His soft smile left Charlotte with no doubt.

"You looked so gorgeous at the country club dance on Saturday night in your low-cut black dress. I could barely take my eyes off you. And when I saw Billy Price pawing you, it took every ounce of restraint I had to keep from going over to your table and giving that pervert a black eye. Being with Susan was agony. All I could think about was holding you, touching you, kissing you..."

"Wanting you," she said in a voice so soft it was nearly a whisper.

Brett stood. He pulled her off the chair and into a tight embrace. His tender kisses brushed her neck and sent a ripple along her skin that ignited a yearning she felt all the way down to her toes. His warm hands found their way under her blouse. The sensation of his caress on her bare skin made Charlotte quiver. She melted into his arms.

Her moist, eager lips met his in a hungry kiss, and suddenly nothing existed except the softness of Brett's mouth. He kissed her fiercely. Long, hard, deep kisses. Kisses that lifted her up and made her tumble into a sensual, tumultuous place. A place only *he* could take her.

Charlotte's heart nearly burst with the intensity of her feelings for him as he scooped her up in his arms and, with a loving gleam in his eyes, carried her into his bedroom.

It was after two in the afternoon when Brett pulled his car into his assigned parking space at Longbourne and Payne.

He turned off the car's engine. Charlotte unbuckled her seat belt and sat in the passenger's seat waiting for him to say something, anything that might give her some hope for their future together. After several moments, he finally said, "Well, here we are."

"Where, exactly, are we?"

"Back where we started."

"You're right. We are back to where we started. I guess I'll have to get to know you all over again, as Brett Stalworth, FBI agent."

Brett smiled. "You already know me. I'm the same guy. Just a different name."

In her heart, she knew that was true. But he *was* different, she was different. Everything was, and they could never go back to the way they were when she thought he was just her boss.

"I have to admit," Brett said, "You're a pretty good detective."

An embarrassing warmth rose to her face. "I was only playing Watson to Jane's Sherlock."

"But you searched the shipping office to investigate Blanchard."

Charlotte lowered her gaze. "You're right, I did go down there to investigate Blanchard, but it was *Miss* Blanchard I was interested in."

"In what way?"

"I went down there to see if I could find something that might implicate her in Carlton Witherspoon's murder. Unfortunately, I couldn't find a thing."

Brett flashed that brilliant, white smile she loved so much. "I see."

"However, I did overhear a conversation between Susan and her father about how she could control you once you were married. I tried to warn you, but you wouldn't listen. Now I realize she was just playing her part."

"It was thoughtful of you, anyway."

Charlotte stared at her shoes. "Thanks."

Brett lifted her chin with his knuckle. You don't have to be a brilliant detective to make a fantastic partner."

What's he getting at? Charlotte tugged at the hem of her skirt. In her rush to get dressed at Brett's, she hadn't noticed that she'd put it on backwards. "Do you mean you want me to join the FBI?"

"No, of course not." His smile seemed to lessen the cut of his words. "But I've been thinking about quitting and opening my own detective agency in Virginia. You could move into my condo there, and we could share an office as business partners. Our motto would be, 'Danger and Excitement at Every Turn'."

A sudden ache shot through her heart. She gazed at his handsome face. "I don't know, John. I mean, Brett. Leaving town and moving in with you is a pretty big step." The thought of it actually frightened her. "What if you got tired of our relationship? Or what if you fell in love with one of your clients? What if the business didn't work out? You could always go back to the FBI, but what about me? I'd be heartbroken and alone in a strange city with nowhere to live and no job. I couldn't come back here. I'd be too ashamed."

Brett stared at her in that intensely masculine way of his. "Everything is a risk, sweetheart. There are no guarantees."

"It's not only that." She sighed. "The kind of life you're talking about has always been Jane's forte, not mine. While I admit I've picked up tidbits about crime solving from Jane, I wouldn't want to do it for a living. I loathe danger, and I'm frightened of violence. I can't have it be a part of my everyday existence."

She fought to keep her voice from cracking. "There was a time when I hated this town and desperately wanted to leave it behind, but after what's happened, I just want to go back to living a normal life again. I've had my fill of danger and excitement."

Brett dropped his shoulders. The lines around his eyes deepened. He couldn't have looked more distressed if she had told him his favorite dog just died. "I've tried working a nine-to-five job, but I can't. I would suffocate being stuck in one place, doing the same job until the day I retired. I like to travel and live on the edge. Detective work is the only thing I'm really good at."

"Couldn't you be a detective in *this* town? I could occasionally help you with your cases part-time, like a consultant."

"There's no future here." Brett sounded adamant. "Can't you see that?"

The determined look in his eyes told Charlotte he wasn't going to back down. She turned away. Her world was unraveling, and there was nothing she could do to stop it. With her heart crushed, sadness engulfed her like a shroud. "Why does everything have to be the man's way or no way?"

She opened the car door, jumped out, and slammed it behind her. As she raced toward the space where her Mustang was parked, Brett called out to her, "Charlotte, don't go."

Her heart begged her to turn around and run back to him, but her disappointment and stubborn pride forced her keep running.

Chapter Twenty Nine

Charlotte descended the stairs from her apartment early Monday morning to find her mother in her pink polyester bathrobe, pacing the driveway and clutching a white coffee mug. She approached Charlotte with one hand held straight out to brush her daughter's cheek. "How are you feeling dear? Are you sure you're ready to go back to work?"

Charlotte shrugged her off. "I'm fine, Mother." *Why does she still treat me like I'm ten years old?*

"So, I hear your girlfriend is running off to Virginia with that FBI agent to open a detective agency." Her mother's ability to change the subject in an instant always caught Charlotte off-guard, but this time, the words nearly caused her to knees to buckle as well. Steeling her back, she held her head high. "Where did you hear that?"

"Rumors are flying, and there's usually a grain of truth behind them."

"I doubt it." Charlotte slipped the car keys from her purse. "Jane emailed me last night. She's at the Eldridge Inn working on her next novel. She said she'd be there for a couple of days, and she'd let me know when she was leaving."

"I wouldn't be so sure if I were you." The smug look on her mother's face made Charlotte wonder where the woman had gotten her information.

"Vivie Eldridge called early this morning—"

"Why does that woman dislike me?" She interrupted.

"It's because you introduced her sister to that horrid man she married."

Charlotte rolled her eyes. "He worked in my office and he seemed like a nice guy. I thought they'd make a cute couple. How could I know he was only marrying Sophie for her money?"

"Indeed, how could anyone know." Mrs. Ross cleared her throat. "But getting back to my phone call. Vivie mentioned that Jane has checked out. She heard from her cousin, who works at the airport as a reservation sales agent, that Jane's already reserved her seat on the next plane out of here. The same plane your ex-boss will be on."

Charlotte struggled to conceal her surprise. *Jane's always been a last-minute person. Maybe something came up and she had to leave. I'd better check my email this morning.* Jane had admitted she was attracted to Brett, and the idea of his entire persona fascinated her, but would she tag along hoping to catch him on the rebound?

It couldn't be true. She wouldn't do that. But then, there were a lot of things about Jane she still didn't understand. She swallowed the lump in her throat. "Sounds like the rumor mongers have been awfully busy this morning."

"You were hoping he'd ask you to marry him, weren't you?"

"What!" *How could she know? Was I that obvious?*

"Don't bother denying it. I know how you act when you're in love. Don't you even care what they're saying about Jane running off with him?" Her mother sounded perplexed.

"No. There's probably a very good reason why Jane checked out. Maybe she had a meeting with her publisher. There's no proof she's running off with anyone. It's only rumor." But the green-eyed monster inside was twisting Charlotte's half-empty stomach into a tight little knot. Determined not to give an inch, she added, "Besides, you should be grateful to Jane. She saved my life."

Mrs. Ross's eyes narrowed into that squint Charlotte recognized whenever her mother was getting ready to spit out an accusation. "Well, it's the least she could have done after she got you involved in this mess. I hope you're happy now that you and your friend have practically ruined this town. To say nothing of Longbourne and Payne."

"We haven't ruined the town." Charlotte had taken about as much as she could this morning. She unlocked her car door and slipped into the driver's seat as her mother's withering glare followed her every move. Charlotte curved her lips into the most serene smile she could muster. "This town will go on in spite of everything that's happened, and so will Longbourne and Payne. As a matter of fact, Jim Longbourne is making a speech this morning to brief everyone on the future of the company."

The president's new executive administrative assistant checked her watch. "We'll have to discuss this some other time, Mom. I have to go now, or I'll be late for the meeting."

Charlotte sped out of her driveway and onto the street, leaving her mother standing alone with a look of frustration on her unmade face. She was just about to drive past the corner when she caught sight of the new stop sign and slammed on her brakes. Her car fishtailed to a sudden stop.

Tires screeched. *Bam!* The impact threw Charlotte forward, but the seatbelt held her firmly in place. She was momentarily stunned. A slow hissing noise filled the air.

"Oh great, a flat, too! I knew I should have put air in that tire yesterday."

The sound of knuckles tapping at her window startled her. She pushed the button to open it, and when it came down, she glanced up at Brett. Her breath caught in her throat.

"I'm sorry, but the way you were racing down the street, I didn't think you were going to stop."

Charlotte's insides jerked when he spoke, and the sight of Brett's face intensified the ache in her heart as it pounded so loudly, she was sure the sound was blaring out of her ears. "I nearly didn't. It was a last-minute decision."

"Are you hurt?"

She rubbed the back of her neck. It felt a little sore when her head jerked forward from the impact. "I'm fine. I think." She unbuckled her seatbelt and stepped out of the car to check the damage.

"It doesn't look too bad," Brett said. "There's only a minor dent in your back fender, and a flat tire."

Charlotte huffed. "Thank goodness for that. But now, I'll be late for the first day of my new job."

Brett appeared unaffected by this little mishap. "I'll call a tow truck for your car, and then I'll drive you to the office. My car doesn't have much damage." He motioned with his head. "Get in."

It had been three lonely, miserable days since she'd seen him. He hadn't tried to contact her. No phone calls, no emails, no texts. Not a word. But being away from him gave her time to reflect on her life and to dwell on what he'd said. She'd made a decision.

Charlotte put a smile on her lips as she got into the passenger's side of his car. "I'm glad you're still here." Her voice sounded a little shakier than she had intended.

Brett's face was impassive. "The reason I'm still here is because I had to wrap up this drug case. But now that my assignment is over, I'll be on the next plane to Virginia."

The painful realization that he was leaving struck Charlotte's heart with the same force as a lightning bolt. Uncontrollable tears welled in her eyes and rolled down her cheeks in huge drops. "But you can't leave. I mean, we still have a lot of unfinished business to discuss."

Brett reached into his pocket and handed her his handkerchief. "I don't think there's anything further to discuss. You've make it perfectly clear where you stand on the issues."

Charlotte dabbed at her tears as she gazed up at him. *God, he's handsome.* She tried to take in a deep breath to gain control of her emotions, but the lump in her throat made it difficult to breathe.

"I'm really sorry about this outburst," she squeaked. "I don't know what's come over me."

Brett pulled his car over to the curb and put it into park. His eyes looked hopeful as he gazed into hers. "I think I do. Have you changed your mind about going away with me?"

Charlotte sighed. It sounded mournful. She wasn't sure how he would take what she wanted to tell him. "I, I'm afraid..."

"If you have doubts about your feelings," he interrupted, "then, there's nothing more to say."

Charlotte dabbed off the smudges around her eyes. With her heart pounding, and a numbing fear she might still lose him, she said, "You didn't give me a chance to finish."

He folded his arms, resolutely. "Go ahead. I'm listening."

"What I wanted to say," Charlotte began in a soft voice, "was that I've been thinking things over, and because I love you, I'm willing to give up what I want just to be with you."

Brett's face softened. He smiled into her eyes. "You love me that much?"

"I do. I love you terribly." This was the hardest part for her to say. "But I need you to do something for me."

He arched an eyebrow. "What?"

She took a deep breath. "Just living together isn't enough. I need more of a commitment from you." She wanted to say, 'And if you won't give me one, I'll be devastated,' but the words wouldn't come out. She still had a little pride left.

He narrowed his eyes. "Is that an ultimatum?"

"Of course not." Charlotte tried to make her tone convincing, even though her words sounded very much like one. She gazed into the depths of his eyes and pleaded, "Please Brett, it's important to me."

A slow smile spread across his lips and dimpled his left cheek. "Well, if it's that important." He reached inside his jacket pocket. "Is this enough of a commitment?"

He took Charlotte's left hand and slipped an engagement ring on her third finger.

She caught her breath. "When did you get it? It's even lovelier than the ring Susan was wearing."

"When I returned that ring, I remembered the gleam in your eyes when you admired it. But it wasn't your style. Then I spotted this one, and I knew you'd like it. I've been carrying it with me, hoping you'd come around. But when I didn't hear from you, I was sure you weren't in love with me."

"How could you even think such a thing?" Charlotte searched his eyes for an answer.

Brett pressed a finger to her lips. "Let me finish. I was going to return the ring to the jeweler this morning, and then I was leaving this town for good. But now you've changed all that. If you love me enough to give up everything, I guess I can try doing things your way for a while."

Charlotte threw her arms around his neck as he enclosed her in a tight embrace. She felt his heart racing nearly as fast as hers. "Thank you, Brett," she whispered in his ear. "You've made me so happy." But a dark thought put a damper on her feelings. She took her arms down. "What about Jane?"

"What about her?"

"The rumor around town is that you and she were planning to run off to Virginia together."

Brett put his arms around Charlotte again and pressed her close as he whispered, "Rest assured, my love, I never had the intention of leaving town with anyone but you."

Epilogue

Charlotte walked into the company meeting late that morning. She smiled at the employees around her as she tried to inconspicuously slip into an empty chair at the back of the room. Mr. Longbourne, her new boss, droned on about the company's standings when the conglomerate took over, but she couldn't concentrate on his words, being too engrossed in thoughts about her own future...with Brett. She could barely contain her excitement every time she glanced at her gorgeous engagement ring.

Spinning the ring on her finger, she pictured what it would be like—visiting him in Chicago on the weekends, and him occasionally coming back to Eldridge Corners until they were married and settled in. Charlotte sighed in contentment. Life couldn't get any better.

Loud applause brought her back to the moment. She looked around and stood, applauding as well, although she didn't know why. *Guess I'll find out later.* She filed out of the conference room along with her coworkers but resisted the urge to show off her ring. Brett was coming back to the office to pick her up for lunch, and they would make a formal announcement then.

Susan tapped Charlotte's shoulder. "Aren't you going to congratulate me on my new promotion?"

I must have missed that part of the meeting. "Oh sure. Congrats."

Susan walked along beside her. "I know we've been at each other's throats lately, but now that everything's behind us, we'll have to come to some kind of working relationship. After all, you'll be training me."

It finally dawned on Charlotte. Susan was filling her old position. She shoved her left hand into her skirt pocket. Being so happy this morning, she hadn't considered what Susan's feelings might be. This was going to be awkward.

On an unusually easy day at the office, Charlotte sidled up to Susan's desk. "I suppose you've heard about all the people getting their DNA tested to see if they might be related to Carlton Witherspoon."

"Yeah, I heard." Susan looked up from her computer screen. "Why?"

"I was just thinking that since your mom was engaged to the man, you might want to get tested."

Susan glared at her. "Are you insinuating my dad isn't my biological father?"

Charlotte cringed. *Maybe this wasn't such a good idea.* "All I'm saying is that there might be a chance of you being Carlton's only living heir. There's a lot of money at stake."

Susan sighed. "I *could* use the money. My mom and I are just making ends meet. Her treatment and meds are really expensive."

"So, what have you got to lose?"

Charlotte turned and walked back to her desk. She hoped Susan would get the test taken. Despite the way she'd been treated by her in the past, she believed Susan was basically a good person, and deserved some happiness.

After a month of traveling back and forth to Chicago, Charlotte was relieved that Brett had decided to take the train to Eldridge Corners to spend this weekend with her.

As she dressed for dinner, he walked into her bedroom. "Do we have to go out?"

Stepping into her shoes, she glanced at him. "We don't *have* to do anything."

He came up to her, put his arms around her waist and gazed into her eyes. "Good, because I'd rather be alone with you tonight. I'll open the bottle of wine I brought, and we can order takeout from Chez Pierre."

Charlotte cherished her "alone" time with him. "Sounds great."

He pulled her close, and she shifted her head to place a warm, loving kiss on his lips.

Ping.

She turned.

"Ignore it," Brett said.

"But it might be for you, and it could be important."

Huffing out a breath of annoyance, he released her and went into the living room. "It's not *my* phone."

Charlotte followed him in. She grabbed hers from the end table. "It's a message... from Susan, of all people."

"What does it say?"

"She took the DNA test. Her results came back positive. What's left of Carlton's millions will be transferred to her, his only remaining heir."

Brett smiled. "I'm glad she got something out of this mess."

Charlotte gazed into his warm, brown eyes. "So am I. Because if it hadn't been for Susan and her suspicions about her father dealing drugs, *we* would never have met." Without breaking eye contact, she sauntered up to him and slipped her arms around his neck. "Now, where were we before the interruption?"

He tenderly tightened the embrace. "You were just about to kiss me."

Thank you for taking the time to read, Love, Lies and Murder. If you enjoyed it, please consider telling your friends or posting a short review. Word of mouth is an author's best friend and much appreciated.

If you'd like to read more of the Charlotte Ross mysteries, the next novels in the series are: **Masterpiece of Murder** and **Once Upon a Crime**.

About the author

Evelyn Cullet has been an author since high school when she wrote short stories. She began her first novel while attending college later in life, and while working in the offices of a major soft drink company. Now, with early retirement, she finally has the chance to do what she loves best: write full time. As a life-long mystery buff, she was a former member of the Agatha Christie Society, and is a current member of the National Chapter of Sisters In Crime. When she's not writing mysteries, reading them or reviewing them, she hosts other authors and their work on her writer's blog. She also plays the piano, is an amateur lapidary, and an organic gardener.

Made in the USA
Las Vegas, NV
07 March 2024

86822534R00167